Lucile Allen, FAKE GIRLFRIEND

EXTRAORDINAIRE

ISBN:978-1-66783-974-5 eBook ISBN:978-1-66783-975-2

To the four scholarly gentlemen from Modesto who made my life more interesting, especially to the quiet one who made it complete.

Chapter One

I stood nervously on stage in a pink satin gown that was too expensive to wear only once but way too uncomfortable and fancy to ever consider wearing again. I tried not to think about how much the mix of rhinestones and sequins made my arms itch along with the unfortunate fact that sweat was pooling all around my body.

Looking out at the crowd, I was unable to see anything because of the stage lights. I started counting in my head, trying to calm my discomfort. Every uncomfortable moment had to pass eventually and counting gave me something else to think about.

Fifteen...sixteen...seventeen...eighteen...

"And your Prom Queen is...Lucile Allen."

Holy shit. That was me.

My mouth dropped open. I turned to Hunter, my boyfriend standing behind me, in shock. He wrapped his arms around me.

"Congratulations, Luce," he kissed my forehead.

I was still too stunned to say anything and it slowly registered that people were cheering. Sadie Jones, the junior class president, placed a tiara on my head to complement my dumbfounded look.

Within seconds, Hunter was announced as Prom King. It was unbelievable. I had never in my life imagined that moment happening to me. It felt so surreal.

Hunter, always at home in front of a crowd, instinctively took my hand and walked me to the dance floor. Thank goodness he was voted Prom King, otherwise I'd have been even more of a nervous mess dancing in front of everyone.

Hunter Davis had been my rock for the past three years—I'd consider him more of a mountain given how amazing he'd been the last six months. There was no need to think about it then, though. Or any other horrible thing that had happened. In that moment, despite all the itchy pink rhinestones, life was perfect and there was no need to count the seconds away.

⌒⟋⟋⟋⟋⟋⟋⌒

"Well that was pretty freakin' crazy," Hunter laughed as we settled back into his dad's BMW, on loan, because it was prom, of course. I smiled a genuine smile for what felt like the first time in months.

"You ready to go to the after party, m'lady?" he said in a horrible British accent before kissing the back of my hand.

"But of course, your majesty," I joked back—my British accent was far superior.

We both still had our crowns on. However, he had his tilted, making him look slightly ridiculous, but still cute. His shaggy blond hair was sticking out at the bottom, and as disheveled as it looked, I had no doubt it took him at least an hour to perfect "the look" he wanted.

Personally, I was not a fan of his longer hair, but Hunter thought it made him look like Julian Wilson, who he had been obsessed with ever since his parents bought a house in Hawaii two years earlier and he started thinking he could be a surfer. (Never mind the fact that we live in the central valley of California where the closest ocean is over two hours away.) I was convinced that was about seventy-five percent of the reason he chose to go to UC Santa Barbara for college.

Messy hair and delusional surfer dreams aside, I did truly love him and hoped he found happiness there. He definitely deserved it. Not that anyone would ever think of Hunter Davis, soccer star and swim captain, as someone who wasn't already happy. Hunter and I were both incredibly skilled when it came to putting on a picture-perfect act for everyone else. And while he was surely the optimist of our dynamic duo, I was close enough to him to know that his façade of constant cheer was often for the benefit of others and to the detriment of himself.

My fingers were crossed that Santa Barbara could give him a fresh start where he could just be who he was, rather than trying to be someone that would make everyone else happy. I hadn't thought much about what my own fresh start at University of Washington in Seattle would bring me, other than a place to be as far away from home as possible.

"You're doing that weird thing where you stare at me like a girl who's proud she just potty-trained her puppy," Hunter called me out of my train of thought.

"Maybe I'm just thinking about how good you would look with only that crown on," I joked with a wink.

"Ha, yeah right," he brushed me off as he turned down the country road leading to Emily Mason's house—which was more like a mansion. "I bet you were really picturing Chase naked."

"Eww! Was not," I countered, regretting ever telling him that I had thought in the eighth grade that Chase Robertson was cute.

While technically part of our group of friends solely because of being on the soccer team with Hunter, Chase Robertson, was the biggest idiot at Beyer High School. He only got into junior college because of a soccer scholarship. It wasn't that I had anything against stupid people, it was just that he was so proud and unapologetic about it with no desire to correct it. He always used his popularity to get girls to do all his homework. Neither Hunter nor I could stand him, but for the sake of keeping drama relatively low within the group, we kept it to ourselves.

"Ugh, now I'm thinking about Chase being at this party," I lamented.

Hunter reached over and held my hand.

"Hey, four more weeks and you pretty much never have to see him again," he reminded me.

"That is true," I sighed as we pulled into the already crowded driveaway.

"You won't even have to spend time being weirdly fixated on Sebastian Torres getting a better grade in AP Lit than you," Hunter made a point to tease me about my academic nemesis.

"You know my paper on *Wuthering Heights* was far superior to his," I quickly snapped, missing Hunter's point.

"I know, Luce. You've only told me about it like ten times since Monday," Hunter said matter-of-factly, dismissing me. "So, what's the plan?" He turned towards me after parking the car.

"I'm down for whatever," I lied. "But I'm not really up for partying," I backtracked. "If you want to, I can drive," I offered, not wanting to deny Hunter a chance to celebrate his only senior prom with friends he would be saying goodbye to soon.

"Nah, I'll probably just nurse a nasty watered-down beer for a few hours. Save face." He smiled at me then paused.

"What?"

"I have a surprise for you." His grin got wider.

I raised an eyebrow.

"My dad, in his ever-present 'cool dad' fashion, rented us a hotel room downtown. I had your sister pack you a bag and put it in the trunk while we were taking pictures at your house. There's also," he paused for dramatic effect, "an extremely nice bottle of cabernet back there, too.

"So I think we should make our rounds at Emily's and then head out for a romantic evening for two that will leave the whole class talking."

"What about my mom? She's never going to let me spend the night with you in a hotel."

"My dad took care of it. He told her he got a hotel room for our group."

"So does that mean—"

"Yes, my dad is my wingman—a very, very naïve, but rich, wingman."

"Hunter Davis, you are going to give me a reputation," I proclaimed with a laugh.

"You mean the one we both already have?" He shrugged, holding his swoon-worthy smile. "Might as well lean into it, right?"

"Ending the night alone with you and a good bottle of wine sounds like the best ending to senior prom ever. Thank you." I leaned in and kissed him on the cheek, thankful that he was my best friend before anything else.

"No, thank you," he said sincerely before kissing my temple like he always did. "Now let's go have some reckless teenage fun before acting like the lame middle-aged housewives we are."

"Deal."

I felt like I was floating as we walked from the car to the house. It still seemed unreal that I had been voted prom queen and my boyfriend was the most popular guy in school, especially after the way high school began. Hunter looked at me and took a deep breath before bursting through the door.

"What's up, what's up, what's up! The Monarchy has arrived, bitches!" he bellowed into the crowded house and was met by cheers.

"Ohmygawd, Hunt and Lucy! You made it!" Emily gushed as she greeted us, giving me a hug. "You look so beautiful tonight," she complimented.

"Thanks, you do too."

"Hunt, you already need to catch up," Brady, Hunter's best friend, walked over and handed him a beer. "And then you need to watch Chase make an idiot of himself trying to play darts." Brady led him to the tavern-themed parlor. "Lucy, I'll make sure to get him good and wasted for you to take advantage of later," Brady half-joked as they walked away, leaving me with Emily.

"So, is everyone else already here?" I asked as Emily handed me a red Solo cup filled with some sort of mixed drink that I wouldn't be drinking.

"Yeah, I think Olivia, Maddison, and Jill are all outside by the pool. Feel free to go for a swim if you brought your suit. Or skinny dip, you know, whatever. Wooo! Senior prom!" Emily lifted her cup to me.

I smiled and half-heartedly did the same before wandering through the living room to get to the backyard. I started to open the screen door when I heard Olivia say my name.

"I can't believe Lucy won," she exclaimed, the tone and volume of her voice revealing that she was already a few drinks in.

"I know!" replied Jill. "I so thought you deserved it more. I mean, her dress was so obvious and ridiculous. Prom Barbie, much?"

The three of them laughed.

"Ohmygod, you're horrible," Olivia said with a smile.

"For real though, she acts like she's all above everything and doesn't care, and the minute they called it out, she's like, 'Oh my God, me?'" Jill mocked wiping away a fake tear before taking another drink. "It's total bullshit. And you know everyone only voted for her because her dad died."

My heart stopped as Jill's words sunk in. I wanted to unhear them.

"That, and because for some unknown reason, she's Hunter's girlfriend," Maddison added.

"Ah yes, the never-ending question of 'What does he see in her?' that's plagued us since sophomore year," Olivia sighed.

"I think we all know it's not about what he sees in her, but more about what she's willing to do to him," Jill snickered.

"Hey Lucy, you need a refill on your drink?" Emily unintentionally announced my presence, causing the three girls to turn to the door and see me.

There I was, frozen. I felt the sting of fighting back tears. Thankfully the shock of being revealed had helped keep the waterworks at bay. They stared at me, motionless too, all of us unsure of how to proceed. Just then, a completely naked Chase Robertson came running out of the house.

"Caaaaanoooonnnbaaaallll!" he bellowed as he barreled into the pool, causing an enormous splash and covering Olivia, Maddison, and Jill with water, temporarily shifting their sense of shock to something else.

Quickly, a crowd gathered to observe the spectacle that Chase had once again created at an Emily Mason house party. Within seconds, Chase was up and pulling Olivia in, followed by Maddison. Jill had managed to escape.

I began frantically looking for my escape too, pushing through people. Thankfully, I looked up to see Hunter. He followed me into the living room, grabbing my arm before I could get to the door—my one goal was to get out of there since I could now feel the tears brimming on my eyes.

"Luce, what's wrong?"

"I...I need to go. Now." My tone left no room for argument. Hunter only nodded and followed me out the front door, neither of us bothering to say goodbye to anybody.

Chapter Two

"Those girls are bitches, Lucy. Screw 'em," Hunter called into the hotel bathroom while I changed into the t-shirt and shorts my younger sister, Ava, had packed for me. It was always easier for him to dismiss all the gossip that had been said about me. He was a guy, it was never near as damaging to be labeled a slut.

Hunter, while a good listener, had always approached the situation from a matter-of-fact standpoint. He knew how popular and sought-out he was by the other girls at school. He had warned me that dating him meant I would have to deal with the jealousy of other girls. I just never considered how vicious the rumors would be until it was too late.

I started pulling out the thousands of bobby pins that had been holding up my meticulously crafted hair. It was only hours earlier that I was sitting in the salon next to Olivia, discussing our dream playlist for prom, thinking she was someone I was going to miss seeing in the fall. Now I never wanted to see her, Maddison, or Jill again.

I stepped out of the bathroom, my hair spewed from my head at all different angles, the term "curls gone wild" highly appropriate. Hunter paused and then burst into laughter at the sight of me.

"Shut up," I sighed, turning my back to him. "There's still pins in the back. I can't reach them." Not needing further direction, he stepped up behind me and began rummaging through my hair.

"Medusa has summoned me," he joked. I rolled my eyes, but still enjoyed the familiar feeling of my back against his chest, his hands running through my hair.

Hunter was more than a half foot taller than me and over the past three years had grown into his frame. His devotion as an athlete led to well-defined muscles in all the desirable areas. It made perfect sense why he had been given the nickname "Hunky Hunter" by underclass girls.

What did not make sense, as Olivia had so eloquently proclaimed by the pool, was why he had chosen to date me for the past three years. I'll admit on the surface it hadn't made much sense to me either, especially when he'd first asked me to Homecoming sophomore year.

We had known each other since elementary school, even playing on the same soccer team when we were six. As we got older, he got more popular because girls started thinking he was hot and other boys managed to gain female attention just by being friends with him. Also, as I said before, Hunter had always been a crowd pleaser—funny, charming, the friendliest guy in the room.

Given the natural progression of middle school social warfare, our friendship shifted to more of an acquaintance status by the seventh grade. It's not like I was a pariah, but I was definitely never part of the "in" crowd. Making the girls' soccer team in ninth grade was my saving grace to not be a complete loner at lunch time.

The start of sophomore year, Hunter and I were paired up for a month-long project in Pre-AP Lit, and then a week later paired up again for a Spanish project. He was still the sweet, hilarious boy I remembered from grade school. I was absolutely shocked when arguably the most popular boy in our class asked me to Homecoming. Especially after he had spent most of Freshman year dating Olivia Rosen. So, I guess her disdain for me shouldn't have been so shocking.

There was a lot of speculation from people, myself included, if we were or were not a couple leading up to the night of the dance. Thankfully, Hunter had made it official that night when he kissed me on my front doorstep and asked me to be his girlfriend.

From that point, everything changed. Sure, I had to deal with terrible and untrue rumors about how I pretty much did anything and everything physical with Hunter, but it seemed like a small price to pay to be part of the cool crowd. Then again, I had to admit there was part of me that always felt like I never did quite fit in with them. Overhearing the girls tonight finally confirmed it.

"Done," Hunter announced, giving my crazy hair an annoying tousle before handing me the remaining bobby pins. He started to unbutton his shirt.

"What are you doing?" I stopped him.

"Changing out of my tux," he said, now standing shirtless.

"Go do that in the bathroom," I ordered.

"I do believe you made a joke earlier about wanting to see me with nothing but that crown on." He motioned to our crowns sitting on the side table.

"Key word 'joke,'" I exclaimed, averting my eyes as I realized he was not moving and was now taking off his pants. "I, sir, am a lady." My head was now fully turned, looking to the corner of the room.

"You certainly don't fart like one," he teased, throwing his pants to land perfectly on top of my head. Oh, the joys of being together for three years.

"Relax, Luce, I'm not taking off my boxers. Your virgin eyes won't be exposed to any dreaded boy parts."

I knew he was right; it really wasn't that big of a deal, especially when it came to him and me, but from my perspective, me seeing him naked was a little bit more complicated than the other way around.

I suppose it's probably important to mention that Hunter is gay. Like one hundred percent, only attracted to men, gay. He was also one hundred percent totally in the closet with everyone but me.

I had started to suspect something was amiss when, after two months of dating, he had done everything in his power to avoid making out with me, and neither he nor his family were super religious.

Not that I was all that disappointed by his hesitancy. After all, he was my first boyfriend, and I was incredibly awkward. But when I started to notice that the hottest boy in the tenth grade, who lost his virginity to Olivia freshman year, was not only just as awkward, but also visibly disinterested in any physical displays of affection beyond hugging, it left me very confused.

I burst into tears one Saturday night in his living room after his parents had irresponsibly left us alone for the evening and he politely brushed my hand away from his leg. Through my sobs, I proceeded to rant embarrassingly about how he didn't think I was pretty, was still into Olivia, and that the whole school would probably think something was wrong with me if we broke up. Hunter, always a sucker when it came to me crying, ended up coming out to me.

I will never forget that moment.

He looked so disappointed in himself and said he wished he could be different. He had thought sleeping with Olivia would change it, but it hadn't. He had hoped dating me might make him realize he was actually straight, because we were such good friends, but once again it was futile. That moment was the first time he had ever said it out loud and the first time he had shared it with another person. I told him I was proud of him and that I would stand by him and love him no matter what. He said he wasn't ready to tell anyone else and asked me to keep it a secret. Understandably, I had no problem agreeing to that.

Hunter said that he had never trusted anyone as much as me. We concluded that if neither of us was interested in dating anyone else, then there was really no reason to break up. At least not right away, since we were such good friends and no one in high school ever accepted the label of "just friends." I had been Hunter's beard ever since, but I tried not to use that term around him. He hated it. But I didn't have a better word for it—teenage life companion sounded weird.

For the most part, the situation was ideal. I was not a particularly horny person and was completely fine with PDA being kept to hugging and the occasional peck on the lips. Plus, I got to stay in the popular crowd. Not that it was the only reason, but I couldn't deny it was a benefit to sticking it out, along with always having a guaranteed date to every school dance who wasn't at all bad to look at. Plus, at that point, I don't think any nice boys would've dated me, seeing as how the savage rumors about what I was willing to do with Hunter managed to stick around for the rest of high school.

Admittedly, I was surprised we had made it all the way to the end of senior year without Hunter wanting to come out. I never really pressed him about it, and figured he would make the call when he was ready to take that step. Now that both of us were heading off to different colleges, an official break up made sense. Long-distance fake relationships are really hard to maintain anyway.

"You ready for this cabernet, Princess?" Hunter uncorked the bottle.

"Excuse me, I am a queen," I corrected emphatically. "Shouldn't you let it breathe?" I asked seriously, only to receive a smirk from Hunter.

Along with the unconventionality of our fake relationship that kept Hunter closeted, we were both eighteen-year-old wine snobs, preferring a nice dry zinfandel to any sugared-up mixed drink. We had our bougie parents to blame.

Hunter's parents had let him start having wine with dinner as early as ninth grade. (Did I mention his dad's hopeless desire to be the "cool dad"?). My parents, on the other hand, maintained a responsible law-abiding stance, which made sense, given that they were both lawyers—until my dad was diagnosed with terminal cancer and he declared that one of his bucket list items was to ensure I had an appreciation for the complexity of wine, reds in particular. From that point, it was no longer a rebellious behavior, but rather, a way to honor one of the last things he taught me before he died that March.

Hunter swirled the cabernet around the glass before handing it to me.

"Your majesty."

We clinked glasses and took our first sips, pausing and nodding in appreciation to one another. Hunter took his spot on the bed, sitting against the headboard with his long athletic legs stretched out in front of him. He pulled me down next to him with his free hand. I curled up next to him, my head resting on his chest. We sat there in silence for a few moments.

"I love you," he said.

"I know," I responded simply.

We let another silence pass, knowing this would likely be the last time we would ever have a moment like this between us.

"You need to stop thinking about those bitches," he announced, reading me without even looking at me.

"I'm not," I unsuccessfully denied while looking up at him.

He raised an eyebrow.

I sighed. "Easy for you to say. Everyone has always loved you."

"That's only because they don't know me."

"Whatever. That's not true," I dismissed.

"You're trying to tell me I would be Prom King if I were out?" he countered. "That any of the guys would even want to be friends with me?"

I didn't respond, not having a rebuttal, because I knew he was probably right, especially when it came to Chase Robertson, who was unabashedly homophobic.

"There are other kids who are gay at our school," I reminded him, once again wishing he could feel like this one thing did not make him abnormal.

"That's fine. You know there's a difference."

I didn't argue. I knew what he meant.

The kids who were out fit into the stereotypes of gay culture—in the drama club, fashion club, dance team. I loved Hunter, but he was anything but the artsy type—he did not fit into what others in high school would label as gay. It made me sad that he couldn't just be who he was.

"Well, it doesn't matter now, because you are going to go off to Santa Barbara and kill it. All those surfer boys won't know what hit them—pure, unadulterated, Central Valley, lover boy hotness."

"Yeah, we'll see," he sighed, taking a drink. He rubbed his forehead.

"You okay?"

"It would just be so much easier if I were straight."

"You're just saying that because you've never been in love." I looked him in the eye. "Believe me, the minute you meet a guy that you're into and he's into you, you're going to be so thankful that you were never into chicks. I mean, hello, drama." I motioned to myself. "It will be great. No matter how your parents end up feeling about it," I referenced one of his bigger insecurities.

"And what about you? You think you're going to regret any of this?"

"Nah," I said without hesitation. "I successfully avoided ever getting sexually harassed by Chase Robertson and tonight I'm in an incredibly fancy hotel suite drinking really smooth, overpriced cabernet with the hottest guy in school who's also my best friend. Also, I don't know if you heard this, but your nerdy AP study buddy was voted Prom Queen. I'd say I'm doing pretty well for myself."

"Yeah, I'd say so," he smiled.

I kissed Hunter's forehead; he knew I was saying thank you for a wonderful, storybook high school experience, despite losing my dad. But just like with my dad, all good things had to come to an end eventually.

I tried to focus on the exciting possibilities that lay ahead for Hunter finally getting to have the freedom to be himself, instead of the dread I felt heading off to a university two states away where I didn't know a single soul. I had relied on being Hunter's person—his confidant, his advisor, his best friend, for so long—now that I was losing it, I was terrified.

And as Olivia, Maddison, and Jill confirmed that night, without Hunter, there wasn't much else I really had to offer.

Chapter Three

As anticipated, the last four weeks of school flew by, as well as summer. I spent the majority of my days with Hunter, both because I wanted to soak up all my remaining time with him and it was a wonderful excuse to not deal with the continued reality of life at home without my dad. There was the occasional complaint from my mom, but my absences were pretty easy to navigate given that she now spent a ridiculous amount of time at work. Once Hunter left for Santa Barbara, I became fixated on my own impending escape.

However, it only took me one week away from home to question my decision to attend the University of Washington entirely. I don't know why I was surprised. Girl leaves the only home she's ever known to move over eight hundred miles away where she knows no one, only six months after her dad dies—sounds like a plan riddled with success. Not.

The only reason I was there was because it was my dad's alma mater for both undergrad and law school. Even my name, Lucile, paid homage to the first female clerk for a Supreme Court Justice who happened to be one of the first women to attend UW Law. No need to feel any pressure. We weren't even related to the woman! The only reason my mom agreed to the name was because she could tell my Puerto Rican, and very Catholic, grandmother that they were naming me after Saint Lucy.

I knew from a very young age that nothing would give my father greater joy than for me to attend his alma mater and eventually follow in his footsteps to become a lawyer. I still applied to various schools, but when he died, my application, which had originally been done to appease, quickly shifted to my first and only choice for college.

At first, I had felt cool being the only one in our graduating class to have declared the University of Washington. Something else for people to talk to me about besides my dad being sick and eventually dying. As I said before, there was part of me that wanted to run away from home, specifically my widowed mother and anything that reminded me of my dad.

Don't get me wrong, I get that my mom had every right to be sad about her husband dying. But when she wasn't buried in work from her own firm, she dove head-first into any and everything church-related. It was odd and frustrating.

One: we had never gone to church outside of major holidays, and two: why waste time honoring someone or something that decided to kill off a nice guy with a family? At least my younger sister seemed to buy into the whole "comfort of religion" thing. I was grateful Ava had something to make her feel better. And maybe that had been my mom's intention all along. But I was not going to join them in wasting my time hoping an invisible force would make me feel better.

Honestly, it really did seem to be in everybody's best interest that me and my negativity packed our bags and left. A logical person would have realized that this could have been achieved at a college within the boundaries of our state.

What I failed to realize was that running away from anything and everything that reminded me of my dad was ill-fated, given that the last trip I took with him was to visit UW campus the summer before my senior year. I had no memories of Seattle besides the ones I had made with him. And it didn't make me feel thankful—it just made me feel shitty.

So there I sat, one week into my move, nervously stewing inside the student housing office. I fought back tears as some lady named Lonnie tried to find me a place to live.

The original plan, after much goading, (too much, if you ask me) was to appease my mother by signing up to participate in Fall Rush for the Greek System. She had been part of a sorority while in college and regarded it as one of the highlights of her whole experience. She was extremely worried that I would not know anyone, and argued that this was the quickest and easiest way for me to make friends and ensure I got off to the right start.

She got pretty emotional about it when I didn't agree right away and proceeded to send me articles that warned about the risk of depression for first-year college students. Along with other articles about the rates of seasonal affective disorder occurring in the state of Washington.

"Lucy, you've never known anything but sunshine! The rain is really going to bother you." You'd think the woman who insisted on us all receiving therapy would know that it's a no-no to declare someone else's feelings for them, but I digress.

Anyway, since my mother and I could never rationally debate anything (that was always my dad's job), I just agreed to do Rush. I mean, I had spent the past three years pretending to be the picture perfect girlfriend to the most popular guy in school who was really gay, acting like I wanted to join a sorority couldn't be that much harder, right?

I was wrong. No one did anything overtly rude or catty. But when I showed up that first week and found myself surrounded by girls that looked, sounded, and acted like Olivia, Maddison, and Jill—and all I could think about, on top of my dad being gone, was the moment after prom when I heard what those girls all really thought of me.

Obviously it wasn't fair to judge these complete strangers off of things people from my past did, but my gut kept telling me I could never trust any of them. It seemed like a disaster waiting to happen. During all the ice breakers and socials it seemed like I only managed to showcase myself as "random awkward girl from California" at best.

I was the complete opposite of Hunter when it came to pleasing a crowd. Navigating the mandatory social events would've been so much easier if he were with me. But he wasn't. And as much as I wanted him to be there, I needed to accept that I was on my own now.

After the fifth slide show about being vulnerable and learning to lean on one another—complete with stock group photos of a bazillion mostly blonde white girls and the occasional token Asian girl - I determined that rather than trying to win anyone over, it made the most sense to save myself the heartache and reject all the bubbly sisters of AlphaZetaWhatever before they could reject me.

The only problem was, I had no other place to live.

"So, you're saying that there are no dorm rooms available?" I heard my voice crack, attempting to take a deep breath before I fell apart.

One...two...three...four...five...

"What I'm saying is that you may have to wait a bit before a room is available. There is a bed available in a loft space where we place overflow residents until rooms become available," Lonnie answered in a calm voice. I'm sure she had been through this with multiple Greek rejects—excuse me, non-elected students—before. Okay, technically I hadn't been rejected, but me and my bad attitude knew where it was headed.

"How long could that take?"

Ten...eleven...twelve...

"Well, it just depends on how many registered residents we have who decide not to live in the dorms. Sometimes it happens really fast, one to two days. Sometimes it can take up to a month."

"A month?" I said in disbelief.

"Not always," she reminded me. "The important thing to remember is that you will have a place to sleep and eventually a room." She paused for a second. "Let me just double check something," Lonnie trailed off while continuing to stare at her monitor.

I wondered if that would have been a good time to cry about having a dead dad. Would it have helped anything? Probably not. It would have just made things awkward for Lonnie. Should I have punished Lonnie by making things awkward? No, it wasn't her fault my insecurities prevented me from being a good candidate for sorority sisterhood.

"Good news," Lonnie announced a few moments later. "There is a spot for you in Lander Hall. You can move in a week from today. Two days before the quarter starts."

I breathed a literal sigh of relief. Grateful that I successfully withheld my tears again. A skill I was getting pretty good at.

Navigating crowded hallways with three oversized suitcases and trying not to get emotional seeing all the other kids getting moved in by their parents was anything but enjoyable. I told myself I really didn't want my mom there because all it would do was highlight that my dad was not.

I took a breath when I finally reached my door. Thankful to finally let go of the heavy load, I fumbled with the key and opened the door. It was a standard dorm room, from the little I knew about dorms, not necessarily spacious, but not as cramped as I had feared. Half the room was already decorated.

I shuffled inside and tried to gather what information I could about my roommate based on her chosen décor. If I had to guess, and I realized I was totally making assumptions, it appeared that she was artsy...maybe goth? If people were even goth anymore.

Really that take-away had only come from the fact that her bedspread was black and all of the photos and posters she had put up were black and white. My mind quickly filled with images of a pale girl with long black hair and heavy eyeliner. I heard a flush followed by the bathroom door opening. Out walked a tall slender girl that did not match the description in my head at all.

Her straight light brown hair was up in a ponytail. She was dressed in athletic clothes and running shoes.

"Wow, that's kind of creepy," she commented, staring back at me, referring to the fact that she stepped out of the bathroom to find a stranger standing in the middle of her room.

"Oh, hi, I, I'm—um—your roommate, Lucy," I reached out my hand to shake hers. She looked briefly down at my hand before deciding not to return the gesture. She walked over to her desk to pick up some AirPods.

"Cool. I'm Danica." She did not sound like she thought anything was cool. "I was about to head out for a run." She paused to put the pods in her ears. "So, I guess I'll leave you to unpack."

"Sounds good," I smiled politely, trying my best to make a good first impression.

"So, like, you were rejected from the sororities, right?" She started stretching her arms. Which, personally, I thought was a little extra to do before a run. Maybe she saved the quad stretches for later.

"Uh, not technically. I dropped out before Bid Day. It just wasn't for me," I shared...possibly justified.

"Right," she nodded, moving towards the door. "Okay, so, don't touch my stuff and I guess I'll see you later?"

"Sure thing," I affirmed with a smile, trying to appear like a worthy roommate to a person who clearly would never be convinced.

Danica headed out without a second look. It was obvious that there would be no sense of lifelong sisterhood developed in room 734 of Lander Hall, but at least I didn't have to worry about her being fake.

I began to unpack, getting used to the idea that this space was now my home. The color scheme I had chosen was quite the contrast from Danica's décor. I felt like my stuff was going to destroy the whole vibe of the room. I'd never felt so self-conscious about liking pastels before. I sighed loudly as I realized for the millionth time how much I missed Hunter.

After I finished unpacking, I was starving. I decided to just go get food from the cafeteria on my own. There was no sense in thinking that Danica had any interest in eating with me. Hopefully there would be some sort of ice cream in the cafeteria to distract me from my feelings. I locked up my new home and headed down the hall, then was immediately caught off guard by who I saw walking down the hall towards me.

Sebastian Torres.

What on earth was he doing here? I attempted to make eye contact with him and smile welcomingly, but failed miserably as evidenced by his making eye contact and then quickly looking away before I could say anything. His pace quickened slightly as he entered a room and closed the door before I could get to him. Thank God I didn't wave at him like an idiot.

I vividly remembered him making a point to let everyone at school know that he and his valedictorian girlfriend, Amelia Yang, were both going to Stanford in the fall. You would think if I was the only person he knew at this university, he would at least be happy to see a familiar face, even if we weren't the best of friends...or even really friends at all.

But didn't an academic acquaintance, or maybe more appropriately labeled, academic adversary, at least deserve a polite hello in this circumstance? Okay, so maybe I had a hunch why he didn't give me a warm welcome.

Chapter Four

I met Sebastian Torres in the ninth grade. He and I had every single class together that year. That wasn't highly unusual; all freshmen who took a full Pre-AP course load were in the same core classes, the one variable being their elective. Sebastian and I both ended up in Band—where he not only instantly played the trumpet perfectly, but also managed to play both the piano and guitar occasionally and with just as much annoying ease. Meanwhile I floundered to make a single correct note on the clarinet. Given the lazy, almost retired, director, it was a lot easier to fake proficiency in Band than the alternative options of Choir or Art.

Having taken a whole year of classes together, you'd think I would have spoken to him at some point, but I don't remember having one single conversation with him that year. He was the silent boy with the dark hair that sat in the back of class and always, and I mean, ALWAYS, annoyingly set the curve. It was the most aggravating when it happened in Math.

By sophomore year, Sebastian and I no longer had identical schedules— for the benefit of everyone's ears, I had put my clarinet to rest and replaced Band with Creative Writing. Sebastian skipped Algebra 2 and went straight into Calculus. Whatever. We still had four classes together and were even put in the same lab group for Chemistry, much to his obvious disappointment.

You know how there are just some people who look annoyed anytime you open your mouth? By the tenth grade, this was how all my interactions with Sebastian seemed to end. It's not like I was an idiot—I maintained a

3.89 GPA with a full AP schedule, thank you very much. I just wasn't, as one might say, overly scholastic when it came to my schooling. My philosophy for learning was to do what was asked of me, remember the info needed to pass, and move on from there. I saw no sense in getting hung up on the big question of "why" for things.

Okay, so I'm seeing how I might not be the best partner to have when it came to unpacking scientific theory. But it was JUST high school. The answer about why the lab results were the results was all explained in the textbook and by the teacher. I didn't need to tell you what I thought the symbolism in the *Odyssey* meant, because the teacher would wisely tell me exactly what it meant. Why waste my time pondering when there was someone with authority over my grade that could tell me the answer they wanted? There was no need to be so deep about everything at that age.

The permanently furrowed brow that appeared whenever he was around me made it clear that Sebastian felt passionately about the importance of the quest for knowledge. So other than the required conversations around lab assignments, I refrained from talking to him. Adolescence was hard enough already, I didn't need some stoic, pseudo-academic making me question my intelligence all the time.

Other memories of Sebastian included seeing him very clearly roll his eyes when I beat everyone in Mr. Rolland's Geography Jeopardy junior year. And him snickering when I shared that I was a quarter Puerto Rican during a presentation I had to give in Spanish class. I'll give that one to him. My Spanish accent was horrendous, providing much shame to my ancestors, according to my mother.

You'll never guess who I saw in my dorm

I texted Hunter after I sat down alone with my sad bowl of macaroni and cheese. I'd hoped comfort food would provide actual comfort, but I would argue the dish was only a step above boxed Kraft and three times as expensive.

The news of seeing Sebastian was significant enough to break my original rule of not initiating texts to Hunter (because I was committed to not being the needy ex-girlfriend). And also it was a good distraction from being one of the only people in the dining hall eating alone.

Russell Wilson

He responded within a few seconds.

Who?

Wow NM

Sebastian Torres

Huh weird I thought he went to Stanford.

I know! Why do you think he's here?

Idk. He probably wants to set the curve in all your classes. Drive you crazy.

More than you already are obvi

Did you meet your roommate yet?

Yeah. Briefly.

I stopped myself. I didn't want to get into the little amount of hope I had about that situation. For three years, I had been the pessimist in our relationship when it came to people. I wanted to try my hand at being an optimist. But after the afternoon I'd had of being dismissed first by Danica and then by Sebastian, I didn't have much in the well to pull from.

And?

I sighed. I guess the benefit of texting was Hunter couldn't see my face or hear my voice.

Haven't talked to her much. She went for a run when I moved in. I'm getting dinner rn.

There. A factual, non-emotional statement.

Let me know how it goes. I'll let you eat. Miss you.

Miss you too. Have a good night.

Darn it. That exchange was supposed to last longer than it did. Apparently, Sebastian being here wasn't nearly as interesting to Hunter as it was to me. Hunter did tell me that I was borderline obsessed with Sebastian when I declared beating him at that geography competition was the highlight of my year. (I think Hunter was slightly offended that his asking me to junior prom in front of the whole school didn't make the cut.)

But my interest in Sebastian's unexpected presence there had nothing to do with obsession. Just natural curiosity that anyone in my position would have...and slight concern that he may also end up in one of my classes.

I headed back to my room, trying hard not to notice that it seemed as though everyone but me was grouped up. In all my fantasizing about leaving everything and everyone from home behind, I never stopped to think just how lonely it would actually be.

"Hey!" a girl's voice called me out of my head before I got to my door. I looked up. She was standing in the door across the hall from my room. She was wearing ripped up jeans and a crop top. Her bright red hair stood out against her pale skin.

"Are you our neighbor?" She smiled, pointing at my door.

"Yeah, one of them. Hi, I'm Lucy," I smiled and held out my hand.

"Veronica," she introduced herself while shaking my hand. "You should come in and meet some of the other girls from the floor," she waved me in. "Hey, guys, this is Lucy from 734."

I stepped in to find five other girls casually sitting around the room. They all greeted me warmly.

"You just moved in, right? We've been waiting to see who would be our other neighbor," Veronica said. "This is my roommate, Hattie," she introduced a petite girl with black hair sitting across the room.

"Hi," I nodded to her wave.

"And this is Corine, Jenna, and Sophie—they're in the triple down at the other end of the hallway," Veronica shared as all three girls smiled.

I felt a nervousness in my stomach that always comes with meeting new people, but this was different than when I met Danica earlier. These girls gave off a vibe of friendliness and willingness to bond over the shared experience of being a freshman in the dorms, even if just momentarily.

"So where are you from?" Hattie asked.

"California." I held back from the city, because I doubted they knew any other cities besides LA, San Francisco, or San Diego.

"Oh cool," Corine spoke up. She gave off the same confident and friendly energy as Veronica "What part? I'm from Oakland."

"The Central Valley, Modesto." I waited to see if she was going to make fun of it, being that she was from a bigger city.

"Awesome, another NorCal girl," she held up her hand to high five, which I reciprocated.

The group humored me with some more get-to-know-you questions and before I knew it over an hour had passed. After the past two weeks, it was a relief to finally feel something other than lonely. Not wanting to overdo it my first time hanging out with them, I decided it was best to call it a night. My mom had wanted an update on how my move went anyway.

"Hey," Veronica stopped me as I went to make my exit, "a couple of us were going to head over to campus tomorrow to make sure we know where all our classes are for the first day. Wouldn't want to be the lost, wandering freshman, you know? You want to come?"

"Yeah, that'd be great." I refrained from showing how much relief and excitement I felt at the invitation.

"Okay, great, I think we'll probably head out about eleven. I'll come get you."

"K, I'll see you all tomorrow," I nodded and said my goodbyes calmly, but inside I was giddy.

I knew it was far from having made lifelong friendships, but I felt hopeful that I might still have the ability to make friends with people—I hadn't realized just how much of a crutch Hunter had become for me over the past three years.

Danica must have come back from her run and left again while I was down at dinner, because I went to bed without seeing her. It wasn't that I expected a welcoming party from her, but I thought she'd be a little more interested in getting to know me. Didn't it make sense to try and figure out if you were living with a crazy person as soon as possible?

Maybe it would work in my favor. I had never shared a room with someone, besides the dreaded remodel of my house that forced my sister and I together for six months. And given Ava's overall dramatic, bossy nature and obsession with K-Pop from an early age, I didn't rate the experience as something I particularly enjoyed.

Luckily, I managed to fall asleep before Danica came home—the whole concept of dormmates is kind of odd, isn't it? Here's a person you've never met, now sleep in the same room together—cross your fingers no one is weird. However, I would say based on our two-minute interaction, Danica seemed more of the aloof type than a strange type, so that was something to be thankful for...unless that meant she was a murderer...

I woke up to see Danica in her bed, back turned to me, still asleep. We were approaching twenty-four hours as roommates, and it was odd that I still had really no impression of her. Maybe later I would ask about the black and white photos she had up on her side of the room, and if she was into photography. I was never that great at initiating questions when it came to getting to know people, an area that Hunter very much shined in. It seemed like he could walk away from a first-time encounter with someone and have their whole life story in under twenty minutes.

I got up as quietly as I could and showered. Was it okay to hang out there if she was sleeping? Okay, clearly, I had to get over that reservation, otherwise it was going to be a long year. It was around ten thirty when Veronica knocked on the door, saving me from having to sit in my state of hypervigilance for another thirty minutes.

"We're all going downstairs to grab coffee before we head out," she announced. I stepped outside quickly so as not to disturb Danica. "Your roommate doesn't want to come?"

"She's still sleeping and I didn't get a chance to ask her about it before I went to bed," I shrugged, closing the door quietly. Jenna, Corine, Hattie, and Sophie joined us in the hall.

"Yeah, she hasn't seemed super interested in getting to know anyone on the floor," Corine shared. I refrained from saying anything else, but it was good to know it wasn't just me who had trouble getting a warm reception from Danica.

Once we got downstairs to the cafeteria, the line for coffee appeared overwhelmingly long, but thankfully the baristas moved through orders quickly. I was grateful I wasn't the only one who didn't drink my coffee black, otherwise I might have felt guilty for holding everyone up.

When we all finally had our various craft coffee orders in hand, we headed out, greeted by the wonderful feel of the northwest sun. I felt the cool breeze—a nice change from the one hundred and five degree heat of California's Central Valley.

We wandered around the massive campus and located the buildings of our various classes, unfortunately, but not surprisingly, finding that none of us had classes together. I gradually started to feel more relaxed around the group of girls as the day went on. They were so friendly and easy to be around in comparison to the high school clique I had defaulted to by dating Hunter.

Before I knew it, we were having dinner together at the dining hall across campus. Everyone was more interested in using their food card funds over having to use actual money at a real restaurant. However, it would likely only be a matter of time before we got sick of campus food.

"Aww, guys, Tony just texted," Sophie announced happily as we sat down with our meals. She looked down at her phone. "'Hope you have a great first day tomorrow. I know you'll do great.' That's so sweet." The table erupted in quiet sentimental agreement. "He's my boyfriend," she filled me in. "But we're doing the whole distance thing while he goes to University of Portland."

"What about you, Lucy? Do you have anyone special, or are you living the single life like the rest of us?" Veronica inquired.

"Currently single," I informed before taking a bite of my mediocre teriyaki.

"Currently? Does that mean you have plans not to be?" Jenna laughed.

"Oh, I just meant I had a boyfriend, but we decided it was best to break up because he's at UC Santa Barbara."

"How long y'all date?" Corine asked in between bites of her pizza.

"Three years."

"That's a long time for high school," she reflected with a shake of her head.

"So, what? Like three years and now it's just over?" Sophie asked in disbelief.

"Oh no, it's not like that," I tried to clarify, not wanting anyone to feel sorry for me. "We're still friends. We still talk. I mean, I miss him, but it's just like how you miss any of your friends from high school."

The group looked at me skeptically.

"You got a picture?" Veronica asked. "I've got a feeling that you're going to be talking more about this ex-boyfriend of three years who you don't miss, and I'm going to need a visual."

I pulled out my phone and opened Instagram, embarrassed when I realized that the entire grid was a shrine to Hunter and Lucy. There was no way that they were going to believe that breaking up with him wasn't a big deal, especially when they saw what Hunter looked like. I selected a picture from the last night we hung out together.

We were both dressed down in our college T-shirts hanging out in his family's pool house, which by senior year, his parents let him treat like his own apartment. That night we had pizza, wine, and binged The Real Housewives of New York—you know, exactly what you would expect of a high school couple on their last night together. I'd hoped the dim lighting and his post-swim hair would downplay how good-looking Hunter was.

It did not.

"Whoa," Veronica exclaimed. Before I could stop her, she started scrolling. Unfortunately, the next picture was taken by the pool earlier that day. And of course, Hunter was shirtless—what once felt like something I was proud to show off on social media was now a record of something people would think I had somehow lost. I reached for the phone, but wasn't quick enough before she handed it across the table to Corine.

"Damn," she responded coolly. "That's a good-looking white boy." She looked back up at me, giving the other three a chance to ogle. They all had similar reactions.

"You guys didn't even want to try to make long distance work?" Sophie handed back the phone, trying to wrap her brain around the situation.

I knew what it looked like on the surface—I had swung above my batting average and was getting left in the dust by him so he could chase tail in Santa Barbara. How could I explain it without outing him? I was pretty sure that was still against the rules, even if Hunter was over a thousand miles away and they were all strangers.

"Maybe it would've made more sense if we were only a few hours away from each other, but it just seemed like a lot to deal with, especially when we're both just trying to figure out how to be in college, you know?"

"Wow," Corine deadpanned. "I do not think I could be that mature about letting go of a guy I dated for three years. Especially with those abs," she joked. "I saw your prom pic in there. You guys were the king and queen, too?"

"Um, yeah," I confirmed sheepishly, holding back from explaining my dead dad as the likely reason for my short stint as teenage royalty.

"That's ridiculous," Veronica laughed.

"Yeah, it kind of is," I agreed.

"No, not in a bad way," she clarified. "I just think of the prom queen at my school who was a total bitch—and you seem so nice. I guess you're breaking down stereotypes."

"Well, give me time. I'm sure I'll change your mind about how nice I am if we see each other before my eight am class tomorrow."

The table laughed.

"You're funny," Corine commented. "I'm glad you didn't let Abs McGee persuade you to go to Santa Barbara."

"Me too," I agreed, surprised to realize that it was a genuine statement.

After taking advantage of the free soda refills, we headed back to Lander Hall. Everyone admitted that even after locating their classes, we all still had some first-day jitters for the next day. We set up the plan to get together for dinner again the following night and I exchanged numbers with all of the girls, only after Veronica pointed out that everyone needed my number now. I was grateful to have met someone so concerned about making everyone feel included. Taking initiative on friendship was never my strong suit.

I headed into my room to find Danica sitting on her bed, leaning up against the wall, scrolling through her phone. She had her hair down and looked more made over than my last encounter with her.

"Oh good, you're back," she sighed.

I raised an eyebrow, not expecting her to sound so relieved to see me. Especially since we hadn't spent more than five waking minutes together.

"So, here's the thing," she started as she got up from her bed. "I met this guy when I moved in last week. From the fifth floor, and like, totally hot. Like seriously," she paused, making eye contact to communicate the significance of the boy in question. "Anyway, we hooked up in his room last night. But tonight, he's going to come over here, like, soon."

She paused. I didn't say anything.

"So," she finally spoke again. "I'm going to need you to go."

I stared at her blankly for a moment as her words registered.

"So...you can hook up again..." I filled in.

"Yes." She smiled. "I'm so glad you get it." She sighed and ran her hand through her hair. "I was totally going to text you, but like, you never gave me your number." Her tone conveyed that this was my oversight. "So, what is it?"

"My number?" I was...befuddled...yep, that was the word, befuddled.

"Yeah, cuz if tonight is anything like last night, I'm pretty sure this is going to keep happening."

She grinned as she looked down at her phone, ready to put in my number.

"Um, 209...457...7899," I answered, unsure of what I was agreeing to.

"Great," she looked up with bright eyes. "I'll text you when we're done. Maybe. Last night, we passed out for like an hour afterwards," she shared, sounding proud, but also maybe annoyed? Never had I expected to be this confused by my college roommate.

"Also, for the future, since I'm not always the most reliable at texting, I think I'll just leave a scrunchy on the door knob." Danica walked over to the door and took the maroon scrunchy off her wrist and wrapped it around the door knob.

"Perfect," she declared proudly.

This had to be a joke. Surely, I didn't end up with the crappy roommate that dorm nightmares were made of. When Danica continued to stare at me expectantly, it solidified how little of a joke it all was to her. Fortunately for Danica, I hated conflict and I found myself obediently picking up my laptop and earbuds at a complete loss for words as I headed out the door.

"Thanks so much, Lucia," Danica called out as I stepped into the hall- way. She closed the door before I could correct her.

Too self-conscious to bother the girls I'd hung out with earlier that day, I decided to familiarize myself with the seventh-floor lounge. Pity was the last thing I wanted when it came to starting new friendships—I didn't want to be the sad girl, far from home, with the dead dad who got dumped by her hot high school boyfriend, who also had the crappy roommate who walked all over her.

What I wanted to be was the cool Californian who ended things with her boyfriend because she needed space for self-discovery and was abso- lutely not insecure when it came to being alone, and overflowing with so much confidence that she chose to hang out in the lounge by herself.

Yep. That was the story I was going to tell myself, along with the hope that Danica kicking me out of my own room would not happen as often as she alluded to. Even if her behavior the night before the first day of school did not give me much faith in her ability to make sensible and considerate choices in the long run.

The lounge appeared empty when I entered. There were a couple tables and chairs in one corner in what appeared to be a kitchen area with no refrigerator. In the center of the room were various sectional pieces and one couch surrounding a large flat screen TV mounted to the wall that was currently off. I quickly determined turning the tv on and watching anything alone would draw entirely too much attention to me should anyone else happen to walk in.

I plopped down on a sofa chair in the corner by the window that was meant to look comfortable, but was covered in industrial grade fabric and was anything but. Trying not to think too much about how many previous residents had puked or put some other bodily fluid on the chair, I turned on my laptop and quickly found I had no interest in watching anything. I settled on old episodes of Watch What Happens Live with my earbuds in. Again, the less attention I drew to myself the better...even if I was the only one there and no one was around to draw attention from.

While Andy Cohen's parade of random quasi-celebrity interviews provided background noise, I toggled back and forth between the internet and apps on my phone. How bizarre was it that for a moment I was actually missing the purpose that homework once gave me? By tomorrow night, I had no doubt that my life would once again be filled with "purpose," based on my quick look through the syllabus from my Intro to Bio class.

After I had made it through my sixth Andy Cohen interview, I let out a yawn and lifted my arms to stretch. Looking up across the lounge mid-stretch I realized I actually was not alone anymore.

I saw him.

Sebastian.

There he sat in the opposite corner of the room reading a book. How long had he been there? Had he met a similar fate with his roommate? Before I could look away, he looked up and caught me staring at him.

I wouldn't fall for it again. I was not going to say or do anything until he acknowledged me first. He didn't look away. He just stared back. Almost as if he was daring me to say something. A few seconds passed. He went back to reading, dismissing me again like a person he had never met before.

Shortly after our stare-down, out of the corner of my eye I saw him look down at his phone. He calmly got up, paused to straighten his zip-up hoodie, and then exited the lounge without a single gesture or word towards me.

I never thought I'd miss him furrowing his brow at me. Turns out being completely dismissed by someone was way worse than receiving a look of disapproval.

Chapter Five

As predicted, I did appreciate having classes and homework to fill my time. However, with only three hours of class a day, there was still so much extra time. I ended up joining Jenna and Veronica on daily runs in the afternoon. While I had been on the soccer team all four years of high school, I despised running just for the sake of running. It seemed so pointless without a ball and a goal. But now I was willing to take a slight interest in the hobby, just so I had something to do. Sometimes I filled my time with napping because I hadn't been allowed back into my room until after two in the morning due to Danica's continued hook-up shenanigans.

To be fair, it only happened about one to two times a week. It seemed to me like it was better to just weather the challenge than confront her and wind up with an unnecessarily tense living situation. Other than being kicked out of the room occasionally, I had no other big complaints about Danica. She kept her half of the room clean, always wore headphones, and had finally learned that my name was Lucy.

Inconsiderate roommate aside, my first round of midterms approached and stress began to pool up around my Biology and Calculus classes. I don't know exactly what I was going to do with an upper-level math and introductory biology credit, but at the time of enrollment I had convinced myself it would look good when it came time to declare a major. I failed to consider how it was going to potentially kill my GPA within my first quarter.

It didn't help that my usual calming strategy wasn't texting me as often anymore. Although Hunter wasn't entirely to blame for that. I hadn't initiated any conversations with him in at least two weeks.

While he may have been too busy to message me, he wasn't too busy to post pics of all his new friends on his Instagram. Our relationship had been reduced to just liking what one another posted. I hated to admit it, as pathetic as it sounded, but I longed to be hugged by him again. There was something so reassuring about him wrapping his arms around me when I got overwhelmed. I knew if I called him, he would make a point to listen and talk me down—but I didn't want to have to be the one that needed him.

"Come on, Lucy, you have to go out with us on Halloween," Veronica pleaded one Tuesday night when I had yet again been scrunchy-sentenced after dinner.

Halloween was that weekend and Veronica, Corine, and Jenna were adamant that we had to hit up the parties on frat row. Sophie, Hattie, and I had been more hesitant. Sophie's reason was because she was still dating Tony; Hattie's and mine was that we weren't into the whole college party scene. We had both avoided going to any frat parties that fall. Veronica and Corine felt that an exception needed to be made because of the holiday.

"So, wearing a costume somehow makes it more enjoyable to dance the night away with people puking around me?" I argued.

"I've been out at least five times and I've never seen anyone puke," Corine countered.

"I have a midterm this week and next week," I provided an additional excuse. Unfortunately, at that moment I was unable to study for my Calculus midterm that was only two days away, because I had stupidly left my stuff in my room before going to dinner.

"Exactly, haven't you ever heard of stress release?" Corine and Veronica were coordinating their flight attendant costumes, the sexy version of course. "You know we already talked Hattie into going."

"Hattie, I feel betrayed," I exclaimed, calling her out of her book.

"Sorry, I cave to peer pressure pretty easily," she admitted nonchalantly.

"I don't even have a costume."

"Buy some cat ears and wear a black dress, problem solved," Veronica said easily.

My reasoning would not be accepted.

"I bet Hunter is going out," she added for good measure.

"Yeah, maybe," I attempted to mirror Hattie's nonchalant tone.

"Come on, you don't want him to win the breakup."

"Honestly, I don't care. I just want to win the Calculus midterm."

I was envious that the other girls were smart enough to have signed up for Business Math, which was essentially basic algebra. Meanwhile I was struggling with matrices, integrals, and various other things I would have absolutely no use for in the future. Admittedly, it had originally fed my ego a bit when the academic counselor placed me in such an advanced math class. Now what little ego I had left wished I had spoken up instead of keeping my mouth shut.

Just then we heard a door across the hallway open. I let out an excited gasp, hopeful that my exile was over and I could actually study. I leaned out the doorway to see a boy heading out from my room. Veronica and Corine peered out with me.

"That was shorter than usual," Corine reflected.

"Maybe things are winding down," Veronica hypothesized.

"More than likely Danica knows the importance of needing to study for midterms, unlike you all. And even if it were winding down, I'm sure she'll have no trouble finding another guy. I mean, there are eleven other floors to choose from."

"Maybe she'll go for that one. I know I'm tempted." Corine nodded her head further down the hall. The boy she was referencing was Sebastian, who had just gone into his room.

"Who? Sebastian?" I scoffed in disbelief as I stepped back into Veronica and Hattie's room to grab my sweatshirt.

"Wait, you know him?" Corine clarified, sounding slightly surprised.

"Yeah, he went to my high school."

The level of interest in their eyes seemed unwarranted.

"You went to school with him and you're just telling us now?" Veronica exclaimed.

"This really doesn't seem like that big of a deal," I dismissed. This was Sebastian Torres we were talking about.

"So, I understand that you might be a little underwhelmed, given that your last boyfriend looks like a Gap model, but that boy is cute," Corine declared.

"Icgh," I reacted. "Maybe if you're into guys who constantly think they're smarter than everyone."

They looked at me like I was crazy.

"If you're looking for an introduction, don't look to me. For some odd reason, he has yet to acknowledge that he knows me. And he might still be with his girlfriend anyway."

"Sounds like you know quite a lot about him for someone you just happened to go to high school with," Veronica teased.

"We had a bunch of AP classes together. I had to be his lab partner in Chemistry one year. I only know about him and Amelia because they were so freakin' showy about it—she was the valedictorian and he was salutatorian. They did this whole rhyming skit during graduation. Only like ten percent of the people got the jokes."

I realized I'd ended up dumping even more information about him. Before I faced more questioning, I stepped out and headed to my room.

"If you're trying to get his attention, you might want to go with a profession that requires an advanced degree," I joked about their flight attendant costumes. "Have a good night."

Despite studying more than I ever had in my life, I did not feel confident about my Calculus midterm. My doubts about my performance were confirmed when I got my results back Thursday night. Sixty percent. I suppose I should've been pleased that I passed, but I had never received such a low score on anything before. It was aggravating, considering how much time I had devoted to studying for it. Was there even a point to putting the same amount of time in for my Biology midterm the following week?

The disappointment grew Friday night when I opened Instagram to see Hunter's post pop up first thing on my feed. There he was with a group of his new friends all dressed up as various superheroes from The Avengers.

Hunter was Captain America and there she was—some random girl, wearing a skintight Black Widow costume. Sure, there were other people in the photo, but I was fixated on whoever that red-headed rando was, leaning in, pushing her chest up against him—oblivious to the fact that he could care less about breasts.

Rationally, I knew jealously didn't make sense—Hunter was still gay and we were never really together—but I had fooled myself into thinking he wouldn't go off to Santa Barbara and keep dating girls. All he had talked about the whole summer was how the minute he got there he was going to act as if he had been out all along. I never bothered to ask him if he followed through on the plan. It wasn't because I was being self-centered in our conversations, I just didn't want to put pressure on him.

I stormed out of my room, frustration and jealousy bubbling up inside me. I pounded on Veronica's door. I held my phone up to her face when she answered.

"Guess I'm going out tomorrow."

She drew her face back, trying to see what I was shoving at her.

"Oh," she replied. "Well, don't be too upset, it's hard to resist a red-head," she consoled matter-of-factly.

My expression was still one of irritation.

"Come on, let's get your costume put together!" Her eyes lit up as she pulled me into her room.

Ultimately, I ended up going with the simple cat idea Veronica had presented earlier in the week. I must admit I did look rather cute in the black skirt and sweater I pieced together from Jenna and Corine. Although it was considerably shorter and tighter than anything I would normally wear.

My anger towards Hunter wasn't just about jealousy. It also had to do with the fact that he never agreed on wearing cute couple costumes when we were together. Last Halloween he'd gotten so jacked up and amused about being a banana that I'd conceded and had to be a monkey.

Do you have any idea how hard it is to find a cute monkey costume? He couldn't even understand why I was completely uninterested in getting a full-body ape costume like he suggested. And then I had to deal with all the blow job innuedos people made on social media regarding me eating Hunter's banana and of course all the whispers about how that was the only reason he was dating me. I realized all of that wasn't technically Hunter's fault, but it would've been one less thing to deal with if he would've just let us be something cute.

Now some girl he just met in Santa Barbara got to be a sexy Black Widow to his Captain America? It was completely unfair. As the memories and the current reality filled my brain, I was met with the urge to yell or throw something. A sensation that was unfortunately becoming more fre-quent in the past few months than I cared to admit.

If I thought this through correctly, all I really needed was a nice picture of me in the costume to post—there was no need to follow through with going to the party. Although, arguably, going to a frat party was something to check off a college experience checklist. Regardless, my expectations of having a good time were exceptionally low.

The allure of underage drinking had faded for me a while ago. (See Hunter's hopelessly "cool" dad and other parents who conveniently never locked up their liquor cabinets.) Also, I wasn't a huge fan of overly loud music and "dancing" when it was really just dry humping. Not that I had any experience with the second part. Unsurprisingly, it wasn't really Hunter's thing either, at least not with me.

"Don't worry, Lucy, all you have to do is give guys a bitch face and they'll leave you alone. They are all too scared to go for anything that seems like too much work," Jenna explained as we walked up to an opulent house.

The music was blasting to the point where I felt the reverberation in my chest. I braced myself for an entire night of screaming, "What?" when anyone said something to me.

My bitch face expression came quite naturally to me since no one bothered to come up to me within the first few minutes of our arrival. Hattie and I stayed back, while Veronica, Corine, and Jenna went in search of drinks. They resurfaced, red Solo cups in hand.

"Girl, you need this more than me," Corine handed over her cup. "You gotta whole uptight vibe going on right now."

I smirked at her and took a drink, making a face as I swallowed whatever punch it was that had too much Vodka...and maybe Tequila in it? Ugh, why would anyone mix those together?

"You think they have any wine?" I shouted jokingly. Corine shook her head at me. I sighed and took another drink. I thought, *Why not? Carpe diem, and all that crap.*

The answer of *why not* became evident shortly after my third cup of the mystery punch. There I was: enjoying dancing and my newfound state of carefree fun, forgetting to maintain a stony expression to ward off unwanted dance partners. Across the room, I locked eyes with a guy.

I had only been staring because I was trying to figure out what on earth his costume was supposed to be. He was in a tank top and had a bow tie on. It didn't make sense to me. He had taken my extended look as an invitation and came up to me. He leaned in and yelled hello in my ear and possibly something about liking my outfit. I yelled back thanks, which he took as the okay to start dancing with me.

It wasn't so bad. At first.

He was tall, not necessarily bad looking, and it had been a while since I had gotten any sort of male attention, so I wasn't quick to refuse it. My defenses were also down because of the drinking. It felt like my brain was moving in slow motion while things around me were happening faster.

Before I knew it, his hands were on my hips and he had pulled me in closer to his body, quickly followed by putting his mouth on mine, shoving his slobbery tongue down my throat. I pushed myself away, stumbling into Jenna and her dance partner.

The guy shook his head at me like I had done something wrong, said something I couldn't hear, and then walked off. I felt sick. Still having the taste of him in my mouth, I hurried up the stairs and out the door. The cool air hitting my face was a welcome change from that stuffy basement.

"Lucy, are you okay?" I was unaware that Corine had followed me out until that moment. "Are you going to be sick?"

"Nah," I answered back loudly and unnecessarily. "That MFer just shoved his tongue down my throat," I exclaimed, my enunciation confirming that I was very much drunk. I had misjudged the strength of the punch. Never having seen me drunk before, Corine tried to stifle a laugh.

"Did you just say MFer?"

"I try not to cuss. I wanna be a good role model for my sister," I explained. "She's fourteen." I sighed. "And also." I paused. "Very sweet."

I rubbed my sleeve over my mouth, hoping the taste of his tongue and that horrific punch would go away. "Yick."

Corine laughed at my dramatic expression. "Are you ready to go home?"

"Yeeeep," I emphasized with a swooping turn, heading toward the sidewalk.

It was a good thing Corine was with me. I had never been this far gone before and my chances of successfully navigating the walk home in the dark by myself seemed very low.

"Was this your first time drinking?"

"No, usually Hunter and I stick to wine. Which does not mess with you like that crap...Repunchnant." I started laughing, amused by myself. "Get it? Like repugnant?"

I kept laughing.

"Yeah, I got it." Corine did not sound like she thought I was clever.

"Corine. Corine, I'm so glad you're walking me home. I'm sorry you had to leave. I really did not mean for you to babysit me tonight. I don't. I don't normally do this."

I linked arms with her as we walked across Red Square.

"Ah, it's fine. I've had my share of nights being babysat back home. Guess it's time to pay it forward. I'm going to have to peace out if you start puking though," she warned.

"Shit, it's cold!" I yelled, shaking off a shiver, realizing it had been stupid to think that the nylon thigh high socks I had borrowed from Veronica were going to provide any sort of shield from the fall Seattle night air.

"Shit, I cussed. Don't tell my sister. But Jesus, I should've worn pants!"

"It's all right, Valley Girl, we're almost there."

"You know that's the wrong valley."

I saw Corine's grin and knew she was messing with me. We had had conversations about how clueless the people around us were about the differences between Northern California and Southern California.

"Oh, thank God, we're inside!" I exclaimed the minute we stepped into the lobby of Lander Hall.

"Shhh," Corine coached, not wanting me to get written up for being drunk. Trying to be quiet only led to me start snickering as we stepped into the elevator.

"Okay, we're almost to our floor. Can you do this?"

I nodded. "Ima be as quiet as a cat," I tried to say in my best resolute tone. Corine raised an eyebrow at me. "Meeeeoowww." My self-amusement continued as the elevator stopped.

Corine shook her head, leading me out by the hand. We started down the hallway.

"Okay," Corine stopped at her door. "Are you good getting back into your room? You have your key?"

"Hid it in my shoe," I announced. "Like a boss!" I swung my arm down proudly to provide flourish to my statement.

"Okay then, Boss, you have a good night. I'll see you tomorrow. Make sure you drink some water." She opened her door as I started taking steps backward.

"Happy Halloween. Safe travels!" I referenced her flight attendant costume.

As I trekked down the hallway, I noticed that Sebastian's door was open as I passed it. Then as I got closer to my own door, I saw that stupid scrunchy on the door knob.

Again.

I halted in the hallway, my shoulders slouched and I let out an exasperated sigh, maybe Corine and Sophie wouldn't mind if I slept in their room until Jenna got back. I turned and started my way back down the hallway, walking more crookedly than I would've liked.

The moment I walked by Sebastian's room, I happened to see him walking towards his door. We once again made eye contact, and he again provided no verbal or physical response. I took two steps and then felt the alcohol trigger my impulses.

"You know, what? No," I proclaimed loudly, turning back around to his door, which he had not yet closed all the way. "This is absolutely ridiculous!"

Sebastian stood frozen in the entryway, staring at me.

I went off.

"What is your problem? What on earth did I ever do to you that would make you refuse to even say hi to me? What? Do people have to have a certain SAT score to be worthy of common human decency from you? Well excuse me for not making it into the coveted 1500 and above crowd."

I tried my hardest not to sound like a rambling drunk, but I know I slurred the word 'excuse' and I was uncharacteristically bobbing my head.

"You don't have to be so snobby about everything. You would think the fact that we are the only two here from home would earn me the occasional smile or head nod, but nooooooo—"

Just as I was on the brink of dredging up past offenses committed by him, Sebastian pulled me into his room unexpectedly...where I then, also unexpectedly, spent the rest of the night.

Chapter Six

My eyes opened slowly, revealing a wall that was not my own. The events of the night slowly pieced together in my memory, not quite distracting enough to pull attention from the pressure pulsating in my head. Still in my black-on-black Halloween outfit, I slowly sat up with a groan. The sunlight on my face was extra obnoxious. I started to rub my forehead.

"Good morning, Sunshine." I looked over to see Sebastian sitting at his desk reading a book, looking smug as ever in an old high school engineering club shirt. He had on his glasses, which I had not seen him wear since sophomore year. I hadn't blacked out, but it was a little fuzzy how I had ended up in his room...and in his bed.

"I'm sorry," I paused, now I was the one furrowing my brow at him. "I remember coming here and telling you off, but how exactly..."

"I pulled you in because the RA on rounds was coming down the hall. I didn't want you to get written up for being so obviously drunk."

This surprised me. He'd actually done something nice for me?

"Had I known you were going to come in here and vomit, cry, and pass out I probably would've chosen differently."

And there was the Sebastian that I knew.

"Ugh, I did throw up," I remembered with disappointment. "But you didn't have to—"

"Clean it up? No, you're remembering that part right." He turned a page, not even bothering to look up from his book at me.

"I'm sorry. I only had three drinks, but I have no idea what was in that punch. I've never been this hungover before." All my joints ached as my head pounded.

"Shocking. I would've thought you'd have quite the hollow leg by now with all the time spent with Hunter Davis and the other future community college drop-outs."

He continued to stare into his book. I didn't have the energy to correct him about his assumption.

"You're lucky you decided to harass me instead of another guy more into..." he paused, finally looking up at me and lifting his hand in a circular motion, "that whole situation."

I tilted my head and glared at him.

"Yes, you're quite the hero for not sexually assaulting me. Someone should give you a medal."

I hopped down from the bed. Looking around for my shoes and room key.

"They're over on the windowsill." He went back to looking at his book. "Along with your room key, which only someone 'devastatingly brilliant' would've thought to hide in their shoe."

I grimaced as he reminded me about the stupid gloating I'd done regarding stowing my key without having a purse.

"I mean, it's true, not since the Hide-A-Key Rock have we seen such American ingenuity."

I decided to ignore him as I slipped my shoes on and grabbed my key. There was no recovery from this situation.

"Well, please extend my apologies to your roommate."

"No need to. Warren is from here. He goes home every weekend."

"Okay, well, sorry again for the puking and the crying."

I walked to his door.

"And the passing out," he added.

"Yeah, anyway, despite what you may think, I don't really have a habit of doing this, but...thank you," I half-mumbled.

"You're welcome." I opened the door and started to step out. "By the way," he stopped me. "I can help you with your Calc if you really need it."

I knew I cried about that stupid class!

"K, thanks."

"No problem, we in the 1500 and above crowd like to take on some charity from time to time."

And I had met my quota of talking to Sebastian for the day, possibly the whole quarter.

Sentenced to feeling shitty for the rest of the day, I showered and then proceeded to lay in bed with my computer. Studying for Bio could wait until Sunday. I answered texts from the girls letting them know I was fine, but not in the mood to eat anything.

By late afternoon my phone rang. It was Hunter. Being that I hadn't gotten an actual phone call from him in some time, I made a point to pick up.

"Hello?"

"Hi, Luce," he greeted with his usual peppy tone. "So, strangest thing," he started. "Last night I got a voicemail from a 206 number. Lots of music in the background, and an incredibly shrill voice shouting about how I would someday regret not staying with her hot ass when I died alone without any hair? I think the crazy person also said something about Captain America being the worst, least sexy Avenger."

Groaning was now my number one form of communication.

"Which you and I both know is false. Captain America is, in fact, the hottest Avenger. So, this drunken insane person calling me from someone else's phone, it couldn't possibly have been you. Right, Lucy?"

After my second drink, Veronica got me all hyped up about not having closure with Hunter. She emphatically and very convincingly encouraged me that it was something I needed. Right at that moment.

Unfortunately, Hunter's phone number was one of the four I had memorized besides my own. When I was remembering my night earlier, I hoped that I had misdialed the number and it had ended up on a stranger's voicemail instead. That would have been less embarrassing.

"I'm sorry," I offered meekly.

"What brought all that on, Luce?" He laughed coolly.

"I don't know," I sighed.

"Yes, you do," he challenged.

"Fine, we haven't been talking that much, and I saw your stupid Halloween picture with that girl shoving her boobs into you and I got jealous."

"Jealous of what? You think I suddenly started liking girls down here?"

"No...I just thought maybe you're still pretending to like girls, and..."

"Oh, I see. You don't want anyone else to be my cover."

I didn't confirm or deny the statement.

"Well, you don't have to worry about that. I mean, I'm friends with her, but I...I actually did it, Luce, I'm out down here." He sounded so proud when he said it.

"That's great. I'm really happy for you."

Which was the truth. I was happy. But there was another feeling, too. Not necessarily jealousy anymore. Maybe sadness? Or even frustration? There were all these people down in Santa Barbara who now knew something about Hunter that, for so long, I was the only other person he had told.

Suddenly our friendship didn't feel so special. It was like he was finally getting to live his dream life and I was stuck in the past, delusional about some random redhead he took a picture with and he probably could care less about who I was hanging out with at school.

"That was the other reason why I wanted to call, besides making fun of you for drunk dialing me from someone else's phone," he poked. "You saw the dude in the pic dressed up as Black Panther, right?"

"Hang on," I paused my resentment for a moment and pulled my phone away to open the app. "Let me pull it up."

I found the group pictures, suddenly paying more attention to the other people present in the pic—realizing there was one girl, surrounded by five guys. It became clearer that more than likely, the mystery girl was surrounded by gay guys. Black Panther was standing right behind Hunter, unmasked and quite handsome. He had large brown eyes and dark skin with a similar build to Hunter.

"Yeah, I see him," I put the phone back up to my ear.

"Well, his name is Justin, and I totally made out with him last night," he gushed proudly.

"What? Shut up." I felt genuine excitement for him and found myself smiling for the first time that day.

"Yeah. It was awesome," he laughed.

I spent the next hour catching up with him on everything going on in his life. Classes, new people, Justin being ONLY a friend.

I did my best to reciprocate the same level of contentment, but inside I knew I was faking it. While I had made a couple of good friends, I was not by any means "winning the break up" as Veronica had termed it.

I was struggling through two of my classes, had an inconsiderate roommate, and completely embarrassed myself by drinking too much last night. Worst of all, I had wasted my first real kiss from a straight guy on an unnamed frat boy with too much saliva.

It was in the middle of Hunter's detailed account about his workout regimen that I realized that our differing realities made me more irritated than sad. It wasn't fair. I was just as deserving as him to be living my best college life.

Thankfully before I got too entrenched in my stupid feelings, Hunter started asking me about the party I went to, making a point to compliment how good I looked in the pictures that were posted. I made a point to recount the version of the night where I had the best time and definitely did not pass out in Sebastian Torres' room after crying about my Calculus grade.

Chapter Seven

After pretty much failing that Calculus midterm, I decided it was in my best interest to study at the library. While it was positive that I had become friends with the group of girls on my floor, I had shown myself to have very poor boundaries around studying when socializing was so readily available.

The lounge had proven unideal because it had become the hangout for a group of gamers. Calculating derivatives and integrals was only made harder when guys were routinely shouting out how "wicked sick" their KDR was about to get.

Although Odegaard Library was quieter, it didn't seem to help me much with understanding my homework. After staring at the same problem for ten minutes...and looking through useless notes for fifteen...I resorted to people watching.

It was just as helpful to my academic success. I was in the process of hoping that the hot boy a couple tables over would look up and make eye contact with me, when I noticed Sebastian was sitting two tables behind him.

There was another quiz coming up on Friday that I really wanted to pass. He did say he would help me if I wanted him to. Would he remember offering? Of course he would. It was a moment highlighting his intellectual superiority.

Just as it had happened that one night in the lounge, Sebastian looked up and caught me staring at him. This time I looked away, still debating whether I was willing to ask for his help. My overall current class standing of sixty-five percent flashed through my mind. When I looked back up, he was no longer at his table.

"Are you going to ask me for help, or just keep staring at me like a stalker?" he asked quietly as he put his backpack down while sitting down next to me. Whispering didn't hide his curtness.

"You're assuming I need help."

He looked down at my homework.

"No, your answers to one and two are confirming you need help."

I glared at him but he didn't bother looking up at me. "Where are your notes?"

I handed my notebook over to him. He started scanning the pages. "Your notes aren't even right." There was that furrowed brow.

"I take the notes in lecture and then when I go to the quiz section people start asking questions and the TA starts explaining things and it seems to be completely different from the lecture," I justified, trying my hardest not to sound like I was whining.

Sebastian sighed. "There's no way I'm going to be able to explain all of this while whispering."

He handed the notebook back to me. He stood up and put his backpack on. Well, he'd given up on me rather quickly.

"What're you doing?" he crossly asked me. "Grab your stuff. We'll go over it back at Lander."

While I didn't appreciate his commands, that sixty-five percent flashed larger in my head. I started packing up my things, but made a point not to move with the haste he was expecting of me. I guess there was just something about Sebastian Torres that made me want to be a dick back to him... even when he was helping me.

The walk back to the dorm was interesting—given that he didn't say a single word to me the whole time. I assumed we'd worked our way up to at least making small talk when walking together. Sebastian's brisk walk and stony face communicated otherwise. Since his legs were longer than mine, my focus was entirely devoted to trying to keep up.

Sebastian selected an open table in the seventh-floor lounge—thankfully the gamers had not made their appearance yet. I got out my textbook, notebook, and calculator, and prepared myself for a night of him being irritated with me. He didn't seem to have much patience for lost causes.

"Okay, so they're asking you to take the derivative of $\sin(x^2)$," he started to go over the first problem, writing in my notebook. "Because it's two functions, you have to use the chain rule. Since sine is the outer function, start there. The derivative of sine would be…" he paused, expecting me to answer.

"Cosine," I said tentatively, even though I knew I was right.

"Yes, so now it's $\cos(x^2)$. Now you get to the x^2, the derivative of that is $2x$. Again, use the chain rule and you would get $\cos(x^2)$ times $2x$ as the derivative of $\sin(x^2)$. Okay, your turn, do number two. Hint, use the chain rule again," he said flatly.

I put my pencil to the paper, trying not to be nervous while he looked at me.

"Tell me what you're doing."

"I'm doing the problem like you told me to," I responded, not hiding my irritation.

"No, tell me the steps you're doing while you're doing it. If I know what you're thinking, it's easier for me to tell you what you're doing wrong."

"Fantastic, just how I wanted to spend Tuesday night."

"I'm sorry, would you prefer me to give out gold stars just for trying your best? Last I checked, the university has higher standards for passing people than Mrs. Finley did. Or we could ask your professor if he, too, gives out extra credit for math-inspired art projects?"

I pursed my lips.

"You weren't even in that class with me."

"Yeah, 'cause I took it sophomore year. But I can speak with confidence when I say that there was nothing in that curriculum that helped anyone pass the AP test. Case in point." He waved his hand at me.

I ignored him, because I knew he was right. I hadn't bothered to take the Calculus AP test because I'd known I had no shot at passing it. Even if that Taylor Swift parody song Hunter and I made about Taylor polynomials turned my B into an A—and was obviously brilliant—it was of no use to me now.

"The derivative of $\cos(x^4)$. Split it into two functions...first the derivative of cosine is negative sine. Then the derivative of x^4 is..." I stopped, unsure of the next thing I should do.

"Power rule. Move the four in front of x, since there is no number there, you multiply it by one, which is..."

"Four," I rolled my eyes because Sebastian actually paused for me to answer that.

"It's important to remember that you don't just move the number in front, because if they were to give you $2x^4$, you would multiply four by two, and it would be eight in front of the x.

"Anyway, back to this problem and the power rule. So, after you move the four in front you subtract one from the exponent, making it three now. So, the derivative of that is $4x^3$."

"Okay, so the answer is $-\sin(4x^3)$." I said confidently.

"Nope." My shoulders sank. "Chain rule." He wrote out a sample equation with f and g and x and a lot of parentheses. It looked familiar, but still confusing.

"You're forgetting that the x^4 stays with cosine when you're finding its derivative. So, it would be $-\sin(x^4)$ not just -sin. And then, you always, always, multiply the two functions. You just have to put as much energy into remembering these rules as you did with knowing all the ports in Spain and Portugal."

He DID remember me beating him at Geography Jeopardy. From what I knew of Sebastian that was probably the closest thing I would ever get from him that resembled a compliment.

"Okay, on to number three," he announced before I could gloat.

It took over an hour to get through the ten assigned problems. Sebastian managed to keep his condescension in check and I had to admit the brain fog surrounding Calculus was starting to dissipate.

"Thank you, Sebastian," I said sincerely while gathering my things.

"You're welcome." He stood up, grabbing his backpack. He began to walk away.

"Wait," I stopped him. "Would you be willing to meet with me Thursday night? I have a quiz Friday and I've failed the last two," I admitted sheepishly.

"Um, yeah, that should be fine. You sure you don't have a party to go and get drunk at?"

"Now why would I do that when I can hang out with you and get drunk on knowledge?" I responded flatly.

He raised his brow slightly at me, which for Sebastian was almost as good as a half-smile.

"Okay, I'll see you here at eight o'clock." He turned and walked away before I confirmed.

Corine sat with me in the lounge Thursday night. She had been keeping me company after dinner. Unsurprisingly, I had come back to find a scrunchy on my doorknob. Neither of us were doing our best focusing on our respective homework assignments.

"So, do you think the color of scrunchy matters?" she pondered aloud while pulling up her long dark hair into a ponytail.

"What do you mean?" I laughed.

"Like, I noticed it was a pink one for a while. But lately she's switched to black. Once there was a blue one. I'm wondering if it's a code of some kind."

"If it's a code, she hasn't shared it with me."

"What if it's a different guy for each color? To make sure you don't mess up names. Keep them a secret from one another."

"I've never met the guy, or guys. I only saw the backside of the guy that one time when we were in Veronica and Hattie's room and he was leaving. You seem to have the impression that Danica actually talks to me."

"You're not the least bit interested in knowing?"

I shrugged.

"I figure if she wanted me to know, she would tell me."

I was never one to gather gossip in real life. My rationale had been that avoiding it altogether was the best way to protect Hunter. If I asked too many questions about other people, it would naturally lead to other people asking questions about us.

Corine shook her head at me. "Do you have to be so disgustingly mature?"

Sebastian walked up to the table. Right on time. Corine looked at me with surprise when he put his backpack down.

"Did you find someone else who needs help with math?" he referenced Corine before sitting down.

"No, Corine was just getting some other work done. Corine, this is Sebastian. Sebastian, Corine," I introduced. Corine reached out and shook his hand.

"Nice to meet you," she smiled brightly.

"Corine lives in 723 and is from Oakland."

I thought Sebastian might enjoy hearing that there was another Californian on the floor. He nodded, but instead of seeming interested, he went to pull something out of his backpack. He turned back around and placed my cat ears from Halloween on the table.

"You left these in my bed. I've been meaning to get them back to you."

Corine's eyes lit up and the corners of her mouth started to turn, excited to have finally been fed the gossip she had been craving. Unwarranted gossip. But I knew what the situation looked like.

"Um, yeah," I scrambled for the ears, trying to get them out of sight and mind as quickly as I could, but knew I could not make Corine unhear what was just said.

"Okay," Corine announced with a smile. "I'm just gonna pack up my things, and give you two a chance—"

"To study," I filled in firmly. "He's helping me study for my Calculus quiz."

She nodded, but her expression only displayed doubt. Sebastian continued to sit, settling himself in, looking at my textbook, completely unaware of the drama he had triggered.

"When you're done, Lucy, make sure you come by my room and uh, tell me more about the thing, you know, that thing we were talking about?"

By this point, she was standing behind Sebastian walking backwards mouthing the words "so cute" with a silent scream. We hadn't reached the point in friendship where we could communicate with eye contact, but if we had, I would've been telling her to shut up.

"Okay, so, where should we start?" Sebastian asked, both hypothetically and cluelessly.

How about the part where he inadvertently alluded to me sleeping with him? I bit my tongue and let him determine that reviewing the chain rule was the best place to start.

The study session was not as painful as the previous one. For as many character flaws as he had, Sebastian did explain Calculus in a way my brain could grasp for longer periods of time. Not that I was anywhere near feeling like I was going to ace tomorrow's quiz, but I had a little more confidence that I would at least pass.

"Can I ask you something?" he asked once we had wrapped up for the night.

I looked up at him as I closed my notebook.

"Why are you even taking Calculus? I didn't figure you for the engineering type."

I sighed. "Well, when I talked with the academic counselor, I said something about being interested in environmental law once I got into law school and then she got so excited, it somehow turned into me working towards an Oceanography major, hence the Calculus and the Bio for this quarter."

"Do you want to be an Oceanography major?"

I shrugged again.

"Did I mention the lady got excited? It was like her third week on the job and I could tell she really wanted to be helpful."

"So, by not correcting her, you let her be the complete opposite of helpful?" he clarified.

"Well, she'll never know that," I muttered.

"Are you seriously telling me that you'd rather let your GPA suffer than tell someone they're wrong?"

"At the time I didn't know my GPA was going to suffer. I guess I figured since I had taken Calculus last year it was going to be more like a review."

"Really?" Sebastian laughed in disbelief. "You really thought Mrs. Finley's Calculus class would be on par with one taught here? You do know this isn't Modesto Junior College, don't you?"

I felt like I was back in Chemistry class with him critiquing every little conclusion I made for one of our labs. He always demanded I share my reasoning and it was never well thought out enough for him. His brow looked like it was starting to furrow, which apparently pulled some sort of trigger in me now.

"Look, Sebastian, I don't know. Half the time I don't even know why I'm here other than trying to fulfill a dream of my dead dad's to eventually become a lawyer at his old school. Not everyone has every second of their academic life planned out. Some of us are just trying to get through the day," I snapped, momentarily surprised at my tone. Normally I was so skilled at keeping any and all irritation I had with people under lock and key.

"You do know UW Law is one of the harder law schools to get into, right?" he asked, completely missing the context of what I just confided.

"And then there's academic inbreeding that you have to worry about now, too," he went on. "If your intention was to go to UW Law, you would've been better off going somewhere else for undergrad. Really, Lucy, they don't just let people in because they were prom queen."

"Thank you for all your advice, Sebastian, priceless and tactless as ever." Admittedly I got a little bit of a high from being so blunt with him.

"I'm only trying to help. But, like actually help, unlike that crappy academic counselor you let mess up your schedule."

"What are you even doing here?" I finally exclaimed. "Aren't you supposed to be off at Stanford endearing your annoying self to Amelia?"

"I was waitlisted at Stanford and ended up not getting in," he admitted quietly, briefly looking away.

Great. Now I felt bad.

"But, you..."

"Made everyone think I was going to Stanford? Yeah, I know. Because I thought I was." He shrugged, trying his best to sound nonchalant. "Anyway, that's why I'm here. You and your GPA can thank me later." He smirked, quite pleased with himself.

"Have a good night, Sebastian," I sighed, making my exit.

I knew he was right that UW Law School wasn't going to just fall into my lap. Originally, I had been totally fine with that reality; then my dad died. Now an unfamiliar sense of duty overwhelmed me. Of course, I knew getting in wouldn't bring him back, but at least I would know without any doubt he'd be proud of me.

Chapter Eight

Tolerating Sebastian's snark had paid off. I ended up getting an eighty percent on the quiz. Corine made sure to tell the other four girls about my embarrassing drunken post-Halloween escapade where I ended up in Sebastian's room. They all quickly concluded that I had a subconscious crush on him. I countered that Corine was an unreliable storyteller—not that anyone listened.

My analysis of the situation was that they were alleviating midterm stress by creating some sort of drama to entertain themselves. It didn't help that they took Sebastian's new willingness to acknowledge and help me as an invitation for them to start talking to him. I hoped this would lead to them seeing how unappealing he was as a person.

It did not.

"Sebastian said the most interesting thing yesterday," Veronica casually brought up at dinner. "I was studying for my Archaeology class, and he told me that the Mayans used to drill holes in their teeth and inlay jade and turquoise in them. It's like they invented the grill. Did you know that?"

"Why would I know that?" I asked in a more pointed tone than I probably should have. But did Sebastian's annoying attempts at charm really have to be brought into our dinner conversation?

"Thought maybe he'd told you about it too," she said simply.

"Sorry, I guess he saves all of his Meso-American ancient civilization fun facts for those he really likes."

"Don't you think it's crazy that he knew that off the top of his head? He's not even taking the class. It's insane how much he just knows, you know?"

"Oh, believe me, that's not something that just happens. He's devoted his whole life to ensuring he'll always be the smartest person in the room. And making sure everyone knows it, too. It doesn't make him interesting. It makes him an ass."

"Mmm, someone's feeling feisty on a Tuesday," Corine joked.

"How does being intelligent make someone an ass?" Veronica laughed.

"It's not the being intelligent part. It's the being smug about it. It's him thinking that little Mayan fact is somehow superior because he read some boring history book compared to learning on the Today Show how many lights they put on the Rockefeller Christmas tree. By the way, it's fifty thousand."

Corine and Veronica exchanged a knowing look and began to smile.

"You don't seem to mind his smarts when it comes to helping you with your math."

"Calculus is completely different. Don't get me wrong, Sebastian totally thinks understanding how to do Calculus makes him smarter than me. That's nothing new. But him explaining how to do it is not the showing off I'm talking about. He knows he can't wow a crowd with talk of derivatives and integrals. But if he catches any of you with any classic literature, I guarantee he's going to launch into some BS discussion points about how Shakespeare could be viewed as a feminist for the time. I'm honestly shocked that he's yet to conveniently drop into a conversation with you that he knows how to play the trumpet, guitar, and piano," I shared with annoyance.

"Sounds like someone's spent a lot of time thinking about someone else," Veronica teased in a sing-song voice.

"It's understandable. That happens a lot after you spend the night with someone,"

Corine grinned widely at her jab.

I rolled my eyes. She knew nothing happened that night, but it didn't keep her from making it sound like it was all more salacious than it was.

"I'm curious, what does Hunter think about your new tutor?" Veronica asked airily.

"Nothing. There's nothing to think about."

"Does that mean you haven't told him?" she prodded.

"There's nothing to tell," I scoffed.

"Oh, so you won't mind if I text him about it right now?" Veronica pulled out her phone.

I raised a brow at her.

"Yeah, remember when you called him from my phone on Halloween? We text occasionally now. He's super friendly," she remarked pleasantly.

This did not surprise me at all. Hunter might as well have had that Yeats quote about strangers being friends tattooed on his forehead.

"We also follow each other on Insta now," she winked. "Any thoughts on Sebastian tutoring Lucy in Calculus?" she said as she texted.

I tried to look unaffected. Hunter's response came almost immediately. Veronica chuckled.

"'Hopefully they don't kill each other,'" she read to the table. Her phone chimed again.

"'Don't tell me, she's obsessing over him again?'"

Corine and Veronica's eyes widened. My mouth dropped open in offense.

"Hmm interesting," she reflected playfully.

I impulsively pulled out my phone and texted Hunter.

What's that supposed to mean?!

"So where do you think the obsession comes from?" Veronica spoke her message as she typed again.

There was a pause. I was dreading what his possible response would be.

"'I don't know, beats me.'" Veronica read.

Another ding.

"'If you figure it out let me know. Maybe I should've tried to be better at math.' And a winky face!" she exclaimed. "Lucy, is he still into you?"

"No, he's just being funny," I deflected.

I understood her confusion. Hunter had yet to come out over social media. For now, it was only me and his friends at Santa Barbara who knew the truth. I guess our charade was still going on, at least partially. More than likely, Hunter knew I was irritated and was trying to make up for saying I was obsessive when it came to Sebastian.

Maybe I should've feigned interest in being hung up on Hunter still? Then they would've all shut up about Sebastian. However, since Halloween, I was beginning to like my newfound status as a single person. Despite their unexplainable interest in my non-existent love life, I had a sense of pride that I was able to become friends with these girls outside of the honored title of "Hunter's girlfriend."

Now if I could just get them to stop teasing me about Sebastian. Perhaps I could play matchmaker? It seemed that both Corine and Veronica were more than interested in being on the receiving end of his pompous tales of scholarly wisdom.

Then again, I didn't know if he was still dating Amelia. Finding out this information would require having a conversation with him about something other than math. Just as I was weighing the pros and cons of this plan in my head, Veronica's phone went off again.

"'Tell Luce she should come home for Thanksgiving,'" she read aloud. She turned and raised a brow. "That boy is missing you," Veronica sing-songed.

I sighed. A week ago, Hunter had messaged me something about how he couldn't wait to see me over break. I wasn't very committed in my response, but hinted that I wasn't sure I was coming home. The truth was that I was absolutely sure I was not going home.

Not only was it expensive to fly home that weekend, I also wanted to avoid the first major holiday without my dad at all costs. I couldn't avoid Christmas, so why torture myself with Thanksgiving if I didn't have to?

"He's just an only child and doesn't want to be bored," I responded nonchalantly.

"And how exactly is he accustomed to being entertained by you?" Corine nudged me. I shook my head.

"You know you are both ridiculous? At what point do we get to talk about who you all dated or are supposedly obsessed with?"

"The minute you start acting less flustered," Corine explained simply. "It's hella entertaining." She smiled good-naturedly. "By the way, if you're not going home for Thanksgiving, what are you going to do?"

"I don't know, maybe Danica will want to take me home and introduce me to her family. We are best friends now, after all," I sighed and they laughed. I was relieved to have distracted everyone from the subject of Sebastian.

In order to avoid further teasing, I committed to only get Calculus help from the TA. But after leaving my second visit to office hours and feeling more confused than when I entered, I found I had no choice but to go to Sebastian for help again the afternoon before another quiz.

I peered out in the hallway, first confirming that Veronica and Hattie's door was closed. I began my cautious walk down the hall, ready to abandon it immediately if I caught sight of Corine. Sophie and Jenna didn't seem nearly as invested in the razzing, but more than likely I'd ditch my plan if I saw them as well. Yes, this was all very elementary school. To my relief, the hallway remained empty while I made my way to Sebastian's door.

I knocked and waited. No answer. I looked down the hallway, making sure the coast was still clear before returning to my room. At that moment, Sebastian turned the corner. He was soaking wet and in athletic clothes.

"Did you just go running?" I asked in disbelief.

"Yeah," he said unaffected as he approached.

"It's pouring outside."

"Oh. Wow, really?" he said flatly.

He pulled his key out of his pocket and went to unlock the door.

"I thought about stowing it in my shoe, but I figured that only made sense when dressed like a slutty cat." Sebastian pointedly locked eyes with me as he opened the door.

Left without a clever retort, I glared. He walked past me.

"Did you need help with something?" He gestured at my laptop I was holding.

"Um, yeah," I stepped inside his room and pulled up the practice problem I was having a hard time with. "So, it's asking for the integral of this one. I split it and did the summation rule. But now the second term doesn't converge."

I looked over and was surprised to see him peeling off his shirt. My brain started flashing.

Sebastian has a six pack. Sebastian Torres has a six pack. Shut up. Shut up. Get your eyes back on the screen.

Thankfully, I successfully moved my attention back to the laptop before there could be any interpretation of my reaction. He stepped forward as he was rubbing his neck with his shirt. My brain was firing again.

Sebastian is shirtless. No shirt. Naked chest. Six pack. Biceps. Shit.

My shoulder and arm muscles tensed. I couldn't bring myself to look at him. He took the computer from my hands and placed it on his lofted bed, examining the problem closer. I made a diligent effort to stare at the screen and not his shoulders that I suddenly appreciated the broadness of.

He let out a sigh and shook his head. Maybe he caught my three second stare and I was about to get scolded for checking him out?

"I hate it when they do stuff like this. The solution to the original integral is that it does not converge because of the second term, which is pretty straightforward, if you were actually taking Math 126. I don't know why they're giving you something like this as a practice problem when it has polar coordinates."

In my head I was shouting, *"Keep your eyes on his eyes. Do. Not. Stare at his chest! Math! Numbers! Converge! Converge!"*

"And they're being all cute about it, which is annoying. Anyway, let me shower and then I'll come by your room and show you, even though you will literally have no use for it in Math 124." He handed the laptop back to me.

Dumbfounded by the new information that Sebastian thought a math problem was annoying and that he had a runner's body, I could only bring myself to nod.

"You okay?" He raised his brow.

"Oh yeah, just you know...math, man," I awkwardly mumbled as I backed out of his room, earning myself a furrowed brow from him before I turned and hustled away.

I managed to continue to string along a steady pattern of low Bs and high Cs with my Calculus assignments. My sixty-five percent made its way to a seventy-nine percent. I had never been prouder of a C plus. If I could keep my momentum up for the second midterm and the final, there was potential that I could get out of the course with a final grade of a B, thanks to all the homework points.

Luckily, Sebastian had given me his phone number, so I was now able to be more inconspicuous about getting together with him. We set up a midday meeting in the student union building twice a week. It worked well because it was right after my Calculus lecture, when all my misunderstandings were at their highest. Sebastian even gave me the slightest bit of encouragement by stating I was not entirely hopeless after seeing a homework assignment I had completed all by myself.

Yes, it was silly to be hiding the tutoring. But after seeing Sebastian shirtless, I knew my cheeks would turn red if my friends started teasing me again. Ever since that encounter, I'd found myself noticing other features one could consider attractive if one were to evaluate Sebastian in that way.

For example, his dark brown eyes...and maybe, maybe, those brows he always furrowed at me, had a nice shape to them. This was only when he wasn't arrogantly evaluating my intelligence, which didn't feel like it was happening as much as it had before.

The last thing I needed was to be distracted by analyzing his or my behavior like a ridiculous Buzzfeed quiz. What I needed to do was get that B and prevent this stupid, unnecessary math class from destroying the rest of my GPA. I had recently gone to a Pre-Law informational meeting, which unfortunately, confirmed everything Sebastian had warned me about. It was insanely competitive, especially when being affiliated as an undergrad. I had managed to get my Biology class under control, but Calculus remained an anchor.

That Tuesday before Thanksgiving, instead of celebrating my coveted seventy-four percent on my second Calculus midterm, I found myself in my room scanning potential majors and their prerequisites. Maybe I was getting ahead of myself. But when I thought about the other students at that informational meeting, it was like a room full of Amelias and Sebastians. And after hearing all their questions rooted in humble brags, it seemed abundantly clear that I needed to start making a serious plan if UW Law was really my end game. Just as I had determined that Economics was the driest field of study I had ever heard of, my phone rang. It was Hunter.

"Hello?"

"You're really not coming home?" he started.

"You know how expensive it is to fly this week, especially tomorrow night. Also, for a three-day trip, it hardly seems worth it." My reasoning was well-practiced at this point.

"You know my parents would've paid for it if you needed them to."

I loved Hunter, but unfortunately, he tended to think he could solve most problems with money. It wasn't his fault; he learned it from his dad.

"I know and I didn't want them to."

"What about Ava? I'm sure she misses you."

He tried to use my sister against me. I had already made my peace with her and promised to make up for it when I came home in December. When I didn't take the bait, Hunter's voice dropped lower.

"Luce, I'm thinking I might tell my mom and dad and I really want you there."

I was silent. I didn't know what to say without sounding heartless.

"I'm really sorry," was all I could muster. "I'll be home in December."

"Are you mad at me about something? This isn't still about Black Widow-gate, is it?" he searched. His inability to realize why I didn't want to come home for Thanksgiving confirmed the reality that my dad's death was something that everyone else seemed to have gotten over.

"Believe it or not, Hunter, not everything I do has to do with you." My tone was even, but I still wondered if it was going to trigger a fight. We had never had a real argument. I waited to see if this would be it.

"Yeah," he sighed, "I know."

Hunter paused.

"It's about him, isn't it?" He didn't have to clarify who the 'him' was. He finally got it. "You know, putting it off doesn't mean December is going to be any easier."

"I know," I affirmed quietly.

He let a silence pass; it was comforting.

"Do I need to get Brenda on this call with me?" he jokingly referenced my old therapist.

"No," I said emphatically. "I already had to negotiate with my mom that I would see her over winter break."

"So that's it? You're just going to be up there, eating a sad turkey sandwich from the dining hall all by yourself? Probably crying into some apple cider, making people think no one cares about you."

His pathetic scenario made me laugh.

"Well, I was planning on crying into a pitifully small pumpkin tart, but you've essentially described the vibe, yes."

I could sense him smiling on the other end of the phone.

"You know you could be crying into a very bold 2008 zinfandel at my house."

"Last I checked, wine usually keeps," I deflected his last attempt to persuade me.

"I'm still going over to your house and eating all the peanut butter cookies your sister's going to bake."

"Oh please do. I'm sure Ava misses you." There was no doubt in my mind that my younger sister would revel in having Hunter come over just to see her.

"You owe me all the hangouts when you come down in December."

"Of course. Good luck with your parents."

"Ha, yeah right, I'm not coming out until I'm thirty now. How's that for passive aggressive?"

73

"Perfect, Real Housewives of Beverly Hills level drama," I joked.

"That was my intention," he laughed. "Love you, Luce."

"Love you, too. Good night."

Chapter Nine

I woke up Thanksgiving morning after a night of some of the best sleep I'd had since moving to Seattle. The promise of Danica's absence for four days left me in an almost tranquil state. There was a break in the rainy gray skies that had been a steady presence for several days. Uncharacteristically, I decided to go for a run of my own volition on the Burke Gilman Trail. It was freezing, but the sun had never felt better.

I took the usual route I ran with Veronica and Jenna, all the way to the top of the hill at Gasworks Park before heading back to the dorm. It was a wonderful feeling, running and having the sense of nothingness in my brain. No Calculus problems, no Biology assignments, no holiday family stress. Just the cold air, the sun, and my breath. I should've known better than to have gotten comfortable with that sense of serenity.

"On your left," I heard a male's voice behind me. The runner came into view as he passed.

Sebastian.

He made eye contact and smiled. Someone else might have taken it as a greeting, but in my opinion, it was a look of bluster. He assumed he had left me behind, but I suddenly felt the need to beat him back to the dorm. I willed my legs to pump faster, taking advantage when he slowed down at a turn as some bicyclists approached.

"On your left," I mimicked, not bothering to look at him as I passed.

My lead lasted for no longer than a minute. I could hear his feet nearing behind me. He didn't bother to call out this time as he sped up in front of me. I stayed on his tail. The dorm came into view, about a quarter mile away.

If I paced myself, and stayed slightly behind, I could take off at the very last moment once the cross walk leading to the building was in sight. My absence of thought had shifted into one thought and one thought only: beat Sebastian.

The exit point of the crosswalk came into view, triggering me to sprint faster than I had in the last six months. Apparently, Sebastian had been pacing himself too, because despite my sprint, his legs quickened and he kept the lead. Not having agreed on an endpoint, I concluded that the front door to the building was it. I noticed him start to slow as he turned the corner to the face of the dorm. I took off, flying up the stairs, triumphantly tagging the door.

My heart was pounding in my throat and I felt like I was going to vomit, clearly a sign of some sort of victory. Sebastian calmly walked up the steps and coolly opened the door, no sign of being nearly as out of breath as I was. He patted me on the shoulder.

"Good run. Maybe next time," he consoled simply as he walked by me into the building.

"Excuse me?" I asked with disbelief, following close behind him.

"The run," he gestured outside. "That I just beat you at. I was saying better luck next time."

"Who says we were racing? And anyway, I beat you to the door."

"Yeah, because I let you," he laughed. I continued to follow him and realized we were walking towards the dining room. "Hungry?"

"I don't have my food card on me."

My stomach was now growling from the last two miles of exertion I had not anticipated when I had left that morning for a leisurely holiday jaunt.

"Really? Are you sure you didn't stash it in your shoe and forget it was there?" He maintained a serious face.

"Will you stop with the shoe jokes?"

"No. It's been forever added to my top Lucile Allen memories. Come on, I'll spot you. Think of it as a consolation prize."

My stomach growled again. I figured he already considered me a charity case; I might as well get a meal out of it.

The dining hall was practically empty. There were extremely limited breakfast options compared to a normal day. I scrounged up a yogurt and banana along with an orange juice to include on Sebastian's tab. He took his tray of plain oatmeal and scrambled eggs and sat down at a table. I figured it would be rude not to join him after he had paid for my food.

"Don't be surprised when your blood sugar crashes in like twenty minutes after eating all that," he commented.

"Oh, I'm sorry I didn't know you moonlighted as a dietician when you're not eating boring old man breakfasts," I snapped at him in between a spoonful of Yoplait.

"Good nutrition has no age limits," he replied calmly.

I determined it was in his best interest if I curbed some of my hunger before I spoke again.

"So," I started as I was half way through my banana, "what are these top Lucile Allen memories you speak of?"

"It's nothing really. They're primarily made up of any time you spoke out loud in Spanish class. Te ah-coo-er-daz?" He mocked my Spanish pronunciation and then laughed.

I rolled my eyes and went back to my orange juice. "So, no Thanksgiving for you either?"

"Nope."

I refrained from asking him why he didn't go home, because I knew it would ultimately lead to him asking why I didn't go home. After running 3 miles, mostly in a sprint, I had no desire to talk about anything feelings-related.

"How'd you do on your midterm?'"

"Seventy-four percent." I waited for him to make fun of me.

"Good job." He nodded in approval. "I know you worked hard. We should celebrate. Dinner tonight?"

I looked at him with confusion.

"I mean, it's the least you can do after all that free tutoring I gave you...and this breakfast," he backtracked on his original consolation prize agreement.

He didn't want to spend the evening eating the pathetic dorm holiday meal that likely awaited us. Neither did I. A show of gratitude on my part was warranted, and was also the perfect disguise for us not having to admit we didn't want to spend the holiday alone—or worse, having to tolerate awkwardly sharing a meal with other students we'd no intention of ever becoming friends with.

"Fair enough," I sighed while standing up. "I'll text you later, Old Man Torres."

"Nos vemos esta noche, señorita."

I wanted to be annoyed by his goodbye, as it was clearly another show of pompousness, but unfortunately, his perfectly pronounced Spanish was now included on the list of attractive qualities.

The sun disappeared by the afternoon and it was raining again by six o'clock. I had no desire to walk or take the bus anywhere for dinner. Especially since I didn't know what type of snarky mood I was going to find Sebastian in. It seemed best to avoid prolonged exposure to him.

There was a Taiwanese restaurant nearby that I could DoorDash. Seeing pictures of the dumplings almost made me drool. My conscience stopped me from impulsively ordering. At first, I didn't care about being inconsiderate, but knew I would feel guilty if I found out Sebastian had some sort of allergy. My fingers were crossed that he wasn't going to wreck something I had started to look forward to.

Taiwanese Ok? I texted, not wanting to bother with the short walk down the hall.

Well, aren't you bougie? Is regular Chinese food too basic for you?

I let out an audible sigh.

Din Tai Fung in the Village is one of the few places open with a DoorDash option

Only the finest of chain restaurants for you on Thanksgiving.

DO YOU HAVE ANY ALLERGIES?

No.

I began ordering on my phone. Another message from Sebastian popped up.

Don't skimp on the dumplings. I hear they're amazing.

I swiped the notification away. Then my ordering got interrupted again.

Pot stickers, too.

And again.

And savory buns.

And again.

Pork, not chicken.

Hunter was right. One of us was going to kill the other one. Currently it wasn't looking good for Sebastian. He was lucky food was a good calming mechanism for me. Now, if he would just let me get the freaking order in.

It took over an hour for the delivery to arrive. The aroma was intoxicating, convincing me it was well worth the wait. Loaded up with two bulging plastic bags holding an excessive amount of food for two people, I knocked on Sebastian's door.

"Where do you want to eat this?" I skipped the pleasantries when I saw him.

"I'm fine here, if you are." He pulled back the door and let me in.

After living in the dorms for a few months, I'd come to appreciate that his room was orderly and free of foul smells. Not that I had been in many dorm rooms, but just by walking past open doors, it was a disappointing reality that some of our peers did not make a habit of cleanliness. I placed the take-out on the counter by the window before taking a seat in his roommate's chair.

"You know, I'm starting to think Warren doesn't exist," I joked about having never seen his roommate.

"What does it mean to really exist anyway, Lucile?" Sebastian asked reflectively as he scrounged through the bag.

A scornful look covered my face.

"Relax, I'm kidding." He half-smiled before sitting down across from me in his own chair, takeout box and chopsticks in hand.

"So, you're just going to eat all the pot stickers?" I commented, my objection clear.

"I dunno, I'll have to see how good they are first."

I let out a sigh before starting in on my jindori chicken bun.

"You really think I'm an asshole, don't you?" he laughed.

"You don't often give contradicting evidence otherwise," I said between mouthfuls, beginning to feel less annoyed as the food filled my stomach.

"I guess we can't all have the charm of Hunter Davis," his sarcasm was clear.

I let the comment pass, concluding a silent dinner with him would probably be the wisest decision.

"I guess you could say I've been a bit of a curmudgeon since—"

"Ninth grade," I filled in automatically.

"I was going to say since I moved up here, but some may make an argument for before then, I guess," he conceded, while looking down into the box to gather a bite. "I was so frustrated when I didn't get into Stanford. When I saw you that first day, it was this horrible reminder that there was someone else up here who knew I failed. I didn't want to deal with it." He looked up at me. "I shouldn't have ignored you, but I honestly didn't think you would care."

I let his feedback sink in. There was no obvious defense against it. Saying 'but I'm a really nice person who only talked to you when it came to mandated academic tasks' seemed like it would only support his point.

"Of course," he paused, "you went ahead and made it clear that you cared abundantly when you stopped by here on Halloween looking for a booty call."

"Excuse me, I did no such thing," I raised my voice and stopped myself when I saw Sebastian grinning at my reaction.

"It's almost too easy," he sighed, shaking his head. He put down the box of pot stickers on the counter and moved on to the box of steamed pork dumplings. "So, why didn't you go home for Thanksgiving?" he asked casually as he sat back in his chair.

"It's expensive and honestly, I didn't want to deal with all the family stuff," I admitted, trusting I wouldn't have to go into much detail beyond that. Pretty much our entire high school knew me as the girl whose dad died last spring. "You?"

"Same. I mean, the money," he clarified. "You know, when your parents work in public education there's not always a lot of extra cash for plane flights on top of out-of-state tuition."

"Your parents are teachers?" My tone conveyed my surprise, tilting my head at him as he sat across from me. I guess I had always viewed Sebastian as so mature that I'd never considered he belonged to actual grownups.

"My mom teaches kindergarten. My dad is in the IT department of the district."

"Shut up, your mom is a kindergarten teacher? That's adorable. I wouldn't have guessed that."

"What? Why?" He raised an amused brow.

"Well, you have to be really patient and kind to teach kindergarten, and you're so..."

"So...?"

"Not." I laughed at my answer. He threw a fortune cookie at me.

"I think I've exhibited quite a bit of patience when it comes to teaching you math. I refrained from the use of the word 'obvious,' even when the answer was obvious."

"Oh, bravo, gold stars for you," I deadpanned before reaching over to take my share of the pot stickers.

"I guess it's not exactly fair to expect someone to have the same professional skills as their parents," he threw back pointedly.

"What is that supposed to mean?" I sat up in the chair straighter as Sebastian stared at me.

"Your parents are lawyers, right? And what do lawyers do?" He urged me to fill in the blank.

"Charge people too much money for their time?" I searched before taking a bite.

"No," he laughed. "They argue."

"Yeah, so?"

"Lucy," he started in his familiar smug tone. "You let a woman put you in two courses you didn't need and didn't want to take because you didn't want to hurt her feelings. And you won't even confront your roommate for kicking you out of your own room on a weekly basis. A room that you're paying for."

"How do you know that?"

"Veronica told me."

"Of course," I sighed. She might as well have become my new Hunter, friends with everybody.

"I think I'm one of the few people you've actually ever argued with."

"That's not true. I have a younger sister."

"Siblings don't count. Face it, you'd rather be nice than disagree with someone," he stated definitively. "Well, someone other than me," he added.

"Well, maybe I'm going to be a nice lawyer who gets people to agree on things."

"You mean a mediator? That's usually an additional degree in conflict resolution."

"Ick," I reacted. "Well never mind then," I predictably resigned myself, putting the takeout box down. "We don't need to talk about all that stuff now anyway," I dismissed. "Let's talk about something else."

"I'm shocked you would respond that way," he said dryly.

I gave him a look of indifference—it supported his point, but I didn't give him the satisfaction of a reaction from me.

"Very well," he allowed, crossing his arms. "What do you want to talk about?"

This was the perfect opportunity to find out if I could work my magic as a matchmaker for Veronica or Corine.

"How about Amelia? How is she? Are you guys still together?"

Okay, so I wasn't the smoothest at finding these things out.

"She's fine," he said nonchalantly, then paused. "I don't know," he sighed with a shrug.

"You don't know?" My opinion of this answer, or lack of an answer, was evident.

"I don't know what we are," he admitted. "We didn't really talk about it. She was pretty pissed when she found out I didn't get into Stanford. That took a couple weeks to fix, if I even fixed it. We talk sometimes...I don't know," he repeated with the same tone.

"I can see you have a lot of scholarly passion regarding the quest for truth on the matter."

"Is that how you think I sound?" He raised his brow.

I smirked, passively confirming his question.

"Amelia's fine," he said coolly. "I'm sure we'll figure out where we stand when I see her in December," he added for good measure.

"Come on, man, you're not even gathering clues from her social?"

"Social? You mean like Facebook stalking?"

"Facebook is for sharing pictures with your grandma. I'm talking about Instagram or Snapchat. You know, Sebastian, they say a picture is worth a thousand words."

"I don't have Instagram or Snapchat. And I highly doubt Amy has them either. Neither of us did in high school, because both of those things are complete wastes of time and intelligence."

He continued to sit there with his arms crossed, sounding so smug. I had to prove him wrong. I was sure Amelia would want to stay in touch with all her snobby AP buddies, the small percent that had laughed at her valedictorian jokes. I pulled out my phone and within seconds of searching, found her.

"Cardinal Amyy," I announced her handle. "With two Ys. How clever."

Sebastian furrowed his brow as he took my phone and looked down at the screen.

"Well, where are all her pictures?"

"Her account is private. She's got to let me follow her for me to see anything."

"So, follow her," he said obviously.

I was taken back by the immediacy in his voice. Someone was sprung.

"Yeah right," I laughed. "She's not going to accept a request from me. She didn't like me at all in high school."

"That's not true."

I stared at him, not buying it.

"She may have thought you were a little...superficial...when it came to your processing of academic material."

I nodded at the confirmation.

"But look at you! You're at the University of Washington, getting a C in Calculus, on your way to a B minus...maybe."

Sebastian tried his best to pad the brutality of his confession by leaning forward and patting my knee. The influence of his kindergarten teaching mother was now apparent.

"I'm not requesting her just so I can do the dirty work for you," I said with principle. "You can make your own account. You know, since Cardinal Amyy with two Ys has now declared it a socially acceptable form of communication, and no longer a complete waste of time reserved for us superficial thinkers."

I got up and arranged the takeout boxes quickly on the windowsill, pausing to meticulously place the chopsticks. I snapped a picture. Glancing at it, I was proud of its composition, the raindrop covered window and moon in the background.

"Here, this can be your first picture." I sent it to him. "You can caption it 'Thanksgiving of Solitude.' Continue that cerebral reputation of yours that you hold so dear."

Sebastian looked down at the text and then back up at me, unamused by the suggestion.

"Make sure you get a bank of pictures on the grid and a few followers before you request her, though. You don't want her thinking you're thirsty." I reclaimed my seat as I spoke with a wisdom normally reserved for lecture halls.

"I cannot believe I took AP classes with you."

"We all have our areas of expertise," I said smartly. "Come on, Sebastian, it's time you embrace your youth. No one likes a grumpy old man. Especially when he's only eighteen."

"And what if he's really good at finding derivatives and integrals?"

"Well, I might make an exception for that, but I'm an unreliable source. I've been told I'm prone to being too nice."

"Yeah, there is that."

A small smile appeared on Sebastian's face. It gave me pause. It was the first time a sign of happiness from him wasn't associated with proving me wrong or making fun of me. Because I can't handle any sort of positive male attention that's not from a gay man (or my dad before he passed), I awkwardly changed the subject to concerns about upcoming finals. I sensed he appreciated returning to a more comfortable subject, too.

The night was a wonderful distraction from the holiday and the emotional weight it held. Maybe it was all a fluke, a temporary truce. Once the weekend passed, there was a chance Sebastian and I would go back to our status quo of subtle to rage-filled irritation with one another, but for the moment, it was an appreciated break.

I didn't want to wreck our current streak of friendliness, so I erred on the side of caution, and kept to myself after Thursday night. Sebastian appeared to have the same logic, because I didn't see or talk to him again for the rest of the weekend.

Hunter provided me more than enough entertainment by insisting on FaceTiming while we simultaneously streamed a backlog of movies and shows Friday and Saturday night. While it did make me feel special, I knew he was avoiding having to see Brady and the other guys who would undoubtedly want some sort of rundown of all the girls he had hooked up with at Santa Barbara. Regardless, I hadn't laughed that hard in a while. Hunter was hilariously catty when it came to romantic comedies and I ate it up every time.

I woke up on Sunday disappointed that my stint of having my own dorm room was coming to an end. The peaceful solitude would all be gone by that afternoon...or evening...Danica didn't really tell me when she was coming back. Shocking, I know.

Staying in Seattle over break provided exactly what I wanted, avoiding any negative feelings that would come up around this being my first major holiday without my dad. However, the reality was that I would have to go home for Christmas. There was a gnawing sense that the emotions I had been pushing away for so long were eventually going to surface somehow.

Trying to move myself past thinking about the end of December, I checked my phone before getting into the shower. There was a notification to follow @sm-torres on Instagram along with a text from him.

> Instagram is stupid. I ended up wasting over 2 hours on it yesterday. I think I may have lost a few IQ points.

> *Sounds like you may be ready to be introduced to TikTok then.*

I texted back. Not expecting much of a reply, I was surprised when my phone chimed.

> Mercedes Garcia goes off to Santa Cruz and is polyamorous now? WTF?
> I dated her in 8th grade. She dumped me because she thought I talked to other girls too much.
> Where was the Zen Love then, Mercedes?

I let out a laugh, hearing his curmudgeonly tone as I read.

> *Good thing you transcend the pettiness of social media*

> Yeah. You'll have to tell me which filter to use to let people know IDGAF.

> *Everyone knows it's Arden*

Damn. My guess was Perpetua. Thank you for saving me from complete and utter social embarrassment from which I would never recover.

You're welcome. I'm hoping my help is returned with only your best tutoring so I can get a 3.0 in Calculus.

I should've never assumed pure altruism from you. We'll see. I'm not even sure if I'll be able to do basic algebra now that I'm living dat 'Gram Lyfe.

The vibrating heart emoji at the end of his text made me laugh out loud again. Sebastian may have been most surprised by Mercedes Garcia's big post-high school lifestyle reveal. (Honestly, most of her former classmates were. It's just that we had all known it for a month before Sebastian.) For me, however, the most unexpected news was that I might have become friends with my high school nemesis.

Chapter Ten

I survived finals, and much to my excitement, I did earn a 3.0 overall in Calculus. That, along with working my butt off in Biology, gave me a cumulative 3.56 GPA. I had never been so proud of my grades. Even though I was still anxious about going home and dealing with this being my first Christmas without my dad, I was looking forward to the break from school and getting to sleep on a non-dorm mattress.

My mom, sister, and I knew that the holiday was going to be hard. Fortunately, we were all expecting it to be so terrible, that when the time finally came, it wasn't as bad as we'd thought it would be. Somehow, we made it through the days leading up to Christmas without any crying. From what very little I had learned in therapy, it was the moments you didn't expect where the grief hit the hardest. Never one to accept being caught off guard, my brain decided to fixate on the numerous situations that might trigger an emotional breakdown until it just couldn't think of any more. When I wasn't crafting plans for how to avoid being sad in the future, I embraced all the distractions Christmastime had to offer, particularly spending quality time with Hunter.

After being out at Santa Barbara for only three months, that boy had managed to find himself in the middle of not one, but possibly two love triangles. And neither of these included the same guy that he made out with on Halloween. It was not totally obvious whether it was two triangles, because it was possible that Josh was a one-time make out session and Lucas was still questioning whether he was into guys. However, they both continued to DM and wanted to "hang out" with Hunter.

The real triangle involved Jonathan and Trevor. Hunter had hung out with them both in group settings and one-on-one. Both guys had mentioned to him that they were looking for something exclusive. Personally, from the limited information that I had, I was rooting for Jonathan. He was a pre-med junior that Hunter had met through slutty Black Widow, excuse me, I mean, Hannah.

Jonathan was older and seemed to have the least amount of drama associated with him. Unfortunately, to Hunter, this equated to being boring. Apparently, niceness only worked in your favor with him when earning the title of fake girlfriend.

"Lucy, you're not understanding," Hunter insisted as I was halfway through wrapping presents for his family, something that I had been kind enough to continue doing for him even though I was no longer said fake girl-friend. "They are all so hot."

We were in the safety of the pool house away from the ears of his parents, whom he still had not come out to.

"Then let them know you're not ready to settle down," I responded simply. It was a fair argument to say I didn't understand. I had never had four hot guys trying to make out with me, let alone one.

"But what if that means the making out stops?" He sighed, scrolling through his phone as he laid on the bed.

"Oh, God forbid the making out stops. How will you ever survive?"

He threw a pillow at me, hitting me in the face.

"You're obviously not ready to commit to anything, and that's fine, but you need to be honest. It's not right to string people along."

"You make everything sound so easy. Did I mention they were all good looking?"

"Did I mention you sound like a boy-crazy thirteen-year-old? Seriously, I'm about to call Ava up and have her sub in for me."

It was justifiable why he was acting boy-crazy. For the past eight years, while the rest of us were publicly gushing about our crushes and when we got butterflies, Hunter had locked it all in. He was emphatic that he did not find any of the openly gay guys in our class the least bit attractive and had always been very tight-lipped, even with me, regarding what he thought about any of the straight guys at school. Now it was like he was starring in his own version of The Bachelor.

"Ava would probably be more helpful anyway," he concluded. "I mean, she's had, like what? Five boyfriends? You've only had one. And I heard he was, like, super gay."

He laughed at his own joke. I got up from the floor and stacked the newly wrapped presents on the dresser, more pleased with my ribbon work than was socially acceptable for a young adult.

"You got any other menial girlfriend tasks you want to use me for before I go?" I asked while picking up my jacket from the bed.

"Yes," he answered, holding his phone up to me. "I want you to tell me which one you think is the cutest."

I looked down to see he had pulled up pictures. Letting out a heavy sigh, I grabbed his phone.

"Are looks seriously all you care about?"

He shrugged.

Humoring him, I started scrolling and inspecting. While I was trying to remember which guy was which, a text message popped up. I read it first, then saw it was Jonathan.

"Ooooo," I crooned.

"What? Who's it from?" He reached for the phone.

"Oh, just Jonathan," I turned away and laughed.

"What? Give it to me!"

He reached again as I dodged him, but this time he grabbed my waist and pulled me down on the bed. I kept moving the phone away from him.

"Seriously, Lucy, what does it say?"

"I thought Jonathan was too boring for you?" I challenged while laughing.

Hunter was seconds away from overpowering me and taking his phone back. However, getting an unknown message from Jonathan managed to throw him off his game. Then he remembered his guaranteed offensive move of tickling my armpits. I dropped the phone immediately.

The tickling was nothing like a flirtatious scene in a romcom. Aggressive finger gouging was a better description of it. Thankfully, once Hunter regained the phone, he stopped.

"He wants to know if you have plans for New Year's. I think someone wants to kiss you at midnight," I teased while still pinned under Hunter, his attention more focused on the phone than letting me up.

"See, that's just it. New Year's is over a week away. Who makes plans that early?"

"Yeah, how dare he value your time. The audacity!"

He looked down at me, unamused by me.

"I would much rather have a guy forget to invite me to something until the last minute," I continued with my sarcasm.

"That was one time, and I thought it was implied we were going to Homecoming together," he automatically defended himself.

"Knock-knock," Hunter's mom called out while opening the glass door. We looked over to see her walking in with a laundry basket.

Hunter rolled off me and we sat up in unison. I was unsure if I needed to feign embarrassment for what looked compromising, but couldn't have been more platonic.

"Doesn't walking in before the person answers cancel out the intention of saying 'knock-knock'?" Hunter asked pointedly.

"I just wanted to get this laundry back to you, Hunty," she said sweetly as she went right to putting the clothes into the dresser. Such a spoiled only child.

"Lucy, did Hunter rope you into wrapping all his gifts again?" She commented on the meticulous presents in front of her.

"Oh, it was nothing."

"Well, they look beautiful," she complimented before finally turning to look at us. "I'm so glad you guys are able to be friendly with one another still."

I nodded, not knowing what else to say. She turned back to the dresser.

"You know, Hunter has not told us about any other girls he's met at Santa Barbara. I guess you left some pretty big shoes to fill." Hunter's mom closed the last drawer before turning back to us again.

"Oh, I'm sure Hunter can find someone with big enough feet to fill them," I quipped and quickly received a jab in my side from him. Completely oblivious, Hunter's mom shook her head in amusement.

"It was nice seeing you, Lucy," she made her way to the door. "Oh, and Hunter, make sure you draw the curtains if you two, you know, need a little more privacy," she called out airily before closing the door.

I turned to him and raised an eyebrow.

"So, when are you going to tell her again?"

"She likes you so much. I figured we'd get married and give her a couple of grandbabies first to soften the blow," he joked, but his stalling made me question how much of it was a joke.

"It's like a band-aid," I started to reason.

"Oh, really? Please give me more advice about how to come out to your parents."

"True," I validated. A mischievous grin crept up on my face. "But you know who might have some really good pointers?" He knew I was plotting, but wasn't quick enough to keep me from recapturing his phone. "I bet Jonathan would be more than happy to help out."

Through the wrestling, I managed to enter his passcode. Attempting to text, I was only able to type gibberish. Pushing send, I cackled out in triumph. Hunter's eyes widened and grew even bigger when his phone started ringing.

"You need me to get that for you?"

He didn't respond.

"Just pick it up already," I commanded. "A guy who actually talks on the phone is hard to find."

I stood up and started gathering my things. The lack of direct attention seemed to help Hunter pick up.

"Uh, hi," he greeted sheepishly and paused. "Yeah, um, I must have pocket texted you. Sorry about that. So, what's up?"

He started nervously fiddling with the throw blanket. It was adorable. Since my work there appeared to be done, I bent down and kissed him on the cheek. I mouthed goodbye before showing myself out.

I officially made it through Christmas Eve and Christmas without any emotional breakdowns. My mom and Ava deserved recognition for also making it through. The biggest drama was Oscar, a random clerk from my mom's law firm, finding an excuse to come over on Christmas night. Apparently, he just had to drop off some of his grandmother's world-renowned coquito. Yeah, we get it, Oscar, you're half Puerto Rican like my mom, congratulations.

I was suspicious, to say the least. When Mom and Oscar were distracted in the kitchen getting glasses, Ava read my face and attempted to calm me down, insisting that Oscar had never come by the house before.

Innocently, she asked if it was really that bad of a thing for Mom to have a new friend, especially if it made her happy.

The answer was yes, since it hadn't even been a year since Dad died. Now really wasn't the time for finding new friends who could make her happy in that way. But I didn't want to wreck the end of Christmas, so I didn't say that. Instead, I quietly drank my small allotment of coquito, smiled politely, and pretended that I was super interested in being a lawyer one day, too. A conflict-free Christmas was my reward. All it cost me was a migraine from clenching my jaw the last hour of the night.

I ended up back at Hunter's the next day to have dinner with his parents. It felt like no time had passed at all since high school, particularly since it was very apparent that they still had no clue that their son was gay. After continuing to give his parents false hope about someday being their daughter-in-law, Hunter and I went back to the pool house. We ended up watching back-to-back horribly cheesy Hallmark Channel Christmas movies. He made a point to draw the curtains. I decided not to hassle him about what he was trying to communicate to his mom and dad.

Hunter laid his long body across the couch and rested his head in my lap. Absent-mindedly, I ran my hands through his hair. Did I mention he was spoiled? That was Hunter though. There was something about him that made you want to take care of him. I'm sure the four boys who awaited him in Santa Barbara had become familiar with this phenomenon by now.

The male lead of the crappy movie showed up at the woman's door, a scarf perfectly wrapped around his neck, and I found myself triggered.

"You know what the worst part about that Oscar guy was? He was wearing a Burberry scarf," I added to my litany of critiques that I had shared with Hunter earlier before dinner. "Like, could you try any harder to look like you have money? It's the Valley—it's not even cold enough for a scarf." I felt my jaw tighten up again and forced myself to relax.

Hunter looked up at me. There was a slight smirk on his face.

"You know I will always one hundred percent agree with you, like maybe ninety percent of the time, but we're upset with this person because he was wearing a scarf in the Valley? Or because of the brand of the scarf?"

"Both," I said obviously.

"Mmmkay, just wanted to clarify." He turned back to the movie, wise enough to know he shouldn't tell me I was being harsh.

"I just think it's a status play, that's all. No one wears Burberry because they like the pattern. They wear it because they're trying to show off. And then he tries to act all humble, with bringing his Abuelita's Puerto Rican egg- nog," I scoffed. "You should've heard him say coquito. It was obnoxious."

Hunter folded his lips in, not responding verbally, but still communicat- ing to me that he was judging me more than Oscar.

"What?" I demanded.

"Nothing," he tried to stifle a laugh, but was unsuccessful.

"No, what?" I demanded again.

"You are such a hater," he smiled.

"Am not!"

"Are too, infinity." He shot back childishly, sitting up to pour himself more wine. "But that's okay. I love you anyway." He placated me with a kiss on the cheek before he took a sip.

"Hey look, Burberry!" He pointed out the protagonist's purse with amusement. "Well great," he sighed. "Now we have to hate her."

Hunter reclaimed his spot on my lap, which I didn't reject. He wasn't going to get his head pet anymore though, that was for sure.

"Aspen is pretty dense not to have figured out Ben's the orphanage's Secret Santa by now," he mused.

"She's blind to love, Hunter. It keeps you from seeing so many things," I deadpanned.

My phone chimed. I picked it up to see a text from Sebastian.

You bored out of your mind yet?

In Modesto? Not possible.

I'm seriously regretting booking my flight for January 3rd

What's the matter? I thought for sure CardinalAmyy would be entertaining you with tales of her overpriced education in Palo Alto.

When there wasn't an immediate reply, I worried my last text might have been a little too snarky.

Amelia decided it was best for us to entertain other people.

I paused. I wasn't quite sure how to respond. Although it wasn't totally genuine, I went with the obvious.

Sorry.

Five minutes passed and Sebastian had not responded. I didn't feel good leaving it where it was at, even if it wasn't until recently that I decided that I could tolerate him.

Emily Mason's New Year's Eve party popped into my head. My former classmates had become all kumbaya after graduating and she left it as an open invitation for the entire class. I never thought of it as Sebastian's scene, but at the very least it would give him something to do for one night while stuck in Modesto.

"Hey, did you decide what you're doing for New Year's yet?" I asked Hunter, seemingly out of nowhere.

"I don't know," he sighed, still staring at the TV. "Jonathan invited me to a Cal Poly party, but he'd be the only person there I'd know. I'm not really into the idea of following him around all night like a puppy. I told him I'd think about it."

"Why? It sounds like you already know you don't want to go."

"It's always good to keep a little mystery, my dear."

"You are unreal," I sighed disapprovingly, checking my phone again. Still nothing else from Sebastian. "So, are you going to Emily Mason's party then?"

"I dunno, maybe."

I sighed again.

He finally turned and looked at me. "Why?" He became suspicious of my questions.

"I'm just curious. I don't want to go if you're not going."

He peered over at my phone and then gasped. "Are you making New Year's Eve plans with someone else?"

He tried to reach for my phone, unsuccessfully because he was still lying down.

"Lucy, do you have a gentleman suitor I do not know about? A Secret Santa, perhaps? One who has awakened your cold heart to love?" he teased.

"No," I said defensively.

"Then who are you texting?"

"No one."

He popped up, moments away from grabbing my phone with his long arms.

"I was going to tell Sebastian Torres he should go to Emily's house," I revealed.

Hunter's eyes widened.

"He's bored and he just told me Amelia Yang broke up with him," I quickly explained.

"Ooooooo," Hunter mocked. "I'm going to have to text Ronnie all about this."

"Ronnie?"

"Yeah, your friend, Veronica. I gave her a nickname."

I shook my head.

"What? She likes it. But not as much as she's going to love hearing about you trying to make out with Sebastian on New Year's," he exaggerated.

"Not even. It's a pity invite. And I'm only going to Emily's if you're going."

"Oh, I'm definitely going now. Who else is going to get all the dirt for Ronnie?"

"I doubt he shows up anyway. He probably hates parties," I reasoned aloud as I texted the invite to Sebastian.

"Which is why you guys make the perfect pair. Haters unite."

"I am not a hater and I don't hate parties," I defended.

He raised both eyebrows.

"I just don't like large gatherings with certain types of people. There's a difference," I clarified, looking back up at the movie. "Did Aspen figure out Ben loves her as much as he loves Christmas yet?

I folded my arms, protecting my phone from him. Hunter stared at me for a moment, contemplating whether he was going to continue harassing me. Thankfully, he lay his head back down and saved his teasing for another time.

Chapter Eleven

Sebastian was not entirely wrong about how time drug on while in Modesto. Especially compared to having a full course load at a large university in a large city. As promised, I appeased my mother by participating in a therapy session with the infamous Brenda.

My suspicions regarding Oscar were further confirmed as Brenda spent the whole time probing my thoughts about different family members' grief timelines and reiterating that "everyone grieves in their own way, at their own pace" and "new relationships do not replace old ones."

Yeah, way to go, Mom, have the therapist soften the blow of your plan to rebound with a random guy from work. I played stupid and sat through the hour, successfully putting up enough walls to the point where Brenda didn't know what to do with me. Forty-five...forty-six...forty-seven...forty-eight...forty-nine... Joke's on her for teaching me that coping strategy.

By the time December thirty-first rolled around, I was itching to get back to Seattle, too. If Mom felt the need to inconsiderately move on and start dating before Dad had even been gone a whole year, I certainly didn't need to be present for it. Especially since Ava seemed to be totally more interested in how Oscar being a distraction for Mom translated into her getting to go out with her friends more in addition to having a midnight curfew on the weekend. Which, needless to say, was ridiculous since I had to wait until senior year for that privilege.

"Lucy? Earth to Lucy?" Hunter called my attention back to him as he drove to Emily's house.

He had been recounting different DMs from Trevor and Jonathan. I had not been the most considerate listener and zoned out about three minutes in.

"Yeah?"

"I asked you what you thought Trevor meant?"

"Meant about what?"

"When he texted about getting coffee?"

I looked at Hunter blankly, pretty sure he had given me ample information only seconds ago to formulate an analysis. He sighed.

"He texted that we needed to get coffee when I got back into town. Not wanted to, *needed* to."

"Uh," I rubbed my head, trying to summon enough energy to decode a random person's behavior with him.

"Dude, Luce, what is up with you?"

"Sorry...I'm just tired."

"Wasn't it your idea to go to this party?"

"Yes, I just...I don't know...I guess I'm just ready to go back to school."

"Wow. Good to know you've missed me too."

"It's not that," I sighed. "I miss you. You know that."

"Look, if this is about running into Olivia and her fleet of bitches tonight, don't worry about it. Just hang out with me and the guys."

"It's not about Olivia, but thank you for reminding me about last spring," I laughed.

Hunter parked the car on the side of the road. The large driveaway was already packed with cars. He unbuckled and turned to face me, in no rush to join the party.

"Is it about your dad?" He tried to guess.

"No...yes...maybe," I revealed my own ambivalence.

"Didn't you get some quality time with Brenda this week?"

"You say that like it would somehow be helpful."

"I mean, isn't that what she's supposed to do? Help you figure out whatever's going on in there." He playfully tapped on my forehead before I swatted his hand away.

"That would require me wanting to talk to her."

"Well, why don't you?"

I shrugged.

"You've never been to therapy before. You walk in and there's this person that you're just supposed to tell everything you're thinking. And you know they have an opinion about it, but they won't say what it is. They just sit there and expect you to keep talking even though you never know what they're really thinking about you," I attempted to explain how embarrassing and pointless the whole thing was, but when I heard the words come out of mouth I knew it wasn't sufficient for communicating the nervousness I felt in my stomach anytime I had to go to that stupid office.

"Well, the idea of someone listening to me talk about myself for an hour actually sounds kind of wonderful to me, but that could just be because I'm an only child."

I gave him a half-smile. He smiled back and grabbed my hand.

"You know, you can always talk to me." He reiterated what I already knew.

Hunter had been amazingly supportive when my dad was dying and right after he passed. He sat through hours of crying, along with hours of silence when I didn't want to talk, but didn't want to be alone. He was always ready with a distraction when I needed to laugh. While I would never want to repeat those weeks, at least when grieving looked like sadness, I felt less embarrassed about it.

However, I'd noticed that ever since that first week away when I was rushing sororities, the grief had morphed itself into anger. Ugly, burning irritation that would bubble up and I would have to make a conscious effort to shove down. Up at school I had been able to control it, aside from the occasional snapping at Sebastian when he gave me a smug response.

But this first visit home and having to be around my family for an extended amount of time led me to feel like I was losing my grasp on it. I had spent the past three years faking, very convincingly, that Hunter and I were dating. It was maddening that I couldn't just fake my way through feeling okay about my dad being gone, too.

The first day I got home, I noticed my mom was no longer wearing her wedding ring, and I caught myself glaring at her hand. My dad's office had been redecorated, and I found myself slamming drawers shut. Ava said that Oscar was no big deal, and anytime I thought about it, my jaw tensed. After keeping it all in check for almost two weeks, I was starting to feel like I wanted to scream multiple times a day. You know, just your typical teen angst on steroids.

Hunter had always teased me about being a hater, because I tended to be a pessimist, but he would also routinely fawn over how nice and sweet I was, particularly to him. I wanted to keep him from seeing this angry side. Honestly, I didn't know what he would do if I revealed it to him. I pictured him playfully tousling my hair and jovially saying, "Oh, you don't really mean that, Luce." The very thought of that only made me angrier, even though it was all hypothetical. The last thing I wanted to do was add Hunter to the list of things I was angry at or about.

"Or you can just sit and stare at me in awkward silence," Hunter joked when I didn't respond to his reminder that I could talk to him. "Either one works for me," he laughed.

"Sorry," I sighed and shook my head, trying to be more in the moment. "Let's just go inside and have a good time." I started to open the door.

"Wait," he stopped me. I turned back to him. "Are we kissing at midnight or not?"

"We're broken up. Why would we kiss at midnight?"

He shrugged.

"I don't know. Neither of us is seeing anybody. Wouldn't we kiss at midnight if we're still friends and single?"

I paused, never considering that we would have to coordinate PDA after being broken up.

"But you don't want to kiss me," I stated the obvious.

"No. But I don't want some other girl to grab me and kiss me either."

"What?" I laughed. "Why would anyone do that? Girls don't do that," I dismissed.

"Um, yes they do, especially if they've been drinking," he argued.

"Really? You're like six foot two and one-ninety. You're telling me that you can't possibly keep some drunk little waif from kissing you?"

"Well, I don't want to be mean," he reasoned, giving me a pathetic look.

"Fine," I sighed. "I'll protect you from all the big scary females," I mocked him as I patted his cheek. "But I'm only going to run interference if I see someone going in for it," I stated my conditions.

"Thanks, Bae," he lifted my hand up and kissed the back of it. "By the way, I told Jonathan my New Year's Resolution was to come out to everyone—so, this very well could be the last night that you ever get to enjoy making out with this hotness." He moved his hand up and down in a presentation of himself.

"Riiiight," I dismissed before finally getting out of the car.

Hunter met me as we walked up the driveway, game plan in place, just like old times. I know only roughly three months had passed since we had last been to a party together, but it felt very different.

I no longer cared about the title of "Hunter's girlfriend." Time away from everything allowed me to feel like I was more of my own person. The fact that he wanted to pull me back into the old role was a little frustrating.

I mean, sometimes it felt like he was never going to come out, and at what point was I being more of a hindrance than a help? Of course, now was not the time to bring that all up. More than anything, I knew Hunter needed me to be supportive. At that moment, I guess that meant continued patience and ignoring whatever irritation it triggered. More than likely, the frustration was just spilling over from all the other stuff that was pissing me off.

"You do look very pretty tonight," he complimented, putting his hand on the small of my back as we walked up to the door. "I like your boots."

I had opted to dress down with leggings and a black flowing top, but also a necklace to add a little sparkle. My dark brown waves were also behaving themselves and had not turned into a frizzy mess. Hunter always knew when to turn on the charm. I looked at him and sighed.

"What?" He laughed, knowing I knew he was trying to lure me in.

"We are broken up," I reminded him, trying to be stern.

"Amicably broken up," he specified with a wink and a grin before opening the door to Emily's house. He wrapped his hand around mine, and I didn't pull away. There was still part of me that liked how special he made me feel in a crowd.

Emily's house was packed. I had not expected to walk into a full class reunion, but I guess the holidays made people nostalgic. Well, more than likely it was Emily's parents' willingness to supply free alcohol to everyone.

I followed Hunter's suggestion to hang out with him and his other guy friends. Olivia and the other girls were on the periphery of the group, but Hunter, highly skilled in social warfare, managed to navigate them out of the conversations.

I started to zone out, given the excessive talk of college sports. I had been able to contribute a little about Pac12 football, given the impressive performance of UW that past season, but after that, I didn't have much else to offer. I leaned into Hunter's ear and excused myself to go get a drink, remembering I had spotted wine in the kitchen when we walked in.

Emily Mason was by all the drinks, fulfilling her duty as all-star hostess as usual. She greeted me for the third time that night. Emily had always been one of the sweeter girls on the outskirts of the clique, and I regretted not having been friendlier to her in high school. It was hard to remember the specifics, but I think Olivia had decided for some reason she didn't like her, so I in turn could not be close friends with her. Looking back on it now, it was all so stupid.

"So, what's the deal with you and Hunter?" she asked the inevitable after wrapping up the predictable small talk about how she was liking UC Davis. "You guys have been all over each other's stories ever since you got home and now you guys are here together?" Emily looked like she might actually squeal.

"Oh, it's nothing. Just hanging out as friends."

She nodded, but I could tell she didn't believe me. I felt tempted to fall into the old habit of lying about myself and Hunter, when suddenly I noticed Sebastian standing amongst a group of people in the living room. He looked bored out of his mind.

We locked eyes and he held up his Solo cup in recognition. I gave him a half-smile, amused because it seemed like such an old man gesture. He tilted his head, gesturing to go outside to the backyard. Emily turned to see who had gotten my attention, and then turned back to me, trying to read my expression.

"Uh, excuse me. Thanks for the wine, Emily." I didn't offer more of an explanation as I headed towards the sliding glass door.

Sebastian was already outside and had taken a seat on the bench by the swimming pool. Since it was the winter, he was probably safe from a naked Chase Robertson Cannonball Surprise, but honestly the amount that Chase had to drink would determine that likelihood more than the weather.

Sebastian already looked like he wasn't enjoying himself, so I held back from warning him about the possibility.

"You decided to come."

"Yep," he sighed, taking a drink.

I sat down next to him, enjoying the cold air on my face and how it was remarkably quieter outside. I appreciated the momentary calm away from all the bodies and personalities inside.

"Did you really tolerate this for all of high school?" He nodded toward the crowded living room. We could hear the muffled music and people.

"Parties this big only happened about three or four times a year. Usually, Hunter and I would stop by for about an hour and then head back to his place," I shrugged.

"Is that the plan tonight?"

"I don't know. I didn't talk it over with him." I turned around to see Hunter still holding court in the study, oblivious to the fact that I hadn't come back yet. "He seems to be having a pretty good time catching up with his bros right now."

"And you? Not feeling the need to catch up with Olivia and the other teen queens?"

"Nah. We were never really friends," I admitted.

"Then why on earth did you decide to come here tonight?"

"Free booze and boredom," I said flatly, leaving out the tiny detail that if I didn't have this party as a distraction, I might have ended up screaming at someone in my family. "And you?"

"Same, I guess," he laughed. "Actually, Alex and Kyle were adamant about coming out tonight," he mentioned his two closest friends from high school. "They think their chances of scoring have magically gone up since we've graduated."

"Well, you're kind of being a crappy wingman right now," I observed.

"I hadn't anticipated having to deal with that tonight."

He nodded towards the side living room where people were dancing. It took me a second to weed out the other people in the crowded room to see what he was referring to. It was Amelia and some gangly white guy I didn't know grinding on one another. I'd never really seen Amelia Yang dance, and seeing her dance like that was highly unexpected and just plain weird—like running into your teacher buying alcohol at the store.

"Yep, that's something I can't unsee." I took a sip, giving my brain something else to focus on. "Who's the guy?"

"Paul Sanderson—he went to Downey." Sebastian continued to stare at them, lost in some sort of masochistic trance.

"How do you know him?"

"Cross Country, MESA, Science Bowl..." he listed.

"So he was like Downey's version of you?"

"Yeah, except he got into Stanford."

"Oh, I see."

"You know, I should've put it together. He was in a bunch of her photos on Instagram. It just wasn't as obvious as that," he said, referring to the dancing, never taking his eyes off them.

"Hey, hey, look at me," I successfully directed his attention to my eyes. I took in his large brown eyes that had an unfamiliar look of defeat in them. "You're walking a fine line between wistful and creepy right now," I warned.

"Sorry, just trying to come to terms with her decision to break up with me and immediately date my high school nemesis, of all people."

"I thought I was your nemesis?" I argued.

"Hardly," he scoffed. "A nemesis implies an intellectual rivalry."

"You are so freaking arrogant." I shook my head, no longer feeling entirely sorry for him.

At the same time, I felt an odd urge to give Amelia a taste of her own medicine. There were so many unfair things in the world, and this, although entirely superficial, was a small piece of justice I could provide.

"I have half a mind not to help you." I stood up and held out my hand.

"Help me?" He looked down at my hand then up at my eyes, furrowing his brow, of course.

"Yeah, instead of pouting and being miserable out here, you're going to go back in there, stand in the kitchen where she can see you, and pretend like whatever I'm saying is the most interesting crap you've ever heard. You're not going to let her win tonight," I ordered. "Come on, Old Man Torres, the night is young!"

I wiggled my fingers, encouraging him to grab my hand. Sebastian hesitated a few moments before accepting. It was a little odd to be holding a hand that was not Hunter's, but I was so focused on my intended purpose, I decided not to dwell on it. Or the fact that Sebastian's hand felt much stronger than I anticipated.

"I highly doubt talking to you in the kitchen is going to make her jealous at all," he stated in traditional Sebastian know-it-all fashion.

What Sebastian hadn't considered was that while no one cared who he and Amelia were dating, people did care about whether Hunter and I had or had not gotten back together. Any attention Sebastian and I attracted would ultimately lead to Amelia noticing us. Inconspicuously, I was able to take inventory of three people who reacted to me holding Sebastian's hand just during our short journey to the kitchen.

"Here, stop right there," I said quietly, positioning us in a spot where Amelia could see us, but Sebastian wouldn't be able to see her. I needed him to keep his attention on me. "Did you want a refill?"

"I'm good. I'm driving and this beer actually tastes disgusting," he criticized.

"I'm surprised to see you drinking."

"And I'm surprised to see you not drunk."

"Halloween was extremely out of character for me," I insisted. "I usually pour one drink at these things and sip on it just to keep up appearances."

"Oh, appearances? I had no idea you had such an important image to uphold," he marveled.

"Well, some people actually want to give the impression of liking fun," I said with my friendliest smile, then casually reached out to trail my hand down his arm, briefly squeezing his hand before letting go.

"What are you doing?" Luckily, Amelia could not see Sebastian's befuddled face.

"Proving you wrong," I said confidently, smiling again.

"No, what you're doing is creeping me out," he corrected.

I let out a quiet fake laugh and leaned in to whisper in his ear.

"Amelia has already glanced over here twice and is no longer grinding up on her date." I backed away, giving him a shy smile.

"Don't turn around." I said, anticipating his instinct. "Keep looking at me."

Thankfully, he listened to me for once in his life.

"What do I do, then?"

"How about you ask me about my final grade in Calculus?" I playfully poked at his chest.

"Please don't poke me. That seems excessive."

"I'm starting to think you've never had anyone flirt with you before."

"I'm starting to think you don't know what flirting is," he fired back.

"If I hadn't gotten a 3.0 in Calculus, there's no way I would be doing this for you right now," I attempted to control my facial expression despite Sebastian making me flustered.

"A 3.0?" He sounded happy for the first time that night. "Congratulations," he smiled. "That's way better than I expected."

"Really?" My smile briefly faded. "That's how you congratulate someone?"

He shrugged and took a sip.

"I'm sorry. I meant—" he grabbed my hand and locked his fingers with mine. "Ohmygosh! You are so amazing!"

He waved our interlocked hands in the air. If it had been another time, I would have snapped at him for mocking me, but to his benefit, Amelia and her new beau began to approach.

"You are so funny," I laughed, gently touching his chest, unfortunately just long enough to have a flashback of what he looked like shirtless. I ordered myself to focus. It wasn't like I hadn't posed with my hands on Hunter's naked chest millions of times. The nervous feeling in my stomach was clearly unwarranted. Predictably, he furrowed his brow at my flirty performance.

"Hey Sebastian," Amelia interrupted us. He calmly turned around.

"Oh hey, Amy," he smiled. "Paul, good to see you," he reached out and shook Paul's hand. There was an awkward pause.

"Hi, I'm Lucy," I introduced myself to Paul, since no one else felt the need to. He smiled hello. Poor guy, I don't think he knew the two of us were props.

"So," Amelia started, "Lucy, you're up at Washington with Bastian?"

"Yeah, it's crazy. We actually ended up on the same floor," I shared.

"Oh," she nodded. "He never mentioned that."

"I guess we both have a habit of not mentioning things," he jabbed at her.

"You mean like not getting into Stanford?" Amelia shot back.

I saw Sebastian's brow start to go. He was about to lose it and give her the reaction she wanted. My years of experience of pretending to be one half of Beyer High's Perfect Fairy Tale Couple kicked in. I knew exactly how to control the narrative and show everyone there that Sebastian had won the breakup.

"Oh my gosh," I exclaimed. "Amelia, I'm just so glad you and Sebastian were able to clear things up since we've been back." She locked eyes with me, demanding clarification.

"I mean, the last thing we ever wanted to do was hurt anyone's feelings. I'm so glad you were able to talk, and just finally be honest. We really wanted to make sure everyone was okay and there were no hard feelings, before we became, you know, public. And seeing you here tonight with Paul, it's like everything worked itself out.

"It's just so great," I said emphatically, turning my superficial tone up to the max. "I mean, believe me, it's been so hard to keep our hands off of each other." I wrapped my arms around Sebastian's waist. "I know you know what I mean," I laughed and looked up at him affectionately.

Thank God Sebastian was able to look somewhat natural despite all my likely unwanted touching. I guess revenge was all the motivation he needed to tolerate me getting handsy. Amelia stood there with Paul, speechless.

"You guys make a super cute couple, by the way," I threw in airily, before resting my head on Sebastian's shoulder.

Amelia examined Sebastian's face, trying to determine if we were lying. I could tell we hadn't fully sold it, but it was enough to make her doubt whether he was still hung up on her like she wanted him to be. To me, that was enough of a success for the night.

"I...I need to get some air," Amelia stammered before rushing out to the backyard, followed by a clueless Paul. We had made a bigger scene than I had originally intended, especially with the old AP crowd who had watched the whole exchange from the living room. Sebastian turned to me, committed enough to the farce to not pull away immediately.

"So now what?" he asked.

"Yeah, now what?" Hunter's voice called over from the corner of the kitchen, all of his old friends were standing behind him.

Okay, so I hadn't thought everything out.

"Seriously, what the hell, Lucy?" Hunter exclaimed once we were outside in front of the house. We had moved far enough away where no one could hear, but I knew people were watching us and trying their best to eavesdrop through open windows.

"I'm not doing this out here," I crossed my arms and started down the driveway. "We can talk in the car," I called behind me.

There was no way I could have this discussion—fight—whatever it was, without mentioning that he was gay. The last thing I needed was to be responsible for outing him to everyone we went to high school with.

We both got in his car, forcefully shutting our doors in unison.

"Are you going to tell me what's going on?"

"You're the one that said I was planning on making out with him tonight. Had to give your pal Ronnie all the dirt."

"Yeah, I was joking. And last I checked, I had a right to know if you were moving on to someone else."

"A right to know? We are not together! We never were," I shouted. "This agreement never went past high school. You were supposed to come out to everyone by now!"

Suddenly all my patience disappeared. So much for protecting Hunter from all my overflowing anger. He shook his head.

"You keep acting like it's the easiest thing do. You have no idea." Hunter was on the brink of tears. I hadn't seen him cry since he came out to me sophomore year.

"It's not going to get any easier if I keep letting you use me whenever you want people to think you're straight." Apparently, the small amount of time I spent at that party had now made me a proponent of tough love.

"I just would've liked a little warning that you were with someone. I don't know why you thought you had to hide it from me. And for me to find out in the middle of a party, with everyone else? Lucy, we tell each other everything."

I paused. I knew I couldn't maintain a lie with him.

"I'm not with Sebastian."

"What?"

"Amelia brought her new boyfriend tonight and they were all over each other. Sebastian seemed so sad about it and it was a pretty coldhearted thing for her to do, so I decided I could make her jealous."

"Did he ask you to do that?"

"No," I shook my head. "I just did it because I knew I could...and...I guess I have some sort of pent up anger towards Amelia Yang...and maybe you, too?" I admitted quietly.

"Me?"

"You act like I'm just always going to be here whenever you need someone to be your beard."

"One: you know I hate that term, and two: don't you remember you got upset when you thought I had someone else doing that down in Santa Barbara?"

"I want you to finally be honest about who you are with everyone," I exclaimed.

"Says the girl who just set herself up to be someone else's fake girlfriend," he laughed, thankfully breaking the tension.

"I didn't say I always make sense," I admitted with a sigh. "Anyway, it's different with Sebastian. It'll blow over in a couple weeks. It was just to keep him from looking pitiful in front of Amelia tonight."

"You need to be careful," he advised, catching me off guard.

"Why?"

"It's one thing to pretend with me; it's another thing when it's a straight guy. If he's attracted to girls and you're attracted to guys, seems like a lot of room for getting confused about things."

"It's no big deal," I dismissed.

"There are literally, like, a million movies about it."

"Like I said, it'll all blow over," I assured.

Hunter's concern amused me. Like I could ever misinterpret something Sebastian did. The boy literally had no filter.

"I'm just doing him a favor after he helped me pass Calculus. Hopefully the story reignites whatever spark he and Amelia have, and they can live pompously ever after doing math problems for fun together," I reasoned aloud. "Now let's just head back to your place and watch Anderson Cooper be awkward with Andy Cohen."

"Yeah, right. After that scene, you can't come home with me," he said definitively. "Especially if you want people to believe the whole thing. You, my friend, have to leave the party with Sebastian Torres."

I sighed and rubbed my face.

Ugh, Hunter was right. I pulled out my phone and texted Sebastian asking him to take me home.

"So, what's the story we're going with?" Hunter sought clarification. "Are we fighting? Am I inconsolable?"

"We've been broken up for like three months, should you really be all that sad?"

He reached out and gently ran his hand through my hair.

"I mean, Lucile Allen is no longer in love with me, how could I not be heartbroken?"

Again, always charming.

"I'll let you call the play. Just remember the more girls you get to feel sorry for you, the more they're going to try to make out with you tonight."

"Damn, you're right."

"Just continue the story I started. You're interested in someone else in Santa Barbara and were waiting to make sure there were no hard feelings. I just beat you to it. It's actually pretty close to the truth anyway. But instead of one girl in Santa Barbara, it's like four guys...actually, really any dude with a surfboard and nice hair," I teased.

I got the text from Sebastian saying he could take me home and to meet him at the front of the house.

"All right, that's my ride," I said and started to get out of the car. Hunter didn't follow me. "Aren't you going back to the party?"

"You know, I think I'm just going to go home."

"Really?"

"Yeah...I've got a New Year's Resolution to get ready for."

I smiled, feeling hopeful for him.

"I'll text you." Hunter gave me a small smile back.

"Okay, have a good night." I closed the door and headed back up to the front of the house where Sebastian was waiting for me.

There was still a crowd around the front windows. More than likely, Hunter would have a bunch of texts awaiting him when he got home. Since I considered the majority of those people Hunter's friends first and foremost, I wasn't anticipating any sort of messages.

"I'm over here," Sebastian started towards a silver Camry.

He unlocked the doors and I got in. He remained silent as he maneuvered out of the driveway; the only sound was some random alternative band playing that I didn't know.

"I'm starving," he announced once we were out on the country road heading back towards town. "You mind if we go through In-N-Out?"

"That's fine." My stomach was growling. I guess orchestrating melodrama made me hungry.

"It's so cliché, but I've actually missed being able to have a Double-Double whenever I want."

I didn't respond. I was a rare breed; a Californian who did not feel passionately about In-N-Out. But there was no need to get into yet another meaningless debate with Sebastian.

"Also, decent Mexican food. It's severely lacking in Seattle."

I turned and looked at him. Was he honestly making small talk with me?

"What?" he asked.

"You don't want to talk about anything that just went down?"

"You mean how you bizarrely put your hands all over me to make your ex-boyfriend jealous?"

"That's not—excuse me," I raised my voice. "I was helping you save face in front of Amelia," I threw back.

"Yeah, but then it became very clear that you were just using my situation for your benefit. Don't get me wrong, I'm all for embarrassing Hunter Davis in front of all the other has-beens, but the least you could do is be honest that you're using me."

Suddenly I wished I had let him pathetically pine after Amelia all night. It was so aggravating to hear someone talk like they were an expert on something that they knew absolutely nothing about. Momentarily, I thought about shoving it all down, but then impulsively I found my irritation coming out in full force.

"I wasn't using you! If anything, I was letting you use me! Maybe if you stopped thinking that you always know everything that everyone is thinking, then maybe for once you could recognize that someone was trying to do something nice for you!" I shocked myself by actually yelling.

He pulled into the drive thru and turned to me.

"What do you want?" he asked, unaffected by my tone.

Sebastian's lack of emotional response left me confused.

"Single? Double Double?...Milkshake?" he inquired casually.

"I...I'll just take a chocolate milkshake," I responded quietly.

He nodded and made the order. He parked the car after we got our food. The urge to continue yelling at him about how extremely wrong he was about everything all the time was temporarily silenced by having ice cream available. Sebastian dug into his burger and fries. Some fireworks started to go off in the distance, lighting up the dark winter sky.

"Hey, look at that," he acknowledged. "Happy New Year."

He held up his cup to clink with mine. I paused but then reciprocated.

"Happy New Year," I said quietly. "I wasn't using you," I reiterated.

"Hmm, how so?" As usual, he demanded evidence.

"Hunter and I are fine with being just friends. There's not nearly as much drama there as people think," I assured.

"Then why all the storming off?"

"It just took him by surprise, that's all. I assure you there's nothing here that would ever make him the least bit jealous."

"Harsh," he laughed.

"It's nothing against you," I quickly tried to backtrack, wishing I could explain more, but knowing that I couldn't. I paused, mulling over his argument again.

"I don't know, maybe you're right," I admitted with a sigh. "Not that I was using you to make Hunter jealous...but maybe just to feel more in control of something," I processed aloud.

He didn't offer any feedback. The words started falling out of my mouth.

"I've been so angry about almost everything lately. It's so magnified when I'm home. It feels like my mom and sister have completely moved on from my dad, even though he hasn't even been gone a year yet. It pisses me off so much. And then it just spills over into other things that have absolutely nothing to with my dad.

"It's like there's this anger that's always in the background and I don't know what to do with it because I've never been an angry person. So I just constantly feel like I'm screaming on the inside. I guess putting Amelia in her place tonight, in some weird way, felt like I could get some of the screaming out of my system."

He let a silence pass. I couldn't believe I had shared that much. Especially with Sebastian Torres.

"Wow," he reflected evenly.

All I could do was stare back at him.

"That's some dark shit, Lucy. Kind of makes me like you more."

"Do you always have to be such a dick?" I assumed he was mocking me.

"I'm being serious," he laughed. "Look, I'm really sorry you're going through all that. I can only imagine. You know, it's okay to be angry. Emotions aren't a constant. They don't define us. Your dad died and you're angry—that doesn't make you less nice. You know that, right?"

Did I?

"And like I said on Thanksgiving, your tendency to be nice at all costs doesn't always work out in your favor."

Instead of arguing, I stared out the window, looking at the random fireworks.

"How come it doesn't bother you when I yell?" I asked softly, thinking back to how unaffected he seemed only minutes ago.

"I have a mom and three sisters. Fiery women are a constant in my household," he said matter-of-factly. "Also, I was captain of the debate team, remember?"

Sebastian finished up his food and leaned back to take a drink of his soda, joining me in staring out the window. It was the most relaxed I'd been all break.

"Have you talked to anyone about your dad? You know, like a professional?"

"Ugh, yes." My annoyance was clear. "There was someone my mom made me see last year. Even had me go see her this week. I'm not a fan of the whole thing."

He nodded and paused.

"What?" I asked defensively, wondering if Sebastian was going to guess just how embarrassing I thought it was to be considered someone who needed help with feelings of all things.

He hesitated briefly, possibly the first time I saw him appear to choose his words carefully with me.

"I'm just thinking that there's probably more than one counselor out there. Sometimes it's about finding the right fit, rather than giving up on something entirely." He paused to take a drink. "Kind of like finding the right person to explain calculus," he added for measure.

I wanted to argue with him, but he sounded so rational. His usual arrogance that triggered me was gone. Was it going to lead me to start calling up any therapist I could find to talk to about my dead dad? Probably not. But in that moment, I was able to take a breath and the anger and frustration didn't feel quite so overwhelming and unfixable. Even though the whole idea of needing any intervention from a paid professional remained a source of embarrassment for me.

After a few moments he looked down at his phone.

"What the hell? I have like ten messages." He started scrolling. "They are all about you—or us, I guess?"

His attention remained on his phone. My theatrics sparking people's curiosity didn't surprise me as much as it did Sebastian. "What should I say?"

"Don't say anything. Less is always more."

He raised a brow.

"I mean, unless you want to tell them that it was all fake and you were trying to make Amelia jealous."

"It wasn't my idea to make Amelia jealous."

"That's funny, I don't remember you correcting any of my lies or swatting my hands away when they were on your waist."

"True," he granted.

"Here."

I grabbed his cup from him without asking and then positioned it next to mine on the dashboard. I snapped a picture, miraculously timing it right when a large firework lit up the sky. I uploaded and captioned it *"The perfect way to start the New Year @sm-torres."*

"What are you doing?"

"I'm posting this picture and I'm tagging you in it."

His phone went off with a notification. "Now you can share it to your stories."

"Why?"

"I'm solidifying the narrative."

"What are you? A sleazy PR rep?"

"Look, do you want to win Amelia back?"

He nodded with slight hesitation.

"You're not going to get her back by looking depressed and bitter. You have to show her that she's missing out on something."

"But if she thinks I'm with you then she's not going to think I want her back. She'll just think I've moved on."

"Oh, silly Sebastian, that's not how it works at all."

Now it was my turn to be smug. I took my milkshake off the dashboard and took a drink. I expected him to start an argument with me, but instead I held his attention.

"This is what you need to do. Tomorrow afternoon, you should DM her—not call—DM," I made sure to specify. "Then apologize for how she found out about us at the party and tell her that it's really important that you stay friends with her, and more than anything, you just want her to be happy.

"You leave it at that. Then you make a point to like things that she posts, but don't comment, just like. But only like...one out of three posts, enough to make her know that you still like her, but you're not hung up on her, at least not publicly. We'll also have to make sure that we set up some posts to help make her a little jealous, and hopefully refuel her attraction to you," I continued.

"Whoa, whoa," he interrupted. "That all seems really manipulative."

"You're just liking pictures she posts on social media, how is that manipulative?"

"You just said I'd have to 'set up' some photos to make her jealous," he said pointedly. "Also, I probably won't really like all of her posts, especially if Paul is in them. That's disingenuous."

"I didn't say like all the pictures, just every third post. It's being nice," I reframed.

"But if I were dating you, it wouldn't really be nice to you if I was spending all this energy liking my ex-girlfriend's posts, right?"

"That's the whole point. It tells her that you still like her even if you're dating someone else. Then you can tell her I started to read into things and accused you of not being over her. And then she'll admit that she misses you and you guys can go back to being the world's most pedantic power couple, providing hope to nerds all over the world."

He gave me the look of doubt I had gotten used to by now.

"What?" I demanded.

"I'm just surprised you used pedantic correctly," Sebastian deadpanned.

"Or you can just let her be with Paul Sanders. He's probably a better intellectual match for her anyway."

"Sanderson," he corrected.

"Whatever."

"I'm starting to think you have a bit of an evil streak in you, Lucile."

"I do not! It's not evil," I defended. "I'm being nice. I'm trying to help you get your old girlfriend back."

"Yeah, through low stakes fraud," he argued, sounding slightly insulted.

I shrugged.

"It's not malicious. No one is going to get hurt." I stared him down to make my point. "Except for maybe Paul," I admitted.

"He doesn't count." Sebastian stared back at me, mulling over my proposal. "I'll think about it. I'd like to think I can win Amy back on my own without having to rely on something that sounds like it came from a plot from a bad Netflix movie."

"Very well, have it your way. You know where to find me when you change your mind and actually want to get her back."

I let the topic drop, knowing it would be incredibly satisfying when he came back to me and told me I was right. There were few things in life that were more enjoyable than proving Sebastian Torres wrong. My confidence only grew when I looked down to see that my post had already been shared five times.

Chapter Twelve

My winter quarter course load was so much better than the fall. I had wisely loaded my schedule with easier classes that would fulfill general education requirements. There was absolutely no math to worry about. I was literally giddy when I looked over each syllabus I received.

Psych 101 actually offered extra credit. All I had to do was volunteer to fill out surveys for research studies conducted by grad students. Art History was pretty much just remembering pictures and fun facts and terms associated with each image. And English Composition simply consisted of reading essays and then writing a response.

I was riding high on excitement by the end of the first day of classes. The thought of how improved my GPA was going to be by March was something to look forward to, especially since I knew I wouldn't have to completely bust my ass to achieve it.

Although I knew it remained a reach, law school seemed just a smidge more attainable. There was still the question of whether I really wanted to be a lawyer, though. The first step would be to figure out a major—and that decision remained completely overwhelming. My small stint in Calculus and Biology made me hesitant to choose anything in the sciences.

I kept hearing it reiterated that freshman year was about exploring and sophomore year was about declaring. But when everyone around you seemed to have already figured out what prerequisites they needed to take, you couldn't help but feel behind. This was when I took comfort in the fact that my memory recall for all the Art History tests would make me feel like I was at least winning at something.

"What is with you?" Veronica asked me at dinner after our first day back at school.

"What do you mean?"

"You have been talking nonstop about your first day back. I've never seen you so...chipper."

"I guess I'm just excited to not have to take any math this term."

"You sure you won't miss the extra help you were getting for Calculus?" Corine teased.

"Hell no," I scoffed. "The fact that I can handle my classes without any help from Sebastian this quarter is the best news ever."

"Just like how you two had the best start to the new year ever?" Jenna uncharacteristically teased, referencing my Instagram post they had all been obsessing over the past week.

"I think you mean the 'perfect start,'" Veronica corrected with a grin.

"By the way, don't think we haven't noticed that you still haven't explained that to us," Corine called me out.

"There's nothing to explain," I insisted.

"I tried getting the details from Hunter, but he's been surprisingly secretive about her perfect New Year's, too," Veronica shared with the table.

"You know us Californians, we just really like In-N-Out. Right, Corine?"

"Yeah, right," she shook her head. "Such a woman of mystery."

"I swear you guys think I'm way more interesting than I am. I'm just a girl excited about her easier classes this quarter, which will raise her GPA and help get her into law school. No time for any of that boy drama."

Despite my best effort to sound convincing, they all still laughed at me.

The truth was, I had not spoken or texted with Sebastian since New Year's, and he had been absent from social media, making it impossible to decipher anything from his posts. If I had been following Amelia's account, I would have been able to at least see if he was publicly interacting with her like I had suggested. I wasn't about to tell my friends the story because without him being on board, I just looked like a crazy girl.

"Hey, didn't you say Khalil sat down next to you in one of your classes today?" I navigated the conversation off me and on to Corine.

"Ohmygod, yes!" Corine dove into sharing the Khalil details with the rest of the table. I was pleased with myself.

After dinner, I returned to my room and dove into my class reading. In addition to having textbooks that I understood this quarter, I had the extra treat of not being scrunchy sentenced...yet. Although, I was sure it was only a matter of time before Danica returned to her old patterns.

We had said a total of six words to one another since returning from winter break. I thought about bringing up the expectation that she not kick me out of the room as much this quarter, but got too anxious thinking about all the different ways that conversation would be uncomfortable, so I decided to avoid it all together.

"Hey."

I looked up from my Psychology book to see Sebastian standing in our doorway.

"Uh, hey." I sat up straighter at my desk. Danica continued to sit with her earbuds in, unaware of anything else going on around her.

"You got a minute?"

"Sure." I got up and stepped out into the hallway with him, not that I thought Danica would notice if we talked in front of her. "What's up?"

He paused. I stared back at him.

"How was your first day?" he stalled.

"Fine. Yours?"

"Good," Sebastian nodded. Another pause. "Any math this quarter?"

"Nope."

Again, he nodded, but said nothing else.

"Okay then..." I trailed off after there was another long pause.

"I was wondering...if I could—get your take on something?" he finally forced out.

It had to be about Amelia. I stared at him and waited for more information. He sighed.

"I took your advice and messaged her." He handed me his phone. "And this is what she said."

I started reading the exchange of messages.

> **Amy, I want to apologize for the other night. The last thing I ever wanted to do was hurt you, and I'm sure you never meant to hurt me. I would like to stay friends, or even return to how things were before. Please let me know if this is possible. --Bastian**
>
> Sebastian, I'm not really sure how I hurt you, but I am sorry if you've been hurt by your own decisions that have led us to where we are now. I'm so glad you still want to be friends.
>
> But you might want to check with how your new girlfriend feels about that? Then again, she might be all for it, given how friendly she is with her own ex.
>
> I wonder if she might be using you to get to him? I know it's hard for guys to resist a girl who gives attention and other things so easily. I'm always here for you if you need to talk. XO, Amy
>
> **Thank you. Lucy understands how important you are to me. I'm sure she wouldn't mind that we continue to be in one another's lives.**

"She didn't respond. She just liked the last message," he said, taking the phone back. "And then I did that thing you said to do about liking her posts. I was only going to like every third one, but then she posted these."

He pulled up her account and handed the phone back to me. There was a selfie of Amelia. She was in a V-neck Stanford T shirt, and was holding the camera at an angle where you could clearly see cleavage. Sebastian and of course several others had liked the photo.

"Look at the comments," he instructed.

Unsurprisingly, there were a variety of compliments about how good she looked. At least Sebastian followed my advice that time and didn't comment.

"And then look at the next three posts." I scrolled up to find similar poses and a more made-up Amelia than I had been familiar with in high school. Each one earning more likes, including Sebastian's.

"And then she posted that one immediately after the last one."

I looked to see her most recent photo was one of her kissing Paul with the caption *"The perfect way to start the new quarter."* To me, it was a clear reference to the New Year's photo I had tagged Sebastian in. The wording was too similar not to be.

"Hey guys, what's going on?" Corine approached us as she was about to step into Veronica and Hattie's room.

"Sebastian's been caught in a thirst trap by his ex-girlfriend," I informed casually.

"Did someone say 'thirst trap?'" Veronica poked her head out almost on cue.

"Oooo, lemme see," Corine grabbed his phone from me.

"Most boring thirst trap ever," she declared disappointedly after seeing the post of Amelia in a red dress. She held it up for Veronica to see.

"Well, it's an Amelia Yang version of a thirst trap," I clarified.

"What on earth is a thirst trap?" Sebastian finally asked.

"You can't be serious," Veronica laughed.

"No, he is," I sighed and then started to enlighten him. "She posted these photos intentionally for people to like them, specifically you, and tell her that she's hot. It was to get your attention, which she appears to have done very easily. And then once she knew she had your attention, she posted the picture with Paul because she knew you would see it—you'd given her enough likes for the algorithm to work in her favor."

"But you were the one who told me to message her and like her posts."

"I didn't tell you to flat out tell her you wanted to get back together. And I had no idea Amelia had it in her to thirst trap you. Otherwise, we would've covered it," I defended.

"So, I'm not supposed to like the photos that I think she looks good in?"

Poor Sebastian. These things were beyond his understanding.

"That's entirely up to you. Just know if you keep liking the ones she posts like that, it'll reinforce that all her other posts, meaning the ones with her and Paul, will show up in your feed."

"Well, what does that mean? Does she want to get back together?"

"I don't know, but Amelia is clearly looking for some sort of revenge on you. Are you sure the only thing you did wrong was not get into Stanford? Also, I'm starting to wonder what exactly it is she has against me? Since when does having the same boyfriend for the past three years make me easy?"

"She didn't call you easy."

"Oh, I know exactly what she meant by 'gives attention and other things so easily,'" I argued.

"Y'all going to catch us up on what's going on here?" Corine put a pause on Sebastian and my bickering, calling our attention back to her and Veronica.

"Sebastian's girlfriend broke up with him over winter break and very rudely showed up to a New Year's party with her new boyfriend and proceeded to grind all over him in front of everyone."

"You're forgetting the part where you made everything way more complicated than it needed to be," he interjected before I could finish the story.

"Oh please, I made nothing more complicated between you two than it already is," I snapped back.

"She proceeded to put her hands all over me until it got Amy's attention and then goes on to announce to the whole crowd that we're dating."

"I seem to recall someone else placing his hand on my hip and not denying any of my statements when we were in front of Miss Grinds-A-Lot."

"Ooohh, so that's what the post was about!" The dots connected for Veronica.

"Yes, and I presented him with a very clear game plan on how to win her back by pretending to date me over Instagram for a short amount of time, but someone thought he and Amelia transcended all that pettiness and he didn't need my help."

"What was the plan?" Veronica inquired.

"Oh great, just what I need, a committee," Sebastian muttered.

"It's been a week and you don't seem to be doing all that much better on your own," I said matter-of-factly before I began to inform our audience.

"I told him he needed to show her what she was missing rather than just being the guy pathetically hung up on her. Play the whole, 'hey we're both dating other people, but let's still be friends. Also, here's a few convenient reminders of how much fun it is to be with me' angle.

"But instead, he sent her messages flat out telling her he would dump me in a heartbeat if it meant getting back together with her and proceeds to like all of her photos and post nothing on his own account, basically confirming to her he's only on Instagram to follow her," I took a breath once I was done presenting my case to Corine and Veronica.

"Show them the messages," I demanded of him.

He furrowed his brow.

"You said you wanted my take on what she meant. Which I gave you. Why not increase your data pool?"

Sebastian pulled up the messages and handed his phone over to Corine and Veronica.

"Girl is definitely feeling the hate for Lucy," Veronica confirmed.

"You really haven't posted anything on your grid?" Corine confirmed what I already knew was problematic.

"I thought less was more," Sebastian exclaimed the advice I gave him in his car on New Year's.

"That only applies when you give them something. It doesn't apply when you give them nothing at all," I exclaimed back.

"Who is them? And what is it that I'm giving them?" He lifted his hands up, exasperated. "I just want my girlfriend back! And now she hates me even more because she thinks I'm with you."

"Yes, because rubbing her backside into Paul's crotch before she knew anything about me was a sign of true love and stability," I cut back curtly.

"Okay, okay, okay," Veronica broke into the debate. "Sebastian, why did she break up with you?"

"I don't know."

All three of us looked at him with disbelief.

"I got waitlisted by Stanford last spring, but told her I got in. She was pissed, but I thought we were going to do long distance. Over break, she told me she thought it was best for us to see other people, but didn't say why."

"Because she was cheating on you with Paul the whole time," I filled in the blank.

"Who is Paul?"

"His other nemesis from high school," I filled in.

"My only nemesis," Sebastian quickly corrected.

"So, she decided to start dating a guy she knew you had beef with and then brought him to a party that she knew you would be at?" Corine clarified.

Sebastian nodded.

"Damn, that's cold-blooded."

"Thank. You." I said, now validated. "Which was why I thought I was doing him a favor! But he couldn't just listen to me and follow my advice to win her back."

"Do you really even want her back?" Veronica asked the obvious.

"Yes," Sebastian sighed, searching for the words when he was met with our skeptical faces. "You guys don't understand. This is not how she usually is. I have no idea where this is coming from. And all I want to do is have a normal conversation with her, but she seems to have gone off to Stanford and jumped on the social media warfare train that apparently all of you have been riding for way too long."

"Do you want our help or not?" I snapped at his low-grade insult.

"Come on, Lucy," Veronica said softly. "He's had his heart broken. You could be a little nicer." She frowned sympathetically as she reached out to rub Sebastian's shoulder.

"What?" I laughed. "Nice is literally all I'm being!"

"I'd say it looks like she's doing a lot of this to make you jealous," Corine evaluated as she ignored me. "If she didn't care what you thought, she wouldn't show off being with this guy so much. It sounds like she took it as a personal offense when you didn't go to Stanford."

"I had no say in the matter," Sebastian interjected. Corine lifted her hand to quiet him, which he shockingly responded to.

"Well for whatever reason, she took it as you saying you didn't want to be with her. You could play it two ways: go silent and completely ignore her and see how she responds to that, which I think would just reinforce the whole idea that you left her. Or, like Lucy said, put some stuff out there to remind her what she's missing."

"So post pictures making it look like Lucy and I are dating?"

"Well, you don't have to, but I'd say judging by her most recent responses, that's probably the quickest way you're going to get her attention back."

"But keep messaging and being friendly with her. Thinking that you are seeking her out even when appearing happy with Lucy will give her satisfaction," Veronica continued.

"But when do I tell her I just want to be with her?"

"Oh, we'll let you know," Corine assured. "Until then, get ready to look all cute in some pictures together," she grinned, tossing his phone back to him.

"Yay! A project," Veronica hopped up excitedly.

"You really think this will work?" Sebastian sounded slightly less doubtful than he had on New Year's.

"Yes," we all answered in unison.

"Okay," he sighed. "I guess I'll talk to you tomorrow about how to make a thirst trap," he deadpanned.

"Eww," I reflexively responded.

"I'm going to get back to my physics," Sebastian shook his head as he put the phone back in his pocket. "At least that's easier to understand." He turned and headed back to his room.

Veronica and Corine were holding matching cheesy grins as we continued to stand in the hallway.

"Well, I would have to agree that this is the perfect way to start the New Year, don't you think so, Veronica?" Corine laughed.

"Ugh, shut up," I dismissed before heading back to my reading.

The next day I was packing up my things at the end of my morning English Comp class. There was a text from Sebastian.

> Can I meet you today at 2?

> *Sure where?*

Starbucks at the HUB?

K, see you then.

More than likely Sebastian was going to further lecture me about how it was somehow my fault that he had not made any progress on winning Amelia back. I should've known better than to offer up my help. After all, I knew from experience how completely horrible he was at group projects. He never trusted my judgment.

At the same time, I imagined breaking up with a girlfriend, an actual one, of two years, was probably pretty upsetting, especially if he thought they were going to be together throughout college. Lucky for him, I could tap into my tendency to be passively nice and just let him vent at me. It was easier to find some compassion, especially now that I wasn't stressed about my courses. Did I mention that Psych 101 tests were ALL multiple choice?

I got to the HUB a little bit before two and decided to get a start on some Art History homework after I ordered my latte. Although it was only two days into the quarter, I was very clearly crushing it in terms of studying. I didn't even let myself get distracted by people-watching despite the ample opportunity surrounding me.

"Hey," Sebastian said briskly, calling my attention up to him as he stood on the other side of the round table. He put all his stuff down in a chair, but remained standing.

Without further comment, he unzipped his backpack and pulled out his laptop and a textbook, haphazardly laying them down. Then, without saying anything, Sebastian pulled out his phone and snapped a picture of our things on the table. Immediately, he started packing up his things and appeared to be leaving just as soon as he got there.

"What are you doing?" I asked, my confusion evident in my tone, along with my own furrowed brow.

"What does it look like? I took a picture to post like you guys told me to." He then proceeded to type into his phone, probably uploading whatever subpar, sloppy shot he'd gotten.

"You do realize that this is going to take a little more coordination than that?"

"I think you think it will take more coordination than it actually will," he clarified condescendingly.

I sighed.

"So, I guess there's no need for me to tell you that Amelia messaged me last night and requested to follow me?"

"Wait. What?" The color drained from his face. I got satisfaction from his reaction.

"Sit," I ordered, and was somewhat surprised when he obeyed without argument. "Calm down. I didn't accept or answer back yet," I reassured.

"Why did she message and request to follow you?"

"Because she's not stupid and I think she's trying to catch you in the lie right now. But also, if this is real, like we want her to think it is, she's trying to set herself up to be an unexpected wedge."

I pulled up the DM on my phone.

> Hi Lucy, I'm so happy for you and Sebastian. I wanted you to know that he messaged me and let me know he still wanted to be friends. I want nothing more than for him to be happy and I think keeping me in his life is a big part of that for him even though I'm with Paul now. Hope you're having a great quarter! -Amelia

"I am so confused. If I was really trying to date you, wouldn't this piss you off?"

"Yeeeep," I took a drink. "She's making sure I know you still have feelings for her. Her passive aggressive game is impressive," I remarked.

"It always has been," he granted.

"This message tells me she's up for competing for you, but she also thinks she's already won—because we haven't given her any information to prove otherwise since New Year's. She's requesting to follow me to keep tabs on you. But you're going to need to post more than two laptops and a text-book to make it believable."

"What? Like kissing?"

"You wish," I laughed. "Don't you worry, I'm an expert in the art of illusion," I assured.

"And bullshit, from what I remember in AP Lit."

"Rude," I gasped, but knew that was how I'd made it through most of AP Lit. Sebastian gave me a slight shrug in response, offering no retraction from his statement.

"Are you sure not getting into Stanford is the only reason why she's pissed off at you?" I fished. "I mean, lots of people don't get into Stanford. It seems like a weird threshold."

"Uh, well," he sighed, rubbing his forehead, "the lying about it until the last minute was a big factor, and there was stuff leading up to it."

"Like?"

"She was adamant that I needed to do more work on my personal statement and needed to try and get a higher SAT score. I guess I was just done. I didn't want to put even more work into it than I already had. And then she ended up being right. She said that if I really cared about being with her, I would've tried harder," Sebastian admitted, sounding defeated.

"I miss how she always drove me to be my best self, you know? It's a good feeling being with someone who knows exactly what she wants...until she decides you're not it anymore." He paused. "I guess that's why it seems so weird to be putting in all this effort into something that she would think is absolutely ridiculous. I would've guessed my GPA would have more weight on winning her back than whom I'm spending my time with."

"Hey, trust me, based off that DM she sent me, she really doesn't want anyone else checking out your GPA, or any other parts of you for that matter."

He furrowed his brow at me as I expected and I snapped a picture and laughed.

"Come on now," he sighed, unamused.

"What?" I laughed. "I'm trying to allow myself a good stockpile to pull from at the ready."

"You have to promise me you won't post anything bad," Sebastian revealed in a brief moment of vulnerability.

"Sebastian, are you telling me that you are, gasp, a little vain?" I snapped a picture again. "I thought surely someone of your intelligence wouldn't be so concerned with something as superficial as physical appearance."

"Not wanting to be publicly embarrassed on the internet has nothing to do with vanity," he argued.

"Okay, fine. Give me your sweetest smile then." I held my camera out and waited.

He gave me the smallest of smiles. I snapped it and reviewed it.

"Tell you what, we'll practice later."

He looked at me, slightly annoyed.

"You're more than welcome to stay and study with me," I grinned. "I promise I won't even talk. I'm just going to sit here and look at naked pictures from the Italian Renaissance and then write a response essay for English Comp. Full of bullshit, of course."

Sebastian didn't say anything, but responded by pulling out his laptop along with his Physics textbook again. We sat and did our work for the next two hours without saying a single thing. It was oddly comforting, and a nice change from having him attempt to teach me about integrals.

Chapter Thirteen

The week wrapped up nicely, both in real life and on social media. I managed to get some decent shots of Sebastian studying that day at the HUB and the sun setting on our walk back to the dorm, and Veronica talked him into taking a post-run picture in which he was covered in sweat and looked somewhat attractive...if someone were into that sort of thing.

It wasn't necessarily thirst trap material, given that it was thirty-nine degrees out, and he had on long sleeves, but it was the best we were going to do for January in Seattle without looking obvious.

Sebastian was most pleased with his caption, where he gloated about running five more miles than me. It made him especially happy when Amelia liked and commented, "Remember I still can beat you at 10 any day." Winking emoji included. Our plan was working.

Other social media wins included Hunter posting a picture of him with Trevor (I think? I know it was not Jonathan) at the beach, one of the slides included Trevor kissing him on the cheek. The caption read *"Just a couple of bros kickin it beach style."*

Chase Robertson, ever the homophobe, commented. "Dude, this looks super gay." To which Hunter responded. "That's probably because I am, dude." Along with a rainbow emoji. This led to the comments blowing up, most of them positive, in addition to a lot of them being statements of shock, as expected.

After New Year's, I knew it was only a matter of time before everyone else knew about Hunter because he kept his resolution to come out to his parents on January 1st. He called me afterwards and said that it had been incredibly awkward, but more than anything he had an overwhelming sense of relief that they finally knew.

He said his parents took comfort in knowing that he had at least "tried" being in a long-term relationship with a girl. As a result, he asked me not to reveal that I knew he was gay the whole time we were dating. While I wasn't thrilled that it was going to make me look clueless when he came out to everyone else, I figured appearing like I unknowingly dated a gay guy wasn't unheard of. Being that we were all out of high school now, hopefully no one cared enough to form an opinion about it.

Veronica and Corine were predictably a little suspicious regarding my lack of emotion about the situation. Even though it probably wouldn't have been that big of a deal to reveal the truth to them since they were total outsiders, my habit of being overly cautious with keeping Hunter's secret continued. Lies were easiest to maintain the fewer the people who knew the truth.

"Lucy, you know it's okay to be upset about it," Veronica tried to comfort while we hung out in her and Hattie's room. "You guys dated for a long time. It's probably quite a shock."

"Really guys, I'm fine. Hunter and I talked, and I'm just so glad that he's able to live his truth."

This was true. This had been true for a long time, yet I felt like I had to work really hard to sell it. Would the situation be more believable if I were more upset? I didn't think I could pull off crying. However, I might be able to pull off being pissed at Hunter, since the simmering frustration in the back of my mind had become even more noticeable ever since going home for Christmas.

"So you're not mad or sad at all?" Corine sounded skeptical.

"Why would I be upset?" I brushed off coolly, quickly calculating that letting any anger come to the surface, even with a fabricated trigger, was too risky. I still wanted Corine and Veronica to like me and no one liked an angry girl.

"It's not like he can control who he's attracted to," I added wisely for good measure.

They looked disturbed rather than comforted by my rationality.

"Yeah, but, Lucy...he didn't tell you after dating you for three years," Veronica said sympathetically.

"I'm sure that was really hard for him."

"You weren't suspicious? Even a little bit?" Corine searched again.

I paused and looked up like I was thinking.

"Honestly, no. But I'm legitimately happy for him."

They stared at me.

"Guys, really I'm fine," I laughed. "You're forgetting that we've been broken up since August."

My phone lit up with a text.

"Sebastian wants to know where we're going for dinner tonight," I announced.

"TBD," Veronica responded.

I raised my brow.

"I figured we'd just head out on the Ave and go from there."

"Time?" I asked.

"Uh...I dunno, seven, seven-thirty," Veronica offered.

I let out a sigh. Not having a clear plan, especially when going out in a group, was something that I loathed.

"With Khalil and Jackson, it's going to make a group of nine. It's going to take forever to get seated," I pointed out. Their lack of concern clearly meant they had not considered this impending headache.

"Uh-oh, we lost super-chill Lucy," Corine joked.

"I'm just saying, calling to reserve a table for nine people on a Friday night might be a good idea."

"Relaaaaaxx," Veronica encouraged.

"I will let you handle texting Sebastian then. I'm sure he'll find all this going with flow highly appealing."

"You know, you make him sound super uptight and critical, and I don't get that vibe from him at all," Corine reflected. "I think it's his way of flirting with you."

"Or he's trying to fool all of you and make me look like the crazy one," I countered as I headed out the door. "Let me know when you all figure out when we're leaving."

More energy was put into my outfit than normal, but I figured the stakes were now raised. If any pictures were posted, I had to look like I actually wanted to look good when going out with Sebastian. As opposed to the usual sweatshirt and sloppy bun everyone had grown accustomed to seeing me in. Although arguably basic, I wore my brown rider boots with leggings, along with a long navy sweater under my peacoat and scarf.

Not that I put a lot of time into noticing, but Sebastian's outfit of a gray fleece over his flannel and dark jeans was a nice combination. I convinced myself it was more about the jacket, because the two other guys who joined us were also wearing fleece jackets and could also be considered attractive. Yep, that was it, I had a thing for guys in North Face jackets. Not that it mattered what I thought of Jackson and Khalil. It was obvious by seating and overt flirting that they had been paired up with Veronica and Corine.

It ended up being a fun night despite lack of planning. For me, group outings in high school had always been more stressful than enjoyable. Hunter was always an amazing date, but as I mentioned before, feeling like I fit in amongst the other girls in the clique was always up for question.

Dinner that night felt different. Turns out not trying to sell yourself as a suitable girlfriend for the hottest, most closeted guy on campus relieved a lot of stress. Also, it was pleasantly surprising to see Sebastian in a social element when he didn't strike me as completely pretentious. This was probably because he didn't say much.

Once the bill was paid and we started gathering our things. Khalil announced that he and Jackson had a friend throwing a house party nearby. Immediately, the other five girls were on board with going.

"I'm actually kind of tired," I started, hoping my excuse wouldn't lead to chastisement. "I think I'm just going to head back for the night."

"Really?" Veronica asked, her disappointment evident.

"I'll walk you back," Sebastian offered seamlessly.

"Perfect," Corine grinned. "Make sure y'all take some cute pictures! I want thirst trap level material!" she called out in the restaurant more loudly than I would have liked. Sebastian was wisely already at the door making an escape from the teasing.

We stepped out into the brisk air and began the short walk back to the dorm.

"I'm surprised you didn't want to go to that party," Sebastian said after we'd walked a few blocks.

"I told you, parties aren't really my thing. It's too loud and you can never hear what anyone is saying. Not that anyone would have anything all that interesting to say, I'm sure."

Keeping his hands in his pockets, he looked over to me, evaluating what I had just said.

"What?"

"Lucile, I'm starting to wonder if you're a bit of a curmudgeon like me."

"Well, I don't know if anyone else could ever achieve your level of curmudgeoness, but Hunter does like to say I am a bit of a hater when it comes to things that other people usually enjoy," I shared as we crossed the street to Lander Hall.

"You know curmudegeoness, isn't a word, right?"

"You know constantly correcting people is unattractive, right?"

"Obviously I know that. You didn't notice I was on my best behavior at dinner?" He opened the front door for me.

"I did notice you were quiet," I admitted. "But I just figured you were bored being around all of us cerebral underlings."

"No, just a little shy sometimes," he admitted before we stepped into the elevator.

"Huh," I reflected. Now it was my turn to evaluate him.

"What?" Sebastian laughed.

"I just always read the quiet as judgmental and not shy."

"Well, that's probably because you're insecure." He winked before we stepped out.

"Excuse me?" I exclaimed—of course, this was his intended reaction.

"It's okay, Lucy," he chastised as we headed down the hall. "It's a completely normal part of development. I'm sure you'll learn all about it in your Psych class when you get to Erikson's theory."

"You can't, for once, show this horribly unappealing side of you to other people?"

"Well, what fun would that be?" Sebastian laughed again, pulling out his keys once we reached his door.

"Whatever. Remember to post one of the four acceptable photos I sent you," I reminded before starting down the remainder of the hallway. Unfortunately, I made out the sight of a scrunchy on the knob before I was halfway to my room.

"Ughhh," I groaned loudly in frustration.

"Warren's gone again," Sebastian called out. "You're welcome to hang out in here while you wait..." he offered.

I turned around and made my way back to his room.

"...you know, since actually dealing with the conflict isn't an option," he remarked sarcastically as I walked past him. I offered him a glare in return.

The heaters in the dorm overcorrected anytime it dropped below forty degrees, especially once inside the rooms. Even after I took off my coat and scarf, I still felt hot. My sweater, as cute as it was, became intolerable as I started to sweat. I could feel my cheeks becoming flushed.

"I don't understand why they insist on turning the heat up to eighty," I complained while pulling my hair up into a bun. I took off my boots and then looked to Sebastian for agreement.

"Feel free to make yourself comfortable," he said flatly.

"They have heels and I'm done wearing them."

"You make sure your key didn't fall out?"

"Har, har," I responded without amusement. "Ugh, it's so hot. This sweater itches when I sweat."

"It sounds like you made a lot of functional oversights when you chose your outfit tonight," he said unsympathetically, now scrolling through his phone.

"Excuse me, my outfit made perfect sense for walking to dinner in January. I didn't know I wouldn't be able to change when I got back."

"Here." Sebastian walked over to his dresser and proceeded to toss a t-shirt and shorts at me, all while still looking at his phone. "Now you can stop complaining."

If he had sounded more chivalrous or was less distracted, I might have thanked him. Instead, without saying anything I stepped into his bathroom to change.

"Better?" he asked expectantly when I stepped back out in his old Beyer engineering club shirt and basketball shorts.

"Yes," I said quietly. Unsure where I should sit, I continued to stand awkwardly in the middle of the room.

"Amelia sent me a message," he shared.

"Ooooo," I exclaimed and impulsively hopped up on the bed next to him. "Lemme see."

He handed me the phone.

> I started Organic Chemistry. Argh! You know Chem was never my strong suit. I might need to call you this quarter if I need help.

I saw that the message had been sent shortly after I posted to my story a pic of the group going out to dinner.

"Hang on," I said as I pulled up the app on my phone. There was a notification. Amelia had reacted to the story and messaged: *Hope you guys had fun! Sebastian looks great in that jacket I got him last winter.* And a smiley face.

"Fascinating," I evaluated.

"What?"

"You don't see this comment?"

He looked and shrugged. "She said I looked good. That's positive, right?"

"She made a point to let me know you're wearing a jacket that she got you. She's trying to get us to fight."

"So, we should fight?"

"Uh, no, not yet," I determined. "You should tell her that you'll help her with Chemistry, but it's probably better that I don't know about it, because you don't want me reading into anything."

"Okay," he went to pick up his phone.

"Wait, what are you doing?" I reached out to stop him.

"I'm sending the message you told me to send."

"No, don't send it now. Make her wait until tomorrow. We don't want you looking too eager."

"Really?" he sighed. His lack of faith in my expertise was evident once again.

"At some point you are going to have to trust me on this stuff," I declared, giving him a pointed look. "We're supposed to be out on a group date right now. If you want to post anything, post one of the pictures from dinner I sent you," I suggested again. "We look cute in those. Give her a little something to ruminate on tonight while she sits with her Chemistry and boring old Paul."

"I'm starting to understand this hater thing Hunter was talking about."

"I am not a hater," I insisted. "I am just well-versed in developing and projecting a specific narrative via social media that leads to desired outcomes," I reframed with a smile.

"Well that's the fanciest way I've ever heard someone say they're good at bullshitting. Tell me, did they teach you that at the Instagram School for the Vapidly Gifted?" he deadpanned.

Trying to gain Sebastian's trust was becoming exhausting. That boy's commitment to concrete evidence for all things was maddening. Despite making the promise to Hunter that I would continue our secret even after he came out to everyone else, it seemed like revealing the truth to Sebastian was the only way to convince him of my talent. While telling Sebastian was riskier than confessing everything to Veronica and Corine, his constant skepticism triggered an impulse to prove there were certain things that I was smarter about than he was.

"Fine, look at this." My tone was borderline irritated when I pulled up Hunter's post from earlier in the week and handed my phone to Sebastian. He swiped through the slides and raised a brow.

"Hunter Davis is gay?"

"Yes!" I confirmed victoriously.

Sebastian looked at me, not understanding my reaction.

"He's been gay this whole time," I added, excited that I finally was able to present indisputable evidence that I was highly skilled in the area of fake relationships that were convincing.

"Well, yeah. That's usually how it works."

"No," I said, exasperated, annoyed that my big reveal hadn't landed. "I mean, I knew he was gay this whole time. He came out to me when we first started dating, but he wasn't ready to be out, so we decided to just keep making everybody think we were a couple."

Sebastian tilted his head as the reality came together.

"So...this whole time?"

"Yep. Completely fake." I affirmed proudly. The feeling of finally telling someone the truth, the whole truth, was exhilarating.

"Do you know how pissed Amelia was when you guys beat us for Cutest Couple?" Sebastian shared with a half-smile, nudging me with his shoulder.

"In all fairness, we still did a lot of things that a boyfriend and girl-friend do," I argued. "It just involved more Taylor Swift and watching Real Housewives than anyone would've expected."

"So, what're people saying now that they all know our favorite teen-age lovers were a complete lie? It wouldn't surprise me if Amelia asked for the yearbooks to be recalled," he joked dryly as he began to scroll through the comments.

"No one else knows that I knew."

He looked up and paused scrolling.

"And they aren't going to," I sighed. "Hunter asked me to act like I didn't know. It's for his parents," I explained. "For some reason, it's easier for them to accept the news if they think he tried to be straight." I rolled my eyes at the ridiculousness.

"So you can't say anything," I ordered. "Anyway, it works in your favor, because the last thing we need is people thinking I hire myself out for fake relationships."

"Even though that's exactly what you do," he finished with a laugh and returned to looking at the comments on Hunter's post. "Lucy, some of these things people said about you are kind of mean."

"Oh, mean comments from idiots on the internet? Alert the press." I shrugged it off.

Not that I didn't know what he was referring to. There were more than a few people who said it finally made sense why Hunter dated me for so long when he was into guys. Lots of alluding to understanding why he would've been clueless about dating someone less attractive than him when it was a girl.

"Why hasn't he gone on here and told these people to shut up?"

"Sometimes you've got to just let the haters hate."

Sebastian looked at me like my answer was unacceptable.

"I think he's just too busy riding the wave of excitement that comes with finally being out. The comments are overall positive and supportive," I justified.

"Yeah, for him." Sebastian stared me down, tempting me to share more.

If I had given in, I would have admitted that I was hurt and even a little angry. Even after Hunter got to finally be free of the lie, I still had to sit with it. At the same time, those feelings could have been more related to the simmering rage and sadness I felt about my dad being dead, and not really about Hunter at all. When you're not used to being constantly angry, it was kind of hard to pinpoint what exactly was pissing you off.

When I looked at the photo of how happy Hunter looked with Trevor it seemed unfair to project any of my stupid, inconvenient dead daddy issues on him. I took in the genuine smile on Hunter's face and reminded myself we were still Hunter and Lucy, and keeping my promise to him was the priority. That's what best friends did. They didn't let stupid dramatic emotions get in the way of the other's happiness.

"Really, it's fine," I insisted, doing my best to convince both Sebastian and myself, before I quickly moved the conversation on. "The point is, I know what I'm doing here. You need to stop questioning me all the time. Deal?"

My tone and expression were as serious as his usually were. Sebastian searched my eyes, and I found myself wishing I knew how to read him as easily as I could Hunter. Then again, maybe it was for the best. He didn't seem to be the biggest fan of lying and I'm sure I just added to the mental list of critiques he had kept on me since the ninth grade.

"Very well," Sebastian finally spoke. My jaw clenched as I anticipated a statement of arrogant piousness from him. However, if Sebastian was evaluating my less-than-honest high school past, he kept it to himself and instead simply handed me his phone.

"I yield to the expert," he granted.

His face was serious. I assumed he determined that verbally withholding his judgment of me was a sacrifice he was willing to make in order to increase the chances of winning Amelia back. Leaving Sebastian relatively speechless was enough validation that I had provided him with sufficient evidence to trust my abilities. I proceeded to post one of our pictures from dinner to his account. I typed the caption, *"No filter needed for this girl"*

Okay, so it was kind of conceited that I wrote it about myself, but sometimes you need a little boost when you've been torn down—even if it is all pretend.

Chapter Fourteen

After peering down the hallway three times and still seeing that stupid scrunchy wrapped around the doorknob, I accepted defeat. Sebastian tried to talk me into texting Danica, but I could not bring myself to do it. The numerous ways in which the interaction would be anything but positive flooded my head.

It was so much easier to just avoid all the awkwardness and possibility of Danica being mad or rude to me...and of course avoid whatever irrational emotions the interaction could possibly trigger in me. There were certain costs to staying in control emotionally, and I guess not getting to sleep in my own room every night was one of them.

And maybe, just maybe, I preferred Sebastian's company to Danica's.

He didn't fight me too hard on me spending the night. Most likely he was feeling sorry about all the nasty things he had read about me in the comments of Hunter's post. If having his pity meant I didn't have to confront Danica or fall asleep in the lounge, I would take it. Of course, he still made sure to thank me for not puking, sobbing, or passing out like the last time I stayed in his room overnight.

We ended up watching Stranger Things when Sebastian found out I had not seen any of it. Not having the option of a couch and the bed being more comfortable than the desk chairs, we sat on his bed with our backs against the wall and legs stretched out while he held the computer on his lap. Definitely more intimate of a position than I had ever expected to be in with Sebastian Torres, but it surprisingly felt just as comfortable as watching a movie with Hunter.

After three episodes of being kind of confused and slightly creeped out, I started to get sleepy and found myself leaning my shoulder against the wall, and then eventually resting my head on it. Soon I was unable to keep my eyes open. The sound of Sebastian shutting down the laptop caused me to stir.

"Sorry," I yawned.

"It's fine. It's late anyway." He hopped down from the bed.

"Next time, Riverdale," I joked quietly, sliding all the way down on my side. My eyes went back to being half closed.

"Oh, totally," he agreed, but his sarcasm was evident. He picked up one of the pillows from his bed and placed it on the floor.

"You don't have to sleep on the floor." I backed up against the wall, making more room. Based on my experience with Hunter, the idea of co-ed platonic sleepovers didn't seem unrealistic to me.

"Nah, I'm good down here. You strike me as a violent sleeper and you didn't brush your teeth."

Sebastian was already laying down. Too tired to argue, or care that much about his choice to stay on the floor, I quickly fell asleep.

The sound of Sebastian unlocking the door was what finally woke me up after ten the next morning. He worked the key out of the door while balancing the two coffee cups against his chest. I sat up as the door closed behind him, tucking my unruly hair behind my ear.

"I brought you your high maintenance coffee," he announced, handing me the cup.

"High maintenance coffee?"

"Yeah, two pump hazelnut latte with almond milk. High maintenance," he declared definitively.

The fact that he'd brought me unrequested coffee in addition to remembering my order left me too surprised to get offended by his judgmental evaluation.

"If it's so high maintenance, then why can you remember it?"

"Just one of the burdens of my intelligence, I guess." He sat down at his desk with his own coffee. "You ordered it every time at the HUB when we met to go over your Calculus," he explained. "One time you got incredibly fixated on it tasting like there were four pumps of syrup instead of two, but refused to ask the barista to fix it because—"

"I didn't want to be rude," I sighed, taking a sip. "Thank you."

I decided to change the subject before I could get another lecture about being too nice. "So, do you have Amelia's coffee order memorized too, or am I just special?"

"Amelia doesn't drink coffee," he informed simply, completely disregarding the second half of my sarcastic question while he dug through his backpack to get a textbook out. "I have to get started on some Physics homework and your doorknob is scrunchy free, so now you can go back to your room and avoiding conflict at all costs."

He didn't look at me while he spoke, more focused on preparing to work at his desk.

"Was the coffee meant to soften the blow before kicking me out?" I hopped down from the bed to gather my clothes along with my boots.

"I'm modeling assertiveness for you." Sebastian opened his laptop, not even walking me to the door. "I'd like my clothes back later, by the way," he stated the obvious.

"Sure thing, Sweetie, right after I take some selfies to remember our magical night," I joked, assuming he wasn't listening to me.

"Whatever helps you get through the day," he dismissed.

Unfortunately, I did not have a comeback ready before the door closed behind me.

It was the start of the third week into the quarter. Academically, I was absolutely killing it. Operation Fake Girlfriend, as Veronica called it, was also going incredibly well. Sebastian had tutored Amelia via FaceTime four times. I could always tell when it happened because he furrowed his brow less.

One afternoon, I came back to the dorm to unexpectedly find a purple scrunchy wrapped around my door knob. It was 3pm. The irritation started to bubble up and my jaw clenched. I stomped back down the hallway and saw Sebastian's door cracked open.

I knocked harder than I meant to, pushing the door open to reveal Sebastian casually laying on his bed reading a paperback book. Without invitation, I stepped into his room, forcefully flinging the door shut behind me and then dropping my messenger bag to the floor.

"What's the matter with you?" He propped himself up on his elbow, all ease and nonchalance, in complete contrast to my frazzled state.

"I stayed up until two last night studying for my Psych midterm and I was planning on taking a nap, but Danica's now decided it's the perfect time for a freaking afternoon delight," I fumed.

Sebastian, as always, remained unexcitable. His only response was to pat the open spot on the bed. The urge to scream quieted for a moment as I sat down and rubbed my forehead. I sat there silently for a moment.

"How'd you do on your midterm?" he quietly asked, returning once again to his book.

"Good," I sighed. "I'm pretty sure I got all the questions right."

"I guess staying up late and being tired now was worth it then," he stated rationally.

Now that I was in proximity to a bed, my exhaustion further set in. My eyes got heavier as I stared at one of his pillows.

"You can lay down," he sighed, reading my mind. My irritation retreated to its usual simmer as I lay down on my side facing Sebastian.

"What are you reading?" I asked, distracting myself from my annoyance of being banned from my room again.

"Los Ingravidos by Valeria Luiselli." Sebastian adjusted his position to give me more space.

"For fun or for school?"

"Recreation," he answered, because he couldn't just say 'fun.'

"Is that all in Spanish?" I peered up at the pages. I knew he was bilingual, but was surprised to see him reading a book written entirely in Spanish just for the heck of it.

"Yes. I wanted to work on my literacy."

"Recreationally, of course." My tone was flat.

"Sí claro."

Out of the corner of my eye, I saw his lips curve in a half-smile as he went back to reading. It was warm and either his bed or his clothes smelled like eucalyptus. I remembered noticing the scent when I stayed the night.

"Why does it smell like eucalyptus?" I interrupted his reading again.

"Laundry detergent. I thought you were sleeping." He modeled his assertiveness again.

I didn't see the point in bickering, so I happily let myself drift off to sleep.

The same interaction continued to happen over the following days. Like Pavlov's dog, I started heading to Sebastian's room before even checking my own door.

He was usually reading on his bed when I stopped by. Sometimes I would do homework at his desk and sometimes I would join him on the bed and sleep, or at least pretend to. We exchanged few words, there was always the smell of eucalyptus, and it was always the most relaxing part of my day.

One day, while we were lying next to each other, Sebastian pulled out his phone after he was finished with his book. I stayed on my back, but looked over to see he was scrolling through IG.

"Can someone please explain to me why Amy has posted for the third time this week about how smart Paul is? If he's so smart, why isn't he helping her with her chemistry?" he asked rhetorically, his brow predictably furrowed.

"You could always ask her," I suggested.

"Oh, is that allowed?" He mocked the rules I had stipulated throughout the past month.

"It is if you aren't combative when you ask."

He didn't respond and continued to look at his phone.

"Here," I reached over and pushed down the arm that was holding his phone. I pulled out my own phone and held the camera over us. "We're going to take a picture right now, because we look cute laying here next to each other."

Sebastian looked up briefly, not smiling, but at least no longer furrowing or frowning. I snapped the picture. Pleased with my results, I went straight to posting.

"What should I caption it?" I attempted to let him contribute.

"How about 'afternoon delight'?" He suggested sarcastically...maybe.

"Eww, no," I quickly rejected.

"I thought we were aiming to make Amy jealous?"

"We can do that without blatantly insinuating sex. Haven't you ever heard of nuance?" I chided. A text from Hunter popped up, stopping me from completing the post.

Thoughts on Trevor and Valentine's Day? I need something
that says 'I'm not ready to be your boyfriend, but let's
still make out'

You still have not DTR yet?!

No

Making out keeps getting in the way ;)

Ugh

You have two weeks to take care of it

I don't want it to wreck the first time I have a Valentine.

Rude

You know what I meant

Well it's a school night anyway

So maybe going out won't even be an issue

Nerd

"You seem to be having quite the amusing conversation over there," Sebastian commented.

I realized I was smiling.

"Oh, it's just Hunter. He's asking for advice on what to do for Valentine's Day with the guy he's seeing."

I quickly sent a text saying I would think about the whole thing and get back to him later.

Sebastian continued to look at me as we lay next to one another.

"Okay," I refocused on the task at hand, "so we were planning your next message to Amelia—"

"You're really that good of friends with him?" Sebastian interrupted.

"Who? Hunter? Yeah, he's probably my best friend. Why?" I turned on my side to face him, propping myself up on my elbow.

"I guess I just thought that it—your whole set-up—was more of a transactional one." Sebastian turned on his side, mirroring my position.

"Like he was paying me?" I laughed.

"I mean, I guess, maybe...not with money, but with social capital?" He raised his brow as he searched for the words.

"Well, yeah, there were definitely benefits. I'm not denying that. But honestly, I would've done it for him even if he wasn't popular. We've known each other since we were six."

"You're trying to tell me that you were always just friends and never had any attraction to him at all?"

"Well, I didn't say that," I clarified with a smile. "Obviously, he's doing just fine in the looks department."

"So, all the dances, the hand holding, the kissing, all of it—that was never hard to deal with? Being attracted to him and knowing it was all fake?"

It felt strange to have someone finally asking me questions about something I had thought secretly about for so long. I tried to think of the best way to explain it.

"I mean, is it really that upsetting if you get to go to all the dances with your best friend? And as far as PDA, it was all fairly platonic, in my opinion, with the exception of the kissing," I granted. "But that never went farther than slightly parting our lips."

"You guys never made out?"

"Nope."

"Not even once? Just for the sake of, I don't know, practice?" He grinned.

I shook my head and was met with the furrowed brow of doubt. My answer had been deemed insufficient.

"Hunter had already gone all the way with Olivia Rosen freshman year," I confirmed what had been commonly known gossip within our class.

"That boy was not questioning or in need of practicing anything by the time he asked me out sophomore year."

Sebastian didn't say anything, but I could tell his brain was still evaluating.

"What?" I asked.

"I'm just surprised, that's all."

"Well, actually, there was this one time after a party junior year," I recalled. "I talked him into letting me try French kissing, but that was an absolute disaster. I barely put my tongue in his mouth and he immediately started freaking out and saying he felt like he was going to throw up."

"What?" Sebastian laughed out of shock.

I laughed too because it was one of my funnier memories of Hunter... if I didn't focus on how pathetic it made me sound.

"He's always been the dramatic one," I quipped to save face. "What about you?"

"What do you mean 'what about me'?" He backed up a little bit.

"Don't think you get to know all this information without sharing anything," I said.

"I've kissed...a few girls," he said vaguely, rather than divulging the real number. "As for all the big stuff, it's just been Amelia."

"Big stuff?"

"First serious girlfriend, all the bases, however you want to label it," he filled in. "Senior year, she got it in her head that we couldn't go off to college without having sex."

He broke eye contact.

"Don't get me wrong, I love her, and it made sense for her to be my first, but I don't know," he sighed. "It kind of felt like it was more about checking a box for her, rather than how it was really supposed to be, you know?"

Once again, Sebastian's eyes met mine.

"So, you've never really been kissed by someone who wanted to kiss you?" He seemed perplexed by this information.

"No. Not unless you count the random guy who stuck his tongue down my throat at that frat party I went to on Halloween." I shook off a chill.

Somehow it seemed like we were now closer than when the conversation first started, still facing one another on our sides, both of us propped up on our elbows. It registered that our knees were touching. For a moment, I caught him staring at my lips, and I glanced down at his. I didn't know what to say because now all I could think about was what it would be like to kiss him, and I certainly didn't want to say that.

"I suppose if there were ever a time," Sebastian said while continuing to hold my stare, "that you would want to be kissed in a way that didn't involve having a tongue shoved down your throat, I could. I mean, I would be willing to help you out with that matter."

I was transfixed by how brown his eyes were, confused by how nervous but also relaxed I was in that moment. I didn't object, but couldn't seem to form words.

"I'm fairly confident it's not going to make me want to throw up either," he joked quietly.

My heart was beating so quickly I felt it in my throat. I looked at his lips and began to close my eyes as he started to lean in.

"But," Sebastian stopped and pulled back slightly. My eyes flashed open, preparing myself for him to announce he'd changed his mind. "I just want to clarify that first kisses are usually not that great and it's not fair to completely judge someone's skill level entirely off a first-time encounter."

"Really?" I scoffed. "A disclaimer? Well, this sure bodes well—"

Sebastian shut me up by pressing his lips gently to mine. He ran his hand through my hair, tucking it behind my ear. Goosebumps formed down my arm.

Kissing Hunter in public for the past three years had conditioned me to expect a kiss to end just as quickly as it had started. It was a pleasant surprise when Sebastian lingered and our lips began to part slowly.

My heart was still pounding. Sebastian inched closer to me. His thumb moved slowly up and down, rubbing a small amount of skin exposed just above my hip. I felt my breath catch for the first time in my life.

Just as the kiss started to deepen, there was the sound of jingling keys in the door, and a moment later, it opened. Awkwardly, I sprang back, miscalculating how close I was to the edge of the bed. I clumsily fell to the ground with a thud. Above me, a short boy with shaggy brown hair and glasses stood in the doorway. I shot up from the ground, trying to make my reaction less humiliating.

"You must be Warren!" I exclaimed loudly.

He stared at me as he pulled his key out of the door.

Warren had every right to be weirded out by me. I knew I would be.

"It's so nice to finally meet you. I live down the hall." I pointed unnecessarily and turned to see Sebastian biting his lip, trying his best not to laugh at me.

"Okay, then," I announced, again more loudly than I needed to. "I will be going."

I walked out the door, but then quickly realized after a few steps I'd left my bag with all my stuff in it.

"Excuse me," I muttered as I came back into the room, keeping my head down. "Just need to grab—" I didn't finish my sentence as I laughed awkwardly to myself.

Warren's continued stare deepened my embarrassment. Sebastian was smirking in amusement, perfect eyebrows and all. There were still butterflies in my stomach.

So this was what Hunter meant when he warned me to be careful.

Chapter Fifteen

Naturally, I avoided Sebastian for the next three days. I debated back and forth on whether to tell Hunter what had happened. It wasn't like he was going to offer any helpful insight other than saying 'I told you so.' He would probably even encourage me to keep making out with Sebastian. A situation in which you could make out with someone without having to worry about any sort of commitment seemed to be the ideal set-up for boy-crazy Hunter right now.

I immediately ruled out confiding in Veronica or Corine. I had already been doing my best to limit interactions with them because of the upcoming one-year mark of my dad's passing had me feeling on edge—I didn't want to answer a bunch of questions if they noticed I seemed off. And anyway, confessing what happened with Sebastian would just confirm the suspicions they'd had all along.

Yes, as I spent more time with him, I found Sebastian less aggravating and more attractive—did I mention the runner's body and eyebrows? However, more valuable than any physical attraction was that he had started to have a calming effect on me...when we weren't bickering.

Okay, so this made absolutely no sense—why on earth would I decide to make things even more confusing by kissing him?

That kiss was unlike anything I had ever experienced. Of course, I would never tell Sebastian because it wasn't like he needed anything else to feed his ego. Also, he was still very much in love with Amelia. I needed to tap into my rational side—the kiss meant nothing. Just a couple of hormonal teenagers bored on a Tuesday afternoon.

Avoiding him probably wasn't the best thing for Operation Fake Girlfriend, but maybe a little distance could be good for the narrative? The lack of posting could lead Amelia to infer that there was conflict and she could swoop in and reclaim her first love.

Yes, it was the perfect transition. I assumed Sebastian hadn't read into my absence because he had made no effort to seek me out. I wasn't able to decipher through my own social media stalking if he had handled the whole thing on his own and gotten back together with Amelia already. All he had posted was something about a Physics midterm.

I dove into my school work, shoving aside all sad memories of my dad and stupid feelings about Sebastian. Quizzes and midterms offered the perfect distraction. Given that the classes were easier than last quarter, there was something comforting about studying.

Every time I opened the books and could understand the information, it was like a giant affirmation of how smart I was. I had switched back to studying at the HUB in the afternoons as part of my plan to avoid Sebastian at all costs. Like all the cool kids, I was looking over Art History slides that Friday afternoon to get ready for an upcoming quiz. My computer had an image of *Anatomy Lesson of Dr. Nicolaes Tulp* on the screen.

"You know, there's a theory out there that Rembrandt was stereoblind, meaning he was unable to see in 3D. This potentially gave him an advantage when it came to depicting people and objects in the 2D form of painting and drawing," Sebastian stated knowingly as he unexpectedly walked up to the table where I was sitting.

He placed a coffee cup in front of me. "That's for you. A peace offering."

I raised a brow at him as he sat down across from me.

"I didn't realize we were fighting."

"It's been my experience that if a girl stops talking to you for a few days, whether she's your real or pretend girlfriend, you're in a fight," he countered. "At first I thought I'd just give you some space until you were ready to talk, but then I realized I was dealing with you and we may actually never speak again if I did that."

Now it was my turn to furrow my brow.

"Oh, come on, you and I both know you've been avoiding me."

I didn't deny it, but stayed silent. Taking a sip of my coffee, I realized he got my order correct again.

"I wanted to apologize."

I almost spit my coffee out. Luckily, I swallowed it before that happened. But my reaction led me to start coughing. Was Sebastian Torres actually admitting to having done something wrong? He smirked slightly at me, knowing exactly what I was thinking.

"I shouldn't have kissed you. I was feeling shitty about all the public fawning Amy was doing over Paul, and," he sighed, "I haven't done any of that stuff in a long time. I saw an opportunity and took advantage, and for that I am sorry."

He made a point to look me in the eyes. I sat there like an idiot holding the cup to my lips not saying anything. I'd never considered the idea that he had anything to be sorry about. After a few moments, he let out a half-smile.

"Now's the part where you either accept or reject my apology. You can even include what you're thinking and feeling," he jokingly coached.

"Um, yeah, it's totally fine," I brushed it off awkwardly, ready to move on.

Hopefully I would never have to think about how much I wanted to kiss him again. It was clear he did not feel the same way. Sebastian shook his head and grinned at me.

"This is actual torture for you, isn't it?"

"What?" I acted clueless.

"Talking about feelings."

"What feelings? I don't have feelings," I quickly panicked. Sebastian was now chuckling.

"Lucy, chill," he continued to grin. "We don't have to talk about it more if you don't want to. I just wanted to say I'm sorry and I won't do it again. You've been extremely selfless, both with me and what you did for Hunter. The last thing you need is an idiot boy getting handsy with you while he waits to get back together with his ex-girlfriend."

There. I had it.

Kissing me had meant nothing to him other than momentary gratification. He still wanted to get back together with Amelia. It felt like my gut had been punched, and that was certainly an unexpected feeling. Did I want him to want to be with me? Did I want to be with him? What I really wanted was to go back to being irritated with him like before. That was so much easier to understand.

"And hopefully, Amelia will come to her senses soon and you can go back to not having to pretend to like me."

"Just until I have to take another math class," I joked, trying to move past the knot I felt in my stomach.

"Pues, sí," he said before taking a sip of his coffee, looking relaxed as usual.

"And how is Amelia? She hasn't posted much the last few days."

"She's fine. Got a B on her first Chemistry midterm. I had to talk her down a bit, but you know, I'm used to that with women." He paused, anticipating a rise from me. I didn't take the bait this time.

"She asked how you were doing when I FaceTimed her last night. You would've been proud; I alluded to us having a fight. I guess bullshit is a little easier for me to spin when it's not entirely bullshit."

"How did she react?"

"Similar to how she reacted when I was sick and missed a week of school and my grade slipped in Econ. Concerned, but also very happy that she was winning. Maybe a little bit more compassionate. She did take off her sweater during the call."

"Did you guys—" my eyes grew wide. Over the past few days it had taken me some time to get used to the fact that Sebastian was way more experienced than I had ever expected him to be.

"No," he laughed at my reaction. "They seem to overheat the dorms down there too. She was wearing a tank top. However, the angle of the phone was nothing to complain about."

"Ugh," I sneered at him.

"What?" he asked unapologetically. "You're going to have to accept that not all of your fake boyfriends are gay."

"Did she say anything about Paul?"

"I didn't ask." He shrugged.

"Well, that's not helpful," I bluntly evaluated.

I paused for a second, trying to develop the next step in the game plan as a way to distract myself from the unexpected woundedness I felt from his unintentional rejection. I was starting to not want him to win Amelia back, and the remedy for that was to get him back with her as soon as possible.

"Valentine's Day!" I exclaimed excitedly.

"You want me to ask her to get back together on Valentine's Day? That seems incredibly banal and riddled with awkwardness and disaster. Especially if I can't do anything in person," he reflexively started picking apart the suggestion.

"Again, you think I don't know what I'm doing. Obviously, that would be a stupid idea," I shot back curtly. "When you FaceTime her next week, ask her what she's doing for Valentine's Day, then tell her that you're not sure what you should do with me because you're questioning how serious the relationship is and how long it will last. It will set it up for you to break up with

166

me at the end of February or beginning of March, and you can make a plan to go see her over Spring Break."

Sebastian paused, considering what I had just laid out for him.

"That is actually very brilliant," he evaluated. "Bravo. PR firms of the world look out; there's an up-and-comer heading your way."

He held up his cup to cheers with mine. I smiled and obliged, even though I thought it was nerdy.

"I kid," he said. "You're far too smart to waste your time with a degree in Communications."

He smirked and I found myself wishing I didn't know how good his lips felt on mine.

"What are you doing?" Veronica and Corine popped up in my doorway.

"Nothing." I looked up from my computer. "What's up?"

I had gone and gotten myself caught down an internet rabbit hole regarding Real Housewives of Beverly Hills after a recent disagreement with Hunter about Lisa Vanderpump versus Lisa Rinna—but they didn't need to know that. I closed out of the window as they stepped into my room.

"Valentine's Day is this week," Veronica stated knowingly.

"Yeah, so?"

"We need to get y'all's photo now to ensure it's perfect and not rushed," Corine informed.

"Whose photo?"

"You and Sebastian!" they said almost in unison.

"We told you guys the plan. He's going to tell Amelia he wants a low-key Valentine's Day because he's hinting that he's getting ready to break up with me. Which is good because I have two midterms on the fifteenth."

"You still need to post something cute to your account to save face," Veronica argued. Damn group projects.

"Why did you tell me to come here with my guitar?" Sebastian walked up behind them.

"Great," Veronica said inexplicably as she pulled him further into my room.

Thankfully, Danica was out for the afternoon and not present to witness a lie that was starting to become a bit ridiculous to maintain. Sebastian continued to stand there awkwardly with his guitar in one hand, looking like he would rather be anywhere else.

"Hang on," Veronica stepped up to him and started to position his hair. "Lucy, stand up," she directed, and I obeyed. She and Corine took a step back, staring at Sebastian and me as we stood next to each other.

"Lucy, you need to change your shirt. The purple won't look good next to the red," Corine referenced Sebastian's flannel. "You should wear that dark gray sweater you have."

"Yes!" Veronica exclaimed. "That would look really good."

"Will someone tell me why I am here with my guitar?" Sebastian repeated, his irritation evident. They had probably interrupted his Physics homework.

"They want to take a picture of us for Valentine's Day," I shared.

"That's not for another three days."

'They said we have to make sure it's a good shot and they didn't want to be rushed on the fourteenth."

Sebastian sighed audibly in response to the information I had given him. I knew we had about two minutes before he would wreck any chance of a decent photo. The boy did not pander when he was grumpy and he wanted to get his Physics done.

Granted, Veronica and Corine were right about the purple and red combination, so I went to my closet to grab the gray sweater that they suggested I wear. Quickly, I pulled my purple sweatshirt off, revealing a black camisole underneath.

"Ooo, wait," Corine stopped me. She exchanged a look with Veronica and they nodded in agreement with one another without saying anything. "Let's just do the tank top. No need for the sweater."

"Really? It's the middle of February," I protested.

Since reading all the hateful comments on Hunter's coming out post, I was not exactly confident about my body.

"Yes," our stylists insisted in unison.

"I'm cold." Now I was the one getting grumpy.

"Here," Sebastian slipped out of his flannel and handed it to me. I tried my best not to notice how his white undershirt fit snugly, revealing his muscles.

"Ohmygawd, perfect!" Veronica exclaimed. I gladly accepted an opportunity to cover back up. "Lucy, leave it unbuttoned. Otherwise, it'll look too baggy."

The smell of eucalyptus hit me as I stood there waiting for my next direction. Corine walked over and undid the sloppy bun on my head. Luckily, I had a minimal amount of frizz that day.

"Okay, now Sebastian," Veronica continued with her art direction. "Sit down in the chair."

He complied, holding the guitar to the side.

"Now, Lucy, sit down on his lap."

I paused. It shouldn't have been weird. How many times had I meticulously positioned myself in an intimate pose with Hunter? It was all pretend and I had signed myself up for it. No need to get shy now.

"You don't have to do that," Sebastian said in response to my pause. "She doesn't have to do that if she doesn't want to."

Suddenly I felt the need to prove to him that I was above reading into PDA when it was orchestrated.

"No, it's fine." I gingerly placed myself down on his knee. Holding back from putting all my weight on him. It felt and looked anything but natural.

"Girl, sit on his lap," Corine laughed. "Scoot."

Sebastian repositioned closer to the back of the seat, pulling me along with him. My legs dangled off to one side of him. Trying to touch the chair and not him, I was anything but relaxed. It probably had something to do with being aware that all he had to do was turn his head to the right to get a face full of my chest.

"Now hold the guitar in front of her like you're playing it."

Sebastian sighed heavily, most likely annoyed by the fact that this was not proper form for playing the guitar. I had to give it to Veronica and Corine; as far as couple poses went, this was going to be an impressive shot—if we actually got Sebastian to smile and me to look natural. Not an easy feat given that all my muscles were refusing to relax. Then again, maybe a crappy picture would help solidify that we were on the brink of breaking up?

"Okay, now look at each other and smile," Veronica directed as she and Corine positioned themselves with their phones at different angles.

Sebastian tilted his head up while I looked down at him. His deep brown eyes staring back at mine, reminding me what happened the last time I was this close to him.

"It's good to see you also have to rely on your fake smile sometimes," he joked, while I tried to appease our photographers.

"My fake smile is the same as my real smile," I argued quietly, trying my best to pretend that what was currently happening in my dorm room was not bizarre and completely of my own making.

"No. You always open your mouth a little bit more when you're really smiling, like you're on the verge of laughing."

He sounded like he had spent time analyzing this just as closely as the results of a chemistry lab we had once done together. I felt like I had been found out. He continued to hold my stare and neither of us were smiling at that point.

"Come on guys, give us something candid!" Veronica said with exasperation.

"You do realize the definition of candid is to be truthful, and that's the complete opposite of this whole situation," Sebastian shot back.

For once, his curtness resonated with me.

"Just shut up and play a song," she fired back.

Sebastian took a breath and surprised me when I heard chords start to play. Appeasing Veronica was the last thing I had expected from him, especially when he could barely see the chords with me sitting on his lap

The melody was slow and I found myself hypnotized, trying to place the familiar sound of the intro that he was playing. Suddenly my memory was triggered as Sebastian started singing the words softly to me.

It was "Lucy in the Sky with Diamonds".

My dad used to sing it to me during bedtime when I was little.

Suddenly it felt like it was just Sebastian and me in the room as he sang. He got to the chorus and I felt all the emotions I had been trying to keep at bay since the funeral well up in my chest. My eyes began to sting, and despite my best efforts, tears started to form. My instinct was to bolt out of the room, but there was nowhere to go...it was my room.

It was futile, the crying started before I could make an escape plan. Sebastian stopped playing and dropped his guitar to his side. He instinctively wrapped his arm around me and I responded by burying my face on his shoulder. The crying graduated to sobbing, and now it was the only sound in the room. Veronica and Corine continued to stand there, frozen and silent in the awkwardness I had created.

"Give us a minute," he said quietly while my face was still buried in his neck.

Veronica and Corine obliged, leaving without saying anything. They would ask for some explanation later. Their concern would be well-meaning, but I had wanted anything but to be known as "the girl with the dead dad."

Now it was unavoidable.

Sebastian continued to sit there holding me. It took a few minutes for me to calm the crying that had been pent up. The start of February had been hard, filled with the realization that last February was when the discussions of hospice had begun. February sixth—it was always the markers you weren't prepared for that caused the most grief.

Sebastian's breathing remained steady and the silence was comforting. Not that Hunter hadn't been comforting when he held me, but his first instinct was usually to jump to immediate reassurance or problem-solving. The fact that Sebastian could just sit there, letting me cry, and not attempt to immediately fix anything or be weirded out seemed somewhat remarkable.

"So," he started softly as my breathing began to match his and the tears slowed. "You're more of a Rolling Stones fan?"

I pulled back to see if he was smirking. His face was serious, but I could tell by his tone he was attempting to make a joke. My face broke and I started crying again. My ability to get over my dad's death was hopeless. I would forever be on the brink of turning into a blubbering mess, no matter how hard I tried to move past it.

Sebastian pushed back the hair that was clinging to my face. He waited.

"Do you want to talk about it?"

I took a breath. The answer was no, but I felt like I owed him an explanation to avoid looking crazy.

"My dad used to sing that to me when I was little," I managed to get out, the shrillness of my voice embarrassing me further. Hearing how the words sounded out loud triggered another flood of tears. I was an absolute basket case.

Sebastian nodded, affirming that he had assumed my reaction had something to do with my dad. He refrained from saying anything but continued holding me. Although I was quite sure having an emotionally unstable girl positioned on his lap was the last way he'd wanted to spend his afternoon.

"Well, that was a really poor song choice on my part then," he evaluated rationally, breaking the silence.

"Yeah, the worst," I agreed, taking another breath, willing the tears to stop like I had so many other times since my dad died last spring. I hadn't allowed myself to cry, at least not to this degree, since the funeral. Without thinking, I wiped my sticky damp face with the sleeve of Sebastian's shirt I was wearing, making sure to avoid eye contact with him.

"So, how's that counselor search going?"

My silence gave him the answer.

Sebastian maneuvered the chair back up to the desk while I remained on his lap. He refreshed the screen of my laptop and started typing one handed into the search bar. His other arm was now resting around my waist. The tension in my shoulders from just five minutes ago when Veronica and Corine were staging us had disappeared.

"Did you know," he began, as I had heard him start many times before—I prepared myself for some statistics on college students with dead parents—"they actually have a whole center for counseling on campus?"

The website loaded. He clicked on the staff page and started to scroll.

"Look at all these ladies and...one guy, who look like they would be so helpful to talk to."

"Easier said than done," I dismissed.

"I know," he acknowledged. When he said it, it registered that he wasn't just placating me.

Sebastian turned his face to look up at me. "When I was twelve, I went on a fishing trip with my grandpa and he had a sudden heart attack and died."

He shared the memory calmly, not absent of emotion, but steady.

"Sebastian, that's horrible."

I suddenly felt guilty for still being worked up about my dad. Yeah, it sucked, but I had time to say goodbye and I wasn't twelve.

"Yeah, it was horrible," he agreed easily. "And sad, and scary, and all of that. I'm not sure if you've ever noticed, but I like to be in control of things." He gave me a half-smile. "And something like that makes you aware of how much you aren't and can't be...I couldn't seem to just move on from it like I wanted to, no matter how hard I tried.

"After a few months of nightmares and constant anxiety, my parents finally decided to take me to see someone. But I can also be a bit particular. Not sure if you've noticed that either." Sebastian paused, giving me the opportunity to further tease him, but I didn't take it.

"It took seeing about five different therapists before I found one I was willing to talk to. But we found one. And it helped. So, maybe, just maybe, there's a chance that one of these eight people might be the right person to talk to."

My eyes explored the screen as he scrolled back up.

"Based off looks alone, my money's on Janessa. She looks pretty hip. It says Yesenia is fluent in Spanish. She could help you with your accent at the same time. Dos pájaros de un tiro."

My mouth started to form a small smile in response to his dry wit. He looked back over to me.

"I'll take *that* smile as a good sign."

Sebastian turned his head up at me. His eyes looked over my face like he wanted to say more. He then turned away and cleared his throat.

"I should get back to my Physics."

I stood up sheepishly. My cheeks felt hot, the embarrassment of my reaction surfacing in the aftermath of the moment.

"I'm sorry," I said quietly as Sebastian got up from the chair, gathering his guitar.

"Don't be. I love Physics." He pretended to forget what we both knew I was referring to.

I crossed my arms, clinging to the warmth of his shirt.

"Lucy, you don't need to apologize for crying about your dad. And you don't need permission from anyone to feel whatever it is you're feeling."

Always rational.

"Now, getting snot all over my favorite flannel. *That*. That is something you should apologize for."

Our moment was over.

"Make sure to wash it before you give it back to me." Sebastian gifted me with another lesson in assertiveness before leaving my room.

Sharing about my dad with Veronica and Corine was not as uncomfortable as I had worried it would be. They responded with hugs and the common offer of "if you need anything." I didn't hold it against them, but that phrase had frustrated me to no end last year. How can you ask someone for what you need when there is absolutely nothing you need other than to bring the person back?

Veronica said that she was amazed by my strength, confiding that she honestly couldn't fathom handling the transition to college right after losing a parent, let alone a college that was out of state, away from her family. I did my best to accept the compliment, but knew that ditching my sister and mom exhibited anything but courage. I guess presenting a false narrative in all areas had turned into my specialty at that point.

"Do you still want to use the pictures?" Corine asked with hesitation.

"Why? Am I ugly crying in all of them?" I attempted to move them past walking on eggshells with me.

"Actually," Veronica exchanged a look with Corine, "they're like, really sweet. We already picked our top three. Here, I'll send them to you and you can pick."

I thanked her and excused myself to go back to studying. They suggested getting dinner, but the thought of trying to pretend like they hadn't just seen me at my absolute worst earlier that afternoon was overwhelming. My eyes were still puffy and being alone sounded a lot easier. It wasn't until right before I went to bed that I realized I had not changed out of Sebastian's shirt.

Chapter Sixteen

There was no denying Veronica and Corine managed to get the perfect shot of Sebastian and me to post on Valentine's Day. The light was shining behind us, although not smiling, both of us were looking intently at each other. He looked like he was serenading me. I was staring at him wide-eyed, entranced. Luckily the camera didn't pick up that I was really on the verge of tears when it happened.

It took me a long time to figure out what caption to write. A sadness resonated as I stared at it. Not entirely because of the memory of the actual event, but rather because it looked like something I would've enjoyed being real. Knowing that Sebastian had FaceTimed Amelia later that same day and lamented having to do something for Valentine's Day with the clueless girl in the picture left a pit in my stomach.

After typing and deleting multiple times, I finally decided to keep it simple with *"Nothing complicated about this. Happy Valentine's Day to my favorite surprise of the year."* It wasn't until after I posted it that I realized the words also further validated Hunter's story that I was in the dark the whole time about him being gay. People's comments were kind enough to bring it to my attention.

Damn Lucy! Way to bring the passive aggression to the V-Day party @hunter.g.davis

I'm sorry if you think @hunter.g.davis being gay is complicated. It's too bad you can't be more supportive.

My favorite surprise of the year was when we all found out why @hunter.g.davis
didn't seem to care about having a hotter girlfriend.

Are you hurt that @hunter.g.davis' new boyfriend has a better chest than you?

Does this mean Sebastian Torres is gay too?

I knew Amelia saw the post because she responded to that last comment. *"I can assure you @sm-torres is ANYTHING but gay ;)"* I quickly closed out of my phone, dropping it down on my bed. The bubbling irritation started in my chest and my eyes began to sting. Danica sitting at her computer was the only thing forcing me to keep my composure.

*Fourteen, fifteen, sixteen, seventeen, eighteen...*I could've counted to a thousand but it wouldn't have made a difference. Shelved anger and annoyance were a permanent part of me now. I gathered my things and headed off to class.

When I returned to the dorm that afternoon, I checked my mailbox in the lobby, finding a delivery slip inside. When I went to turn it in at the front office, the student worker surprisingly returned with an enormous bouquet of flowers. A slight improvement to the day. While I hadn't expected it, it did not surprise me that the flowers were from Hunter. The card read simply: *"To my first and best Valentine. Love, Hunter."*

The overwhelming bouquet of roses, hydrangeas, and gerbera daisies was quite the attention-grabber during my journey back up to the seventh floor. I had gotten used to being looked at when I dated Hunter, but turns out, I was not a fan of it when I didn't have him standing next to me.

I texted him:

Happy Valentine's Day! Thank you for the flowers.

Hunter called in response to my text.

"I'm glad they made it to you. The florist thought it was weird to send a bouquet to a dorm. I think they thought I was a dirty old man inappropriately propositioning you."

"Well, there are always things to aspire to," I joked back. "Did you figure out what you're doing with Trevor?"

"I'm taking a page out of the Lucy Allen playbook and staying home to study since it's a school night."

"Really?" I was surprised. "Are you no longer boy crazy?"

"No, I'm still boy crazy. I just thought about how it was probably better not to make it a thing just because he was available, you know? It's okay for things to be low key."

"Hunter Davis, you sound like you might be growing up."

"Well...it might have also been because we still did not DTR yet."

I gave him an audible sigh, which was more than enough of a response for him to know what I thought about that. We wisely moved on from the disagreement.

"I saw your post with Sebastian. It was super cute. Very Taylor and Harry."

"Oh, not Taylor and Joe?"

"No, we were Taylor and Joe."

"Jonas or Alwyn?"

"Hello, high school, Jonas, obviously. You can't find your Alwyn until you're at least twenty-six," Hunter stated confidently. "Anyway, as I was saying, Sebastian is clearly a Harry. Moody, brooding."

His analysis made me smile.

"Well, if all goes as planned, we will be heading the way of Taylor and Harry soon. I had him FaceTime with Amelia this week to whine about having to do Valentine's Day with me and hint about breaking up soon. I'll be glad when it's all over."

"I bet. I can only imagine how much bickering is going on."

"Actually, not as much as I expected."

I paused and I thought about confessing what had happened—the frequent trips to Sebastian's room, the kiss, the fact that I felt so calm when I was around him.

"Uh-oh," Hunter finally broke the silence.

"What?"

"I told you to be careful."

He read me without even seeing my face.

"That's not what's happening," I quickly denied. "It's just, it's a lot more fun being a fake girlfriend when the goal isn't to get the guy back together with his ex-girlfriend...and you don't have to keep pretending that you didn't know your last boyfriend was gay." I deflected.

I heard him take a breath.

"I'm sorry," he apologized.

"I know."

"I love you, you know."

"I know."

"And people are stupid."

"I know," I sighed.

In fact, I was starting to feel like said stupid people. In high school, it was a bit easier to tolerate people's hate for me as Hunter's girlfriend because I was protecting him and he needed me. We just reasoned they were jealous. But now, even though it was obvious there was nothing to be jealous of anymore, an inexplicable distaste for me on social media remained. Wouldn't they be nicer if they knew that I had conspired to help and supported him all along? At the same time, why did I even still care what people from high school thought?

There was another pause before Hunter successfully distracted me by bringing up the latest episode of Real Housewives of Beverly Hills. The entertainment of his cattiness successfully shelved the negative feelings once more.

Although, I was surprised he hadn't acknowledged last year's Valentine's Day. Throughout the entire phone call, I kept waiting for him to say something about it, but it never happened. I reminded myself that not everyone was operating under a timeline of milestones marked by my father's gradual, but cruelly quick death.

Not that I wanted to talk about it. I told myself that Hunter's silence on the matter was for the sole reason that he knew me well enough to know I didn't want to talk about it. Thankfully, Danica had managed to shift her afternoon trysts to another location and I was able to dive into getting ready for my midterms at my desk. Studying was my go-to avoidance strategy now.

I didn't know if intense studying could be defined as a thing, but I think I was on to something. I found myself trying to see just how many pages I could read and information I could recall in five-minute increments.

Not since studying for the infamous Geography Jeopardy had I felt this level of clarity when it came to memorizing facts. Yes, Psych and Art History were both intro courses. It was nothing to get cocky about, but there was consolation in knowing that even if I was about to look like a twice-over loser girlfriend on social media, there was at least one thing I was going to win at.

Just as I had impressed myself with correctly identifying the artist, year, period, location, and cultural significance of *The Ecstasy of Saint Teresa*, Sebastian knocked on my open door. I had been so zoned-in, I jumped slightly.

"Hey," he stepped into my room. He was about to say something, but suddenly got distracted.

"That is a very large arrangement of flowers," Sebastian stated the obvious while pointing at the vase on the window sill.

"Oh, yeah," I said sheepishly. "They're from Hunter."

"Shown up by the gay ex-boyfriend. I should've seen it coming." His sarcasm was evident as he walked over to inspect the bouquet, quickly glancing at the card. "I think a better gesture would've been if he had told some of those people on Instagram to shut the fuck up today."

I paused, caught off guard by Sebastian's cursing. It took me a moment to recognize that he was referring to the comments on my post from that morning. He looked over to see my reaction.

"Can't waste time on stupid things people say." I impressed myself with how unaffected I sounded. Perhaps the studying had managed to move the negative feelings from the shelf to the closet.

"Anyway, it made sense that Hunter's many admirers responded that way. I guess I've just gotten too good at facilitating drama. I don't even have to think that hard about it anymore."

He inspected my face. Sebastian didn't know me well enough to know when I was holding back.

"It worked, too. I assume you saw the response Amelia tagged you in. Hashtag caliente. Hashtag Latin lover for life," I teased with a grin.

"You really anticipated that whole reaction from people?"

He crossed his arms and leaned back against the windowsill, brow well on its way to being furrowed. I shrugged to communicate just how effortless it was for me.

"Well, I guess it's good I didn't get on there to tell people to shut up, then."

Butterflies in my stomach.

Yes, my reaction was completely archaic, but the thought of him wanting to protect me, when Hunter had done so little of that the past few weeks, meant more than the overpriced flowers. I played it cool, though.

"Yes, it is good you didn't. That would make it look like you might like me, and you are on your way to not liking me, remember?"

"Doesn't mean I don't think you deserve respect." He held my gaze.

"Oh, it's fine. It's just Instagram," I dismissed.

He wasn't going to get me to cry again, that was for damn sure.

"All right," Sebastian sighed. "If that's what you want. I came over here to ask you if you wanted to go grab an early dinner?"

"Today?" I raised my brow. "On February fourteenth?"

"Yes, I know what day it is," he mocked. "It's what I worked out with Amy. She said go out early before it gets busy, and it's less romantic. Oh, and to pick a place where you order from a counter."

I nodded slightly, granting that this was indeed a good way to communicate to a girl you were dating that it was almost over.

"So, can you pause the studying and head out for a bit?"

"Why?" I laughed. "We don't really have to have evidence that we did that. Just say we did. In fact, not posting any pictures solidifies the story that we're about to break up. Less is more," I reminded.

"I'm kind of over the amount of lying I'm already doing," he admitted. "And I'd rather eat non-dorm food tonight."

I furrowed my brow at him. To which he furrowed his brow back dramatically. It made me break into a smile.

"Come on, Cyrano," he prompted, "take a break. It's far too soon for us to have a fake fight about our fake date on our first fake Valentine's Day. Hashtag couple goals."

He did have a point about the non-dorm food. I shut down my computer and started gathering my things into my tote.

"That's a pretty novel invention, but—" Sebastian paused and I knew where it was going before he could even finish— "have you ever thought about using your shoe?"

"Never gets old, does it?" I held back from the reaction he was hoping for.

"It really doesn't, no."

He followed me out the door for our non-date to eat non-dorm food.

"Did you ever find out what Amelia and Paul were doing tonight?" I asked while we sat down with our respective order numbers. I insisted on paying for my teriyaki. My suspicion was that Sebastian was only offering to do something nice out of pity, like when he let me stay overnight in his room.

"She also had midterms, so they were going to go out this weekend instead. She didn't know what the plan was though. Honestly, I do not envy Paul."

I raised a brow at him.

"Amelia has pretty high expectations," he explained. "For the most part I appreciate that about her, but there's a lot of pressure to deliver for specific things. Holidays, birthdays, anniversaries. She's got me so well trained that it actually feels kind of weird not having anything big planned today."

"But what about her? Did she ever do anything for you?"

He smirked.

"Eww, gross, never mind."

Sebastian laughed and shrugged. Our food was delivered, thankfully offering a distraction.

"What about you?" he asked. "I imagine you are missing some of those grand romantic gestures Hunter used to force us all to witness."

"Nah. I mean, I guess it made me feel special, but when you know both you and the guy would rather be kissing Harry Styles in front of everybody, it kind of wrecks the whole thing." I made him laugh.

I refrained from sharing about how much my last Valentine's Day had sucked. Growing up, my mom would always make a fancy steak dinner with chocolate cake for dessert. She continued to do it even when I was in high school. The rule was I couldn't do anything with Hunter until after dinner.

Last Valentine's Day had coincided with the day they brought in the hospital bed for hospice. Dad was still able to move around a bit. But there it was, in the living room, staring at us, reminding us he was going to start sleeping downstairs. And then die. Did this stop my mom from making dinner? Nope. But Dad didn't really want to eat anything.

Steak was his favorite.

My eyes started to well as the memory sank in. I refrained from looking at Sebastian because I did not want a repeat of the guitar incident in public. I took a deep breath.

Six...seven...eight...nine...ten...eleven...twelve...

"That was a heavy sigh," he observed. "You okay?"

We both knew the answer was no. We both knew I didn't want to talk about it. Thankfully his phone notified him of a text.

"And that would be the fifth message from my mother today." Now it was Sebastian's turn to sigh. "Do you mind if I call her real quick?"

I shook my head, surprised he'd asked my permission.

He held the phone up to his ear and waited. When she picked up, a grin spread across his face. The entire conversation was in Spanish. I understood most of it.

He spent most of the conversation updating her on his courses. It was sweet to hear him ask about her Kindergarten class in return. The conversation shifted to him answering questions about what he was currently doing and who he was with. He raised a mischievous brow at me as he toyed with his mother's curiosity.

I listened intently, silently translating his half of the conversation "Oh, she's just a friend...Mama, don't you think all friends are special in their own way? ...Even the ones who don't cook as well as you...but maybe I should ask her to make pozole tonight and we'll know for sure how special she is..."

Hearing the conversation reminded me of being around my mom and grandma, who always wanted me to speak in Spanish more than I did, hence my horrible accent. Suddenly I felt homesick.

Even though my mom had always made a big deal about Valentine's Day being a family thing, I hadn't planned to call home that night because all I could think of was how sad the last one had been. It wasn't like it was a major holiday anyway. Also, I was worried maybe that stupid Oscar guy would be at the house and I would lose it. Why risk making the day even worse for my mom and Ava?

Sebastian concluded his conversation with his mom, saying he loved her and would call over the weekend.

"Sorry about that." He put the phone down and went back to eating.

"Do you talk to her a lot?"

"I'm the baby, the only boy, and we're Mexican. What do you think?" he asked obviously.

"You were very coy with her. Poor woman."

He raised a brow at me.

"Just because I don't speak it very well, doesn't mean I don't understand it," I reminded. "By the way, I hate pozole."

"That's because you're a quarter Puerto Rican and misguided on what constitutes good food."

I scoffed and he shrugged.

"It's a good thing this isn't real, because my mom would really lose her shit if you showed up to the house with pasteles and not real tamales on Christmas."

He made me laugh.

"I wasn't quite sure if you were going to get that." He grinned, impressed with himself as usual.

My nervousness about calling my family subsided slightly after I saw his response to talking to his mom. As we finished our food, I texted Ava to let her know I would call later.

After maneuvering through all of Ava's continued questions about Hunter being gay and assuring her that she would still get to see him, (which I had already assured her of back in January when he first came out), she moved on to questions about the picture of me with the unfamiliar guy I had posted that morning. I had been wise enough to keep most of my stuff with Sebastian to my stories where I could limit her access to avoid too many questions. Really, there was no need to get my family attached to another relationship that was completely fake. Thankfully I was able to deflect her question by saying it wasn't anything serious, just a nice boy to hang out with.

"It must be hard knowing that no one you date will ever be as great as Hunter," Ava reflected in a rare moment of empathy.

"Yeah," I simply agreed, not in the mood to fawn over Hunter. Unsurprisingly, Ava quickly lost interest in talking to me when I had nothing more to say about boys and she handed the phone over to my mother.

My mom sounded happy to hear from me, and managed to refrain from asking any of her own questions about boys. Likely she was planning to just get the information from Ava later. Despite the welcomed surprise of hearing from me, there was also an obvious sadness in her voice. It was like we had put so much of our energy into making it through Christmas that we had no energy left to get through the one-year mark of Dad passing away. I didn't want to say anniversary...anniversaries were supposed to be for happy things.

We said nothing about what last Valentine's Day had looked like, but we both knew it was at the forefront of our minds. She shared that she and Ava had made a point to continue the tradition with having a steak dinner and invited my grandma over (but no coworkers named Oscar, thank God). I had to commend her for that. I wasn't sure if I would've been able to stomach continuing the tradition.

"When did you say your Spring Break was, again?"

"March twentieth."

"I think I'm going to pull Ava out of school for a couple days and get us a house at the beach."

I could hear my breath on the phone, unable to say anything. I knew exactly what she was planning. We had yet to spread Dad's ashes. He had requested we do it in Monterey Bay.

"I think it will be good to do something with just the three of us." She wisely avoided being direct.

There was a lump in my throat.

"Sure, that sounds good," I forced out.

Five weeks was plenty of time to come up with an excuse for not going. I wrapped up the conversation quickly after that, pleased with myself that I had avoided crying again even though I could feel the water filling my eyes the moment my mom mentioned the beach. She told me that she loved and missed me and wished me luck on my midterms.

After hanging up the phone, I lay down on my bed and stared blankly at the wall on Danica's side of the room. Good thing I had sufficiently studied earlier; my brain felt like mush. Concentration seemed impossible.

"Hey, Cyrano," Sebastian called me out of my stare, standing in my doorway. He walked in before being invited. He was looking down at his phone as he approached.

"Amelia just texted me asking to FaceTime tonight to help prep for her Chemistry midterm tomorrow. I didn't want to risk the wrath of going rogue, so I thought I'd check with you before resp—"

He stopped when he saw my face. The silence led me to prop myself up on my elbow. He searched my face, trying to read me again.

"Where's your roommate?"

"I guess she and her current gentleman suitor made other arrangements for the evening."

"Well, score," he said with a straight face. "In more ways than one, I guess," he joked in his dry tone before taking a seat next to me on the bed. I flipped over on my back to see him looking down at me.

"You were saying something about Amelia wanting to FaceTime?" I reminded him.

Hopefully the plotting would be a good distraction and get rid of the lump in my throat.

"Yeah, I was just going to say," he started as he laid down next to me, now joining me in staring at the ceiling, "that she wanted to FaceTime tonight, but I decided to play hard to get and told her I was busy."

It was obvious that Sebastian had just made that decision on the spot. I held back from telling him that FaceTiming with Amelia that night would only work in his favor for winning her back. Choosing to tutor your ex-girlfriend over spending time with your current one on Valentine's Day was definitely communicating something. I had a feeling Amelia knew that, too. Selfishly, I didn't want him to leave at that moment so I didn't challenge his choice.

"So, is this how one studies for a Psych midterm?" He finally spoke, moving one of his arms behind his head. "I would've guessed this strategy for Philosophy, maybe."

"I hate February," I finally responded, surprised that it came out more angry than sad. A single tear fell down my cheek. I wiped it away. "And yes, before you ask again, I made a stupid appointment with a counselor for next week," I quietly spat at him.

Ever steady, Sebastian continued to lay there in the silence. Several minutes passed. I felt tears coming. Instead of trying to fight them in silence, I decided to try something different.

Before I even knew what was happening, I started recounting my last Valentine's Day to him. The hospital bed, the steak my dad couldn't eat, the cake I refused to eat, the sneaking out to spend the night at Hunter's because I knew from that point on, being at home would be all about waiting for my dad to die, and I wasn't ready for it. I still wasn't ready for it when he died two weeks later.

"Hunter was there for the whole thing...and today...it's like he completely forgot it happened just last year," I finally verbalized something that had been eating at me all day.

Saying it out loud felt like betrayal. For the lie of our romantic relationship to succeed, it depended on Hunter's and my ability to have a strong friendship with little drama. I honestly did not know how to deal with my recent feelings of being hurt by him because it was so unfamiliar. I even questioned whether my feelings were justified. Perhaps I was putting too much on him, given that he was going through so much with recently coming out?

Although tears had welled up in my eyes again, with a few making their escape, I surprised myself with the composure I had kept while talking. It was a rush when I realized that I had gotten so many words out. Sebastian was looking over at me, but I continued to stare forward. If I looked in his eyes, without a doubt there would be a repeat of the sobbing situation from earlier in the week.

"I felt homesick after I heard you talk to your mom earlier, so I called mine. She wants to spread my dad's ashes when I go home for Spring Break."

My voice finally cracked. Without any hesitation, Sebastian pulled me in and held me to his chest. I managed to hold the tears back, focusing on how his chest went up and down. His chin rested on the top of my head.

Sebastian continued his comforting silence, and I felt my eyes get heavy. The emotional drain from the day finally caught up to me, along with the calming effect of his scent, steady breathing, and warmth. He stayed there as I drifted off to sleep. I'm not sure how long he stayed, but there was a part of me that was disappointed when I didn't wake up next to him.

Chapter Seventeen

I'll admit it: I flirted with the idea of being late for the intake appointment I had scheduled. However, ever the rule follower, the biggest defiance I could muster was showing up on time rather than my usual ten minutes early. The waiting room attempted to be warm and inviting with its fake potted plants and old magazines on the table, but was decidedly losing the battle. All the fluorescent lighting, industrial university furniture, and beige carpet was difficult to combat.

I sat in one of the uncomfortable chairs and went to work filling out the paperwork I was handed when I checked in. Making sure to keep my face down, I hoped no one I knew would walk in. Once the forms were all completed, I had nothing to distract me from noticing how sweaty my palms were. I stared at the bulletin board, scanning all the fliers offering various support and resources. Shame settled in my stomach as I recognized that I was one of "those" people who needed help. Being helpful was a characteristic I had always pridefully thought of myself as having...the idea of actually needing someone else's help left me with no pride at all.

The memory of Sebastian sharing about his grandpa resonated in my mind. He was one of the most capable, intelligent people I knew, and even he had a moment in time when he needed to talk to somebody. He was the last person on earth that I would ever think of as clingy or needy. So maybe being here didn't define me in those negative terms I had associated with needing counseling?

A young woman who looked to be a few years older than myself stepped into the waiting room from the hallway that led to the offices. She had the standard PNW winter outfit of riding boots, leggings, an oversized cardigan, and an infinity scarf. She made eye contact with me, since I was the only one in the waiting room, and smiled warmly.

"Hi, Lucile?"

I nodded and got up, gathering my things along with the intake forms. My heart was pounding in my chest.

"Hi, I'm Katrina," she greeted as I handed the clipboard over to her. "We're just going to head back here, down the hall, and then to the right."

She led me into the inner offices.

Her brown hair was pulled back in a sloppy bun, and it amused me that I had actually done my hair for the meeting. I suppose I wanted to look like I had some things in my life together.

I followed her into a meeting room. There was an actual couch that looked quite comfortable and like it belonged in someone's home. The lighting was softer and the room smelled like lavender, successfully achieving the cozy vibe the waiting room aspired to. Katrina invited me to have a seat as she shut the door. She took her spot in the armchair positioned at an angle from the couch.

"How are you today?" She started with pleasantries.

"Good," I said politely.

Katrina looked over the clipboard.

"You go by Lucile?"

"Um, sometimes. Lucy is fine, too," I offered, not really wanting to be called Lucile for the next hour.

"Okay," she nodded and looked up, resting the clipboard in her lap.

"So," she smiled, remarkably more relaxed than me, "Tell me a bit about yourself and why you're here today?"

I paused.

"Isn't...isn't that all on the papers you just read?" I hesitated.

"Yeah," she shrugged, smiling at my point. "Figured it might be good to hear it from you. What's written on paper doesn't always do a great job of capturing everything," she explained. "You're from California?"

I nodded.

"That's awesome. I have some family down in San Diego."

Great, now the California small-talk had started.

"Oh, I'm not from anywhere near there. But yeah, San Diego is great."

"I suppose that happens a lot, right?" she grinned. "It's like when you tell people you go to the University of Washington, and they don't realize how big it is, and they ask you if you know their friend, Tim."

I felt myself smile at the appropriate comparison, starting to feel slightly at ease.

"Yeah, it is kind of like that."

"Well, how are you liking being up here?"

"Um, it's good."

I hated sharing when I didn't know someone, especially in a situation like this when we weren't on equal ground. Katrina nodded, no stranger to pauses in conversation. Good thing I was no stranger to waiting a therapist out.

"So, it says that you've been to therapy before. How about you tell me a little bit about that?"

"I, I, uh, went a few times last year after my dad died."

"And how was that? Did you find it helpful at all?"

No, Katrina, that's why I'm here.

"Um, it was fine."

She smiled. My truncated answers didn't seem to faze her.

"All right, so, you're probably familiar with all of this, but I'm going to go over some housekeeping items from the forms you signed. Limits of confidentiality, informed consent, HIPAA, and all that fun stuff."

Katrina leaned in, showing me the papers I had signed, and began the spiel that she had given many times before. Not as many times as Brenda though, given how much younger she looked.

Katrina made a few more attempts to get to know me better. Asking about the classes I'd taken and inquiring what major I was leaning towards. I answered the questions, but kept it surface and didn't divulge the original intention for Law School. That would require talking about my dad. Which, yes, I knew was the whole point of why I was there, but there was something in me that continued to resist opening up.

Glancing at the clock, I saw there were only forty more minutes left. *One...two...three...four...five...*

"So," Katrina redirected my attention. "What would you say you want to get out of this experience?"

Her question caught me off guard. I had never been asked that. The message I got from my mom and others throughout all the meetings I'd had with Brenda was 'you must go because it's just something you are supposed to do.'

There was a belief that counseling would somehow make me feel better—less sad—but I didn't honestly believe that was even possible. The whole thing had seemed pointless from the beginning. I didn't say that to Katrina, though. I didn't want to be rude and tear down the woman's profession within fifteen minutes of knowing her.

At the same time, I was there because my solution of 'acting fine to feel fine' was no longer as effective as it had been six months ago...but I wasn't sure if I wanted to share that either.

"I guess...I would like to not be sad about my dad."

The sentence sounded stupid coming out of my mouth.

"Do you think that's possible?"

Okay, I didn't see that coming. I stared at her, my surprise evident.

"Sorry," Katrina smiled warmly. "I guess I should clarify. With grief, we can't necessarily make certain emotions disappear.

"Don't get me wrong, it would be great if we could, but the focus is usually on decreasing the intensity of those emotions through various strategies. Would you say the level of sadness you're feeling has gotten more intense than you'd like?"

I nodded, not willing to verbally admit it.

She nodded back.

"So, right now, just for the sake of helping me understand, when you think of that emotion at its most intense, what does that look like?"

She waited through my silence. Brenda would usually just start guessing and filling in the blanks. Not Katrina.

"Crying," I finally allowed.

She still waited.

"Being irritated or frustrated easily." I decided to test the waters. "Wanting to scream."

"Has that happened yet?"

I shook my head. Granted, I had raised my voice to Sebastian a few times, but I knew what I had released was tame compared to what was buried inside of me.

"So, you wrote that your dad passed away at the end of February last year?"

I nodded.

"As the date approaches, have you noticed an increase in those feelings?"

I nodded.

"And I'm sure you've heard this before, but that's all very normal."

I sat there politely and didn't say anything. I felt anything but normal.

"So," she sighed, "sitting here right now, are you feeling any of those things?"

I decided to be honest and nod.

"Over the past year, have you noticed anything that seems to be helpful in regards to coping?"

I waited. Katrina waited.

"Not thinking or talking about it."

I wasn't trying to be clever, just honest. A small smile formed on my lips when it occurred to me that Sebastian would've been amused by my answer.

"How's that working for you now?" Her tone came across more caring than judgmental.

My eyes started to tear up. I shook my head.

Luckily, she didn't offer me tissue. I hated that gesture. It always felt like the person was trying to get you to cry. They might as well say, 'Hey, it looks like you're going to cry. I totally notice it, and I'm going to call more attention to it.'

"It seems like this is really hard for you to talk about. Again, that's completely normal. You've known me all of what, twenty minutes?" She smiled. "Totally understandable to not want to get into everything right now. I wouldn't expect you to," she assured.

"It just helps me to know what goal we're working towards. Otherwise, you might just have to sit here while we fill the time with random questions about California, and then you'd probably really want to scream," she joked, slightly breaking the tension.

"So," Katrina started again. "Please correct me if I'm wrong. You're hoping that meeting with me will make you want to cry and scream less?"

I nodded.

"Okay, we can work with that," she said confidently. "One of my favorite metaphors to use when talking about emotions is that they're like having kids in a car: you don't want them driving, but you don't want to shove them in the trunk either."

I allowed her a half-smile.

The remaining time was not as tortuous as my other meetings with Brenda had been. I'm not sure the exact reason why. It wasn't like Katrina had a magical skill where I effortlessly felt the need to divulge everything. There was security in knowing she wouldn't run and tell my mom everything I said. I'd always doubted just how much confidentiality I had with Brenda.

As Katrina anticipated though, I decided not to share very much during that first meeting. Nonetheless, when I left the office, my muscles felt slightly less tense and my lungs didn't feel like I would start screaming at the smallest trigger. I was still highly skeptical that anything Katrina could say would really help me—but at the risk of sounding like an optimist, I thought maybe this wouldn't be a total waste of time after all.

Veronica had told me earlier in the week that she was planning on getting a group together to go out to dinner on Friday night. Of course, she didn't specify until the last minute that she and Corine had essentially been plotting to put together a triple date with Kahlil, Jackson, and Sebastian.

She probably knew that if we had been so obviously paired up in couples, I would've backed out. Especially since we were now in the end phase of Operation Fake Girlfriend. The report of Paul majorly messing up on Valentine's Day signaled to me that it was time to end our little group project of scheming to get Sebastian and Amelia back together.

Surprisingly, Sebastian was adamant that he wanted to wait before moving forward on our fake breakup. He wanted to see how Paul was going to attempt to redeem himself. In my opinion, an unspoken competition had developed between him and Amelia over whose rebound would be the first to end.

When I asked how Paul had failed miserably on Valentine's Day, Sebastian smirked and said, "He went cliché over meaningful. Big mistake."

I argued that their relationship was under six months old, and it was unrealistic for Amelia to be expecting gestures flooded with deep emotional value.

He shrugged and said, "And yet, somehow, I always managed to deliver."

I, of course, rolled my eyes in response.

Not wanting to overanalyze the group date, I reminded myself that if Sebastian didn't seem bothered by it, there was no reason for me to stress about it. The three of them made a point to tease me when I met them at the elevators bundled up in my peacoat, along with a knit cap, scarf, and gloves. Corine had taken to calling me Valley Girl anytime I said I was cold. I'm not sure why Sebastian escaped her teasing. Probably because he didn't react to teasing.

Regardless of the goading, I felt confident about my choice to be warm because I thought we were walking to dinner. Then I realized the elevator was taking us to the parking garage.

"We're driving?" I asked, confused.

Veronica's parents had agreed to let her bring her car back after winter break. However, because walking and the bus were free—unlike gas—we rarely drove for group outings.

"Where are we going?" I threw out another question when no one answered my first.

"It's a surprise," Veronica smiled, and I swear she looked at Sebastian when she did.

"Are Kahlil and Jackson still coming? How are we all going to fit?"

"Lucy, chill," Corine laughed. "They're meeting us there."

"So, everyone knows where we're going but me?" I asked with exasperation.

"I told you she was going to hate not knowing," Veronica said to Sebastian.

"Yeah, but that's part of the fun," he smiled proudly.

I sighed audibly as we stepped out into the garage.

"If I told you we have reservations, would that make you feel better?" Sebastian knew me better than I thought.

"Yes," I confirmed, getting into the backseat with him.

He didn't respond. Veronica started the car and began to back out.

"So, are there reservations or not?" I demanded, letting Sebastian know I'd noticed that he never officially told me if there were actual reservations. They all three erupted into laughter.

I pursed my lips, preparing myself for a long wait time before we got food. It's not like I felt that horrible, familiar urge to scream, but I'd be lying if I said I didn't feel simmering irritation. I took to staring out the window.

Focusing on body sensations over the thoughts in my head was something that Katrina had suggested earlier in the week. Of course, I'd dismissed it as useless at the time, but at that moment I was thankful for the cold air hitting my cheeks.

Unexpectedly, Sebastian's hand squeezed mine to get my attention. I turned to look at him.

"Hey," he whispered, "it's all good, promise." His large brown eyes stared back at mine. I instantly felt calmer.

I nodded slightly before he squeezed my hand one more time and let go.

After circling around the residential streets off Lake City Way a few times, we finally found parking. Stepping out of the car, the wind blew. It was freezing. Corine and Veronica started to scurry down the sidewalk, trying quickly to escape the cold. Sebastian waited for me on the sidewalk as I moved around the car, shoving my hands in my pockets.

"Isn't it, like, going to be March tomorrow? How is it *this* cold right now?"

I knew he knew the weather was ridiculous by Central Californian standards.

"Do you want an explanation on weather patterns and climates? Because I can give it to you," he offered honestly. "Or was that just an invitation to commiserate?"

"What do you think?"

"You're right, Lucy; it is very cold," he said flatly. "It's a good thing we're going in there." Sebastian nodded his head to the small, brightly colored building coming up at the corner of the street.

"I did some research," he said. "I thought this might be a place you'd like to try."

I raised a brow at him as we approached the entrance, catching up to Veronica and Corine, who had already met up with Kahlil and Jackson. We said our hellos and walked into the loud, compact, and crowded restaurant.

Sebastian gave his name to the hostess, finally revealing that we did, in fact, have reservations. The minute the warm aroma of plantains being grilled along with various spices hit me, I was grateful we were seated right away. The menu listed an assortment of Caribbean dishes.

My stomach growled just from seeing the words empanadas, tostones, and maduros. It wasn't quite Puerto Rican, but it was closer to my grandma's cooking than anything I had been able to find since moving away for school.

This coming Wednesday would mark my dad being gone for one year. I had been steeling myself in anticipation of the likely overwhelming sadness. It was one of those obvious dates you could prepare for. However, the anticipation had left me slightly on edge, much like Christmas.

The edge seemed to soften as I sat there with my friends, next to Sebastian. He was casually resting his arm on the back of my chair, and more talkative than other times we had gone out as a group. I might even admit that he came off a bit charming as he and Corine lamented the lack of good Mexican food in the area compared to northern—well really, all of— California. Veronica and the other boys tried their best to argue Seattle's case.

"Lucy, tell them we're right," Sebastian insisted, smiling, but still serious about the debate. "You know we're right."

"To be fair," I started, "You haven't tried all the Mexican food in Seattle, let alone all of the Pacific Northwest. It's kind of a big claim to say there's no good Mexican food in the northwest."

"We should've known," Sebastian said as he turned to Corine. "She doesn't want to hurt their feelings with the truth about the subpar Mexican food. Lucy, I think Veronica can take it," he stated. "Have my lessons on assertiveness taught you nothing?"

"I mean, Chipotle is on the Ave. Do you really need anything else?" I said honestly.

"Ooooohhh," he playfully covered his mouth like I had insulted him. He shook his head. "I think I can hear my ancestors crying." He made the table laugh. "You play me like that after I found the one place in Seattle that serves sancocho?"

"Well, I guess you should've tried harder and found one that served asopao and had arepas made from flour instead of corn," I joked back.

"Espero que te gustan tus tostones, traidora" he said dejectedly.

I shook my head at him, unable not to smile. Then I realized the table was staring at us.

"Lucy, you speak Spanish?" Veronica asked, her surprise evident.

"Mmm, I don't know if we would define it as 'speaking,'" Sebastian teased with a laugh.

I slapped his shoulder.

"I have a horrible accent," I informed, "but yes, I understand it."

"You guys didn't know? Lucy's Puerto Rican." Sebastian informed what had not even been suspected, given my last name and how pale my skin was.

Of course, the others had to call attention to that now that they knew—which was exactly why I usually chose not to tell people. It always felt like that quarter of myself wasn't enough to check the box.

It struck me when I realized how little it had come up with Hunter or anyone I hung out with in high school. I mean, they all knew I was a quarter Puerto Rican, but it was never really acknowledged. To them I was just another white kid. However, within only a short amount of time being friends with Sebastian, he had brought it up in a variety of ways, albeit mostly teasing me for my lack of a proper accent. Nonetheless, it was like he saw a part of me that no one besides my family had ever recognized before.

After dinner, we ended up back at Kahlil and Jackson's house simply because they had access to alcohol. Since it wasn't a house party, I was more content to follow along and even agreed to play beer pong.

Unexpectedly, Sebastian agreed to participate as well. I had always assumed he would turn his nose up at anything so juvenile. Since the main goal of the activity was to get drunk, everyone started to get tipsy. I couldn't remember the last time I had laughed that much. It didn't even matter that what we were laughing at wasn't really that funny.

Sebastian and I stopped after a few rounds, unlike our four counterparts. After everyone else had finished up the sixth round, it was obvious we would not have a sober driver for several more hours. I got the sense that Corine and Veronica were looking for a sleepover with Kahlil and Jackson anyway. Not wanting to be the fifth and sixth wheel, Sebastian and I decided to take an Uber back to the dorm.

While I was nowhere near as messed up as I had been on Halloween, I was still definitely buzzed when we returned to our floor. To no one's surprise, there was a scrunchy on my doorknob waiting for me. Anticipating this situation, Sebastian had remained in the hallway, standing by his door.

"Is there ever going to be a point when you stop avoiding conflict?" he asked as I was walking back to him.

"Probably not," I admitted and grinned, stepping toward his room.

He held up his arm, blocking me from entering. He peered down at me with his dark eyes and a mischievous grin.

"'Scuse me," I laughed, trying to move past him.

He continued to block me. I was leaning on him, making a weak attempt to get by, my laughter stopping me.

"Sorry, entry is only for people who don't run away from their room-mate problems."

I managed to pause my laughter momentarily to give him my best pouty face, but started to laugh again.

"I know," he sighed. "Sad."

He did not look like he was sorry.

I gave him puppy dog eyes, managing not to laugh at all that time.

"Welp, have fun in the lounge tonight," he said, unaffected. "I'm going to get some rest."

Sebastian stepped into his room. He was very convincing, given my somewhat inebriated state, so I began sulking towards the lounge. Sebastian stepped back into the hallway, laughing before I got very far.

"Lucy, I'm joking. Come back here."

A grin reappeared on my face as I readily skipped back to him.

"I mean, I know you'll never confront her."

The finality in his statement gave me pause.

"Excuse me?"

"I said: I think you're too nice. And I don't think you can do it," he said pointedly, smirking while looking me in the eye.

I scoffed. "Really?"

"Really," he affirmed.

"Oh yeah?"

"Yeah," he laughed, daring me.

"I'm going to do it."

"Do it, then," he egged me on.

I grabbed his arm and pulled him down the hallway with me. Once we made it to my door, I shoved my key in to unlock it. I flung the door open dramatically, and Danica, along with another person, gasped. The lights were off.

"Am I interrupting something?" I called out cluelessly as I stepped in.

Sebastian remained by the door, watching my performance.

"Uh-oh, looks like I am. Don't worry; I'll be quick, unlike you guys every freakin' weekday afternoon. Oh, I'm sorry, Danica, I forgot to ask if this is the same guy or a different one? My bad."

Danica and the random guy, both shell-shocked, stared at me from under the covers.

"Anyway, it's totally cool if you want to stay the whole night. I just needed to grab this."

I stepped into the bathroom and grabbed my toothbrush, too buzzed on White Claw and my newfound assertiveness to remember there were several other things I might need for spending the night somewhere else.

"Hope I didn't make this awkward." I started walking out the door and then stopped to look Danica directly in the eye.

"You know, with getting ready for finals and all, it's so hard to remember everything. And I don't think I'm going to be able to remember what that scrunchy on the door means after tonight," I shrugged. "It is what it is. Peace, bitches. Modesto out!"

I slammed the door shut. Adrenaline was pulsing through my veins like a drug. I turned to Sebastian, wide-eyed, and started to hop up and down with excitement.

"Ohmygod! Ohmygod! Ohmygod!" I kept saying in disbelief.

Sebastian grabbed my hand and led me back to his room where we erupted into laughter once inside, especially when I realized I was randomly still holding my toothbrush. We gradually gained composure and settled into another sleepover arrangement without much discussion. However, this time Sebastian joined me in the bed, a contrast I wasn't about to question.

Unfortunately, for no particular reason, I ended up getting the giggles for the next hour. When I realized how exhausted my stomach muscles were and that Sebastian was yawning, I was able to finally rein it in for the night. Lying next to him, easily relaxed by the slow rhythm of his breathing, my buzz slowly lifted as I blissfully dozed off. The simmering irritation and anger was temporarily forgotten.

I woke up Saturday morning in Sebastian's bed, wearing his engineering club t-shirt and the shorts he had lent me the last time I'd stayed over. His arm was draped over my hip, enveloping me along with the warmth of the covers. Deciding there was nothing important enough to interrupt the situation, I drifted back to sleep. Sometime later, I woke up to him stirring.

"Good afternoon," he said quietly in response to my own shifting.

"Afternoon? Really?" I flipped over to face him.

"Well, that's what happens when someone keeps someone else up with incessant giggling." He propped himself up on his elbow, staring at me.

My mind flooded with concerns over how much of a mess I looked and how bad my breath was. Sebastian didn't seem to care. I tried my best to play it cool.

"I apologize. Next time I'll try to be more stoic when I'm buzzed."

He gave me a half-smile.

My brow furrowed. "Am I...? Am I not wearing a bra?"

I knew we hadn't fooled around, but the fact that the garment was missing left me confused.

"Oh, yes," he stated knowingly. "Shortly after we started to fall asleep, you sat up and declared that you did not want to be weighted down with the shackles of the patriarchy anymore."

"Oh my God," I cringed, putting my hand to my forehead. "Ugh, so basic," I sighed.

"There's nothing basic when it comes to smashing the patriarchy," he said dryly.

Silently, we continued to lay there. It was another moment I didn't want to end. The feeling was starting to become commonplace when I was with him.

"Did you have a good night?"

I nodded, but I didn't tell him it had easily been my favorite night in the past year. Even better than prom.

"Thank you for finding that restaurant," I said quietly. "It was a nice surprise."

He nodded, confirming he had done it for me, but not offering a further explanation as to why.

"Thank you for shouting 'Peace, bitches. Modesto out.' to your roommate after drunkenly grabbing your toothbrush to spend the night in my room."

My eyes widened and I collapsed my head into his chest over the memory.

"It's totally cool," he assured. "I'm sure all of us who were there will only remember it...forever."

I groaned. Momentarily, I peered up at him to glare. He grinned back, but then briefly patted my back.

"Look at it this way, drunkenly bragging about having a key in your shoe while dressed as a cat is no longer the most embarrassing thing you've done in front of me," he dismissed rationally before giving me a wink and reaching for his phone.

We remained in his bed, slowly waking up for the next hour. We spoke periodically as Sebastian read the news on his phone like an old man and I scanned social media on mine. It was comforting and something I could easily get used to.

When Veronica sent me pictures from dinner, I didn't post them. My account was already flooded with things that weren't true. I wanted to remember everything about that night as real.

Chapter Eighteen

Amy called me last night. She broke up with Paul.

I stared at the text notification, but didn't want to open it.

As I continued with my day, trying to think of anything other than the impending reality that Sebastian would soon get exactly what he wanted and I would be left with nothing but the satisfaction of knowing I was gifted at manipulation.

Although my time with Katrina was supposed to focus on my emotions surrounding the death of my dad, she had finagled her way into becoming someone I trusted with all my neuroses. Tricky therapist.

When she started our meeting by asking me how I was that day, I impulsively let out a bunch of word vomit regarding both my past relationship with Hunter and the current predicament I was in with Sebastian.

"And what I really want is to stop feeling like this about him. It was never supposed to be like this," I exclaimed. "This is all a complete mess! I'm a complete mess! I vacillate between this horrible sadness about my dad, and the next minute being all twitterpated around a guy who was never really dating me, and then the next minute I feel resentful about the other guy who won't just let me move on from the last fake relationship I orchestrated. And like ninety percent of the time, I wonder if would feel any of these stupid feelings if my dad hadn't died."

I took a breath, shocked that I had dumped all of that on her. In under five minutes, no less. Katrina, despite having previously shown herself to be experienced in her craft, also seemed taken aback by my sudden truth explosion.

"Okay," she paused calmly.

"Sorry," I immediately apologized.

"No, no need to be sorry," she assured. "I just need a minute to organize all that in my brain. I know this is a totally overused therapy statement, but Lucy, it sounds like you have a lot going on."

"You think?" I asked sarcastically.

We sat quietly for a moment while she chose her words.

"Lucy, in the short time I've known you - and keep in mind I'm not the expert on you; you're the expert on you, so please feel free to correct me if I'm wrong—" she qualified as she always did before sharing her thoughts, "I get the sense that there's a pattern where you choose not to share your feelings for fear that you might hurt someone, disappoint someone, make life harder for someone. Which is a very considerate quality...provided it doesn't turn on you.

"Sometimes people's commitment to kindness can cause them to become *overly* nice. Trying to please everyone and be agreeable at the cost of authenticity. This can lead to personal frustration, resentfulness, difficulty regulating all the emotions that have been shoved down for so long."

I didn't disagree with Katrina's statement.

"With these two guys, it sounds like you've found two people that you care about, but you still hesitate to be completely and totally honest with them for fear of how they may react."

I shifted my eyes away as the truth of Katrina's words set in.

"Which, believe me, is no easy feat. There are people way older than you who still haven't learned how to be productively honest in their relationships. My hope is, that as you get a little bit more comfortable recognizing your own emotions, coping with them, and not being afraid of them, it will become easier to be honest about them with others you care about."

Katrina paused, again no stranger to waiting out silences. I returned my gaze to her, communicating that I was listening.

"Bear in mind," Katrina added, "I fully recognize and appreciate that there is always risk when being honest with someone. As with most things, it comes down to weighing the risk and the benefit of that honesty."

I wanted so badly to trust that I could be completely honest with someone, but the idea of telling anyone how I truly felt about anything that went beyond the surface seemed like a fairytale.

After my session, I determined the risk did not outweigh the cost when it came to being honest with Sebastian. He knew he wanted to be with Amelia. All I knew was that I wanted to keep cuddling with him. It wasn't fair to him to make things more complicated because I had gone and caught feelings that I didn't know what to do with.

The truth was I didn't know the first thing about actually dating someone, and the thought of doing it wrong terrified me. It seemed too selfish to ask Sebastian to give up a chance of getting back together with his first love, especially when we had worked so hard to give him that opportunity.

He would be giving it all up, for what? A girl with daddy issues who needed help with math and had a penchant for Puerto Rican food? Yeah, no thank you.

Best to stay the course, and hopefully get to keep the friendship. Provided I didn't have to hear too much about Amelia once they were back together. During the short amount of time Sebastian and I had fake dated, it had only solidified my opinion that I did not care for her as a person. I was somewhat perplexed by what Sebastian saw in her, especially when I had come to know him as a caring person, underneath all the smugness, of course.

But reaching this conclusion in my head didn't mean I was necessarily ready to respond to his text. I avoided opening the message for the rest of the afternoon. He texted again that night.

How do you want me to break up with you? I've never broken up with someone on Instagram before. Is there a special filter I'm supposed to use?

Sorry. Been busy today getting ready for finals. Let me think about it and
get back to you.

I bought myself some more time. Really, this phase of the plan was
not complicated. He could just message Amelia and tell her that he was single again. With all the processing and rationalizing I had done after seeing
Katrina, how could I still not be ready to let go? Moments later I got another
text from him.

Also, some guys I know from the aerospace track are having a party this
weekend. You want to go?

We are all nerds and don't like loud music, so I promise you will be able to
hear ALL the important things that we have to say.

A party with aerospace guys? Sounds out of this world.

Wow.

Are you trying to get uninvited?

I like to think my humor is both RATIONAL and INTEGRAL when it
comes to CONVERGING and having a good time. COUNT me in!

Done yet?

I think the limit does not exist for the fun that will be had!

Admittedly, I chuckled to myself when I sent the last text.

When a quick response from Sebastian didn't come, I started to wonder if I actually had gotten myself uninvited. Honestly, I would have survived
not going to an engineering party with a room full of Sebastians, but I did like
the idea of him still wanting to hang out with me even after he had no use
for me.

Hopefully you won't be too busy smashing the patriarchy.

PS Probably best to wear your shackles. Not sure if these guys could handle
the distraction. #realtalk

Chapter Nineteen

I accepted the reality of having to let Sebastian go by that Friday. I told him going to the party would be an excellent setting for the fake break-up. No post needed. He could DM Amelia at the end of the night and tell her that I confronted him about still having feelings for her, and that he ultimately confessed it to me. The fact that Sebastian was only willing to partly lie worked in my favor, because I got a chance to enjoy his company at his friends' party.

The party was low-key, but didn't feel all that different from any other low-key house party I had been to. As with most parties, people were drinking and acting more obnoxious than they normally would sober. Granted, there wasn't any dancing or grinding to be had, and in my opinion, the party was all the better for it.

Sebastian was quite the gentleman, introducing me to all his friends. He didn't even ditch me when two other girls tried, with noticeable effort, to get him to play pool. Even after all the time we'd spent together, it still surprised me to see him so laid back in a social setting. It just didn't align with the image I'd always had of him in high school as a stuck-up intellectual.

After a couple of hours, he pulled me into a corner to craft his DM to Amelia. Just in time for our charade to end, he consulted my opinion on every detail and asked for my approval with each word choice. He had finally grown to trust my expertise.

Unfortunately, it was also clear he really loved Amelia and wanted her back even after all she had done to him. I refrained from questioning

Sebastian about it. After all, it wasn't like I knew more about relationships or what he wanted than he did. Once he had read his message several times, Sebastian finally pressed send and took a breath.

"All right. Now we wait and see, Cyrano. Thank you, by the way."

Sebastian kept his eyes on mine. He looked so cute and hopeful, part of me couldn't help but want it to all work out for him.

"Sure, anytime." I looked away, and tried to pretend like I was interested in watching the game of pool in the corner.

"How long do you think it will take her to respond?" he asked only a few moments later. The slight sound of insecurity in his tone gave me pause.

"Oh, I'm sure she's going to drop everything she's doing to call you right away. You'll probably have to talk her out of skipping finals and getting on a plane tonight." I modeled some of his signature sarcasm.

He glanced at his phone. There was no notification.

"Sebastian, chill." I echoed what he and my girlfriends had told me so often. "A watched phone never dings."

I stood up.

"Come on, let's go home." I held my hand out to him. "Before those girls over in the corner talk you into doing body shots and it ends up all over the internet."

"But what if they want to talk *you* into doing body shots?" he joked with a smirk.

"Really? So stereotypical," I dismissed with a sigh as we headed for the door.

"I just think all possibilities must be considered before deriving a conclusion," he explained before revealing a grin.

"Ugh, I can't believe I'm friends with you now."

"That's because you never considered the possibility," he reiterated.

Little did he know I had considered much more.

During the walk home, we talked about our course loads for next quarter.

"I can't believe you're taking American Pop Song," Sebastian mocked. "I bet all you have to do to pass is know how to open Spotify and name all living members of the Spice Girls."

"None of the Spice Girls are dead and they're all British," I quickly corrected with a scoff.

"Can't get anything past you. Sounds like you are well on your way to a B in that class," he marveled as we crossed the street. He was trying to hook me. I decided to play along for old times' sake.

"Oh, and I'm sure you'll find the most boring courses possible to fulfill your VLPA requirements," I fired back. "You're probably disappointed they don't offer a class on black and white foreign films about existentialism."

"But would I really be choosing to take a course like that or would it just be the result of circumstance that was being forced upon me?" Sebastian joked, clearly proud of his own cleverness. "Actually, I'm thinking of taking Art History," he said casually. "Then you'll have to tutor me. Since you owe me for Calculus, you know."

I rolled my eyes at him, but wished he was serious. Deep down, I knew there was no chance that he would ever need my help with anything academic.

We returned to the dorm floor. As we approached his room, I didn't want the night to end. Also, Amelia had yet to call or text. There was part of me that wanted to be there when it happened. Maybe I thought seeing it would help me move on.

"Hey, we should celebrate," I stalled as we stopped at his door.

"Celebrate what?"

"Our break up, of course."

He raised his brow at me.

"It's all part of the Lucile Allen Fake Girlfriend Experience." I tried to come off as cute and breezy.

"I'm not sure you really want to coin that. Kind of makes you sound like a prostitute."

There were still moments when Sebastian could have been more tactful in his word choice. But hey, no one's perfect.

"How else are you planning to distract yourself until she calls?"

"Maybe I'll just call her."

"No, absolutely not. She has to call you."

Yes, part of me was just looking for an excuse to spend more time with him, but I also firmly believed it. Sebastian had already DMed her and said he missed her. Amelia had all the information she needed. It was on her to make the next move.

He didn't argue with me.

I squinted at him for a moment. "I'll be right back."

I hurried off to my room and quickly changed into sweatpants and a t-shirt. Underneath a sweatshirt draped over my arm, I hid a bottle of wine I'd smuggled back from my house after winter break. I grabbed two plastic cups from off the top of my minifridge, too. Undetected by any RAs, I slipped back into Sebastian's room, shutting the door behind me. He met my mischievous grin with a raised brow.

I unveiled the bottle with pride.

"Scandalous," he responded flatly.

"Now, I know it's a twist top," I acknowledged. "But don't let that turn you off. It's a really drinkable malbec. Not too dry, really balanced and smooth."

He laughed at me.

"What?"

"Are you kidding me?"

"No, why?"

"I just had no idea that you were a sommelier in addition to a sleazy PR rep."

"Consider it another one of my hidden talents."

Placing the plastic cups on his desk, I gave two generous pours before handing one over to him. I took a sip while he took a large drink, which was a mistake. Sebastian's face turned.

"What?" I laughed. "You don't like it?"

"I do not," he said definitively.

"But it's so good," I insisted. "You're supposed to sip it, not gulp it," I added pointedly.

"I don't really drink wine. Unless you count Communion wine. And that's like maybe six times a year, tops."

"Okay, well this is probably too bold of a wine to start you off on. Had I known, I would've smuggled back a white or a rosé"

He started laughing at me again.

"Are you for real? You do realize you're a freshman in college and not a fifty-year-old divorcee?"

I put my hand on my hip, accepting his teasing. Without any hesitation, I began to share a memory about my dad.

"One week after my dad was diagnosed, he declared that teaching me about wine was in the top five of his bucket list. He came home from BevMo with two whole cases of all these different varieties. My mom was pissed. But he insisted that picturing me walking around drinking Stella Rosa and thinking it tasted good was too big of a concern for him to overlook.

"It was so unlike him. He was such a rule follower. It was hilarious seeing my parents debate over the ethics of it all. His closing argument was just him looking at her and saying, 'Stella Rosa, Sonia. Stella. Rosa.' Then she let out this huge sigh and poured herself one of the biggest glasses of cabernet I've ever seen."

Suddenly, I realized how big I was smiling. In turn, Sebastian was smiling back at me. More importantly, the memory didn't bring me to tears like it would have a few weeks ago.

"To your dad, then," Sebastian clinked cups with mine, powering through another sip of wine he did not like.

Sebastian pulled his phone out of his pocket to glance at it. Sipping on malbec for the rest of the night, no matter how drinkable I thought it was, would not be enough of a distraction for him. I had no choice but to pull out the big guns.

"Relax. Get comfortable." I handed my cup to him before casually hopping up on his bed. I turned back to him as he stood before me and retrieved my cup before settling in at the head of his bed. My legs were stretched out in front of me, while I sat against the wall.

"Let's watch something," I suggested. "But I get to pick because you picked last time."

He stared at me.

"I'm not letting you call her," I stated. "Come on, we're in the home stretch. Sí se puede!"

"Yeah, not at all offensive to encourage the Mexican kid with the Dolores Huerta catch phrase," Sebastian sighed. "I'm sure this is exactly what the United Farm Workers were talking about," he mumbled before heading to his dresser and pulling out a t-shirt and sweats to sleep in. He stepped into the bathroom and I wished the night could be as fun as the last time I was there.

He was gone long enough for me to open Instagram.

There it was.

The first post in the feed: Amelia with three other girls, all dressed up and ready to go out. The caption read, *"Make them miss what they never really had."*

There were multiple slides, or rather, thirst traps.

Sebastian stepped out of the bathroom, now changed. I knew he had been looking at his phone from the expression on his face alone.

"Okay, so it could be taken several ways," I started before he even had to say anything.

He shook his head.

"I'm done," he said. "This whole game is stupid."

He plugged his phone in for the night and picked up his laptop off the desk before settling in next to me on the bed, his demeanor the perfect embodiment of stoicism.

His brow wasn't furrowed, so I ruled out him being annoyed or confused. It was still unclear to me what Sebastian looked like when he was hurt. One thing was clear, his statement signaled defeat, and I knew him well enough to know he hated losing.

"Now, you don't mean that," I consoled, reflexively wanting to cheer him up.

His only response was to unlock his computer. I immediately logged into my Hulu account as I began to share my valuable female insight.

"Look, she's probably just having a girls' night out because of breaking up with Paul. It was likely planned long before you sent her your message."

"She posted that twenty minutes ago and the message is marked as seen," he countered.

I paused. I didn't have a rebuttal, so I went back to my original plan of distraction.

"Well, I'm about to introduce you to something that will make you feel better. Because no matter how much drama you have in your life, you will never, ever, have as much as the Real Housewives of Beverly Hills—or really any of the cities in which they have Real Housewives."

The episode started with each of the women saying their intro line.

"Are you trying to make my night worse?" Sebastian groaned.

"I feel like you haven't considered all possibilities before deriving a conclusion in regards to what you might get out of this show," I used his argument against him.

"I'm suddenly appreciating this wine more, that's for damn sure," he said before taking another sip.

"You're welcome. Now let me give you some backstory. Those two ladies are mad at each other because that one adopted a dog but then decided she didn't want it, so she gave it to a shelter and I think the dog died and that lady was upset because she's super into dogs, and she leaked it to the press to make that lady look bad, but she won't fess up about leaking it to the press. Actually, I think really everyone is mad at her."

Sebastian had his arms crossed, holding his cup against his forearm, his expression decidedly unamused. He let out an audible sigh.

"And do any of these women realize there are people in the world with actual problems?"

"College is about having new experiences and learning about new cultures. Stop being such a snob and enjoy."

"And what culture is this?"

"Rich, middle-aged, and partially famous women, of course."

Sebastian managed to tolerate one episode. His occasional half-smile told me he was at least slightly entertained by my commentary.

By the end of the episode, we had finished our cups of wine. I decided not to have another drink because I did not want to get sloppy and say something stupid, which had started to become par for the course whenever I drank too much around Sebastian. Obviously, he didn't have more because for as smart as he was, he'd yet to appreciate decent wine when he was served some.

Despite feeling like I was forcing companionship on him that night, I started another episode. I reasoned that if Sebastian had really wanted me to leave, he would have said something.

"So, is this really how you spent all of your dates with Hunter?" he asked as the cheesy intro lines started up again.

"Pretty much," I confirmed. "I told you I was going to give you the complete Lucile Allen Fake Girlfriend Experience. Hunter likes wine more than you do though."

"I think I prefer the experience that includes practice kissing," he said in his standard dry tone.

Impulsively, I decided not to respond in my usual dismissive way.

"I think I do, too."

My pulse quickened when the words came out of my mouth. I felt his eyes on me. I was too nervous to look away from the screen.

"How about we turn it into a game? Every time someone talks about someone else behind their back, we have to kiss."

His proposal made me laugh.

"We would end up kissing during the whole episode."

I finally turned my head to see he was looking at me with a small smirk.

"I know. Exactly," he said quietly, shutting the laptop and placing it at the foot of the bed.

Returning to me, Sebastian gently put his hand to my cheek. I closed my eyes and felt his lips against mine. He took his time before parting his lips. The kiss deepened.

The last time we had reached this point, his roommate interrupted us. There was no Warren to interrupt us tonight, though. At first, I wasn't sure if that was a good thing or a bad thing, but the longer Sebastian remained attached to my lips, I found myself not thinking about anything besides how wonderful it felt to be kissed by someone who actually wanted to kiss me.

I chose to ignore the reality that it had only been a few hours since I helped him craft the perfect reconciliation email to the ex-girlfriend he had been fixated on getting back together with for months. Instead, I focused on how surprisingly good he was at kissing.

Moments passed and we were no longer sitting up. I'm not sure who initiated the gradual change in our positioning. More than likely, it was Sebastian's doing, because I knew I was nowhere near smooth enough to have made the transition to laying on our sides happen so seamlessly. His hand had made its way to my hip, just like before, his thumb gently gliding over my hip bone as he rested his other fingers on the small of my back.

All of a sudden, I heard a loud bass begin to thump through the wall. The beat sounded familiar and when the muffled lyrics started, I couldn't help but snicker. Sebastian pulled away in response to my reaction and then realized his neighbors were blasting "WAP" by Cardi B.

"What if I told you I arranged that to help set the mood?" he joked.

I erupted into more laughter as the song continued to play. Sebastian tried a few more times to kiss me, but my snickering was too much of a deterrent.

"Do you think they'll let us request something you don't find so funny?" Sebastian interlocked his fingers with mine and I just about melted.

"I have some music on my phone," I offered.

"I'll take it."

I picked up my phone from where I had laid it off to the side earlier. Spotify opened and I quickly pressed play, not consumed with trying to find the perfect song. Pretty much anything would be better for the situation than what we were currently hearing. As the random song started playing, the sounds of a piano helped drown out the less than romantic rapping from next door.

Sebastian found my lips again. He trailed his mouth down to my neck, causing goosebumps.

"Oh God. Is this Taylor Swift?" He lamented, his breath on my neck.

"Yeah, so what?"

"So cliché," he sighed, before his lips found a spot behind my ear.

"She just so happens to be one of the most talented musicians ever, Sebastian Torres." I informed sternly, enjoying his mouth on my neck. Simultaneously, he was tracing his fingers along my arm. I didn't know it was possible to enjoy someone else's touch so much.

"And you need to accept that she is being quite the solid wingman for you right now."

Sebastian's hand returned to holding mine, fiddling with my fingers. He pulled back, so I could see his large brown eyes shaped by his dark eyebrows. He furrowed them slightly as if deeply considering my point.

"You're right," he granted. "I must write to Taylor and thank her." He went back to kissing my lips. "And all the Real Housewives of Beverly Hills, too," he added before he deepened the kiss. After a moment, Sebastian unexpectedly broke away, looking at me with serious eyes. "But not that Lisa with a British accent, because she is nothing but trouble," he mocked my tutorial from earlier.

"It's good to know you're capable of retaining important information," I deadpanned.

"I think we've established that I'm good at lots of things," he gloated with a smirk.

"Especially being arrogant," I critiqued in between kisses.

"Hmm," he pretended to think, "Is it really arrogance if it's backed up with results?"

Sebastian returned to my neck, moving his way back up to my ear, while his hand pressed against my back under my shirt. He pulled me closer and I could feel his chest against mine. Unfortunately, the sound of my breath catching was evident. He let out a chuckle.

"It sounds like you can really relate to what your friend Taylor is singing about right now." He referenced "Wildest Dreams" playing in the background.

"Shut up," I ordered quietly.

"Gladly," he obliged before reclaiming my lips.

In the moment, everything seemed worth the cost, which at that point was only hypothetical. I would find out in the morning that I was wrong.

Chapter Twenty

I woke up alone in Sebastian's bed, trying my best to not overthink the events of the previous night that had led me there. Thankfully, there wasn't too much to analyze in the grand scheme of things. Both of us had refrained from doing much beyond kissing and wandering hands.

It had been a few minutes and Sebastian had yet to return. I reasoned that he had gone to get coffee like the other time I had spent the night in his room. However, it did cross my mind that maybe he had left and was hoping I would leave before he got back. But he had never shown himself to be that avoidant. If anything, he would be the type to wake me up and bluntly tell me to leave...if that's what he wanted. Maybe...I didn't know if making out with him changed his normal style of communication with me.

If he wasn't back within the next fifteen minutes, I would take the hint and leave. Fifteen long minutes with nothing but my thoughts to fill my head; not an ideal situation.

Staring up at the ceiling, I reviewed the facts. After seeing Amelia's post and her failure to respond to his message last night, Sebastian declared he was "done." He kissed me first. He very clearly seemed to enjoy kissing me.

Now the less exciting facts. We weren't dating. I didn't know if he would ever even want to date me. I had never been in a romantic relationship with someone and if the choice came down to having to choose between making out with Sebastian or keeping him as a friend, I would choose the latter.

Don't get me wrong, kissing could be added to his list of perfect attributes that usually annoyed me, but there were so many questions about what I would lose when we ultimately broke up. Because that would be the likely conclusion to someone I dated as a freshman in college. How on earth were other people so okay with the casualness that came with all this stuff? There seemed to be the potential for far too much awkwardness and hurt and everything I had grown accustomed to avoiding.

Before I went into full-on freak-out mode, Sebastian returned, coffees in hand as I had predicted. He looked at me and smiled as he handed me a cup.

"Good morning."

He sounded...cheerful? Maybe he thought I was a good kisser, too.

"So, exciting news," he started. My eyes followed him as he went to sit down in his chair. "Amelia messaged me this morning and invited me down for Spring Break, just like we planned."

The words punched me in the stomach. Luckily, years of masking how I really felt about things had prepared me for that moment.

"Oh, wow," I forced a half-smile.

"Yeah, I know! I totally wasn't expecting it after last night."

"Me either," I tried my hardest to sound happily surprised along with him, continuing to ignore the devastation in my gut.

"So, thank you again for all your help."

"No problem. I'm glad it all worked out." I raised my cup to him awkwardly before taking a drink.

"Turns out you were right about everything all along. I have to admit, I'm a little impressed. I will never doubt you again."

"Can I get that in writing?" I managed to joke back, regretting the skill I was once secretly proud of.

"And we're cool, right?"

I assumed Sebastian was vaguely alluding to our making out.

"Oh yeah, totally," I said breezily. "I should probably get going. Gotta get ready for finals." I hopped down, gathering my keys, phone, and sweatshirt.

"Hey, before you go—" he stopped me, "I have some good news for you, too."

I turned to him, hoping he would say that he had been messing with me. That he picked me over Amelia.

"You remember that guy, Caleb, from last night?"

I nodded, remembering Sebastian's friend. Tall, skinny, nice eyes...but not like Sebastian's.

"He texted and asked for your number. Do you want me to give it to him?"

"Uh, yeah, sure," I permitted, already formulating the excuse I would give if Caleb followed through on texting me.

"All right, well, I'll see you around. Congratulations." I smiled at him as I let myself out.

Chapter Twenty-One

I didn't see or talk to Sebastian after that morning, since both of us were consumed with our own finals. More important than any boy drama, I aced all my finals and walked away with three 4.0s. Intensive studying, thank you very much. My term grades added a much-appreciated boost to my cumulative GPA. Too bad I still couldn't figure out what major I wanted to declare.

Unable to come up with a good excuse for avoiding my family, I ended up going home for Spring Break as planned. Meeting with Katrina helped me feel steadier about the impending reality that I would have to participate in the spreading of my dad's ashes. I tried to frame it in the positive—it would just be my mom and Ava (no Oscar to worry about), no forced appointments with Brenda, and no forced church services. (Per Ava's report, my mom had cooled it a bit on that front.)

Hunter had chosen to go to Puerto Vallarta with a group of Santa Barbara friends for the week, leaving no temptation for distraction. It was a chance to finally just be with my mom and sister, whom I had spent the better part of the past year avoiding. Despite how upset I still was about the whole Sebastian situation, the thought of spending time with my mom and sister when there wasn't holiday stress left me more hopeful than anxious.

My mother found the perfect beach house to rent in Monterey. It looked directly out over the ocean cliffs. We made a point to drink coffee every morning on the deck, staring at the overwhelmingly powerful coastal waves crashing against the rocks, the sun beaming down. It was perfect.

On the second morning, Ava slept in after staying up too late FaceTiming with multiple friends. I was recently on a social media cleanse after seeing Amelia and Sebastian all over each other's stories, along with a post of them in front of the Golden Gate bridge she captioned, *"Some things just look better together."*

That was the breaking point. I quietly unfollowed them both and removed them from my followers. If Sebastian ever noticed, I would just tell him it made sense for the narrative.

My mom came out to the deck to join me as I stared out at the water, sipping my homemade high maintenance coffee.

"Well, would you look at that? Is that my eighteen-year-old daughter sitting without a phone in her hand? I almost didn't recognize you," she joked.

It reminded me of something my dad would say.

"I am not the one who was up all-night FaceTiming with my friends," I defended.

She nodded, granting me my point.

"Before you came out here," I started to share, "I noticed that I had been sitting here for the past thirty minutes, not really thinking about anything. It was nice."

My mother sighed.

"That does sound nice." She took a drink from her mug. "Any idea what you want to do today?"

I shook my head.

"Well, we have to think of something or else we will not hear the end of how bored your sister is and how we are ruining her life by taking her away from her friends this week."

"I suppose I could tolerate Fisherman's Wharf or the Aquarium," I acquiesced with a mock long-suffering sigh.

"Okay, we'll see what the boss says when she gets up."

My dad had coined that nickname for Ava when she was about two years old and made it very clear to everyone else that she was in charge. Or at least she thought she was.

"What about you? Are you missing any of your friends? Old ones...or new ones?"

She tried her best to sound unsuspecting, casually taking a sip of her coffee after she asked.

"No, I'm good." A half-smile formed on my face.

She nodded and held my gaze.

"What?" I laughed.

Although not as angry at my mother as I had been in recent months when she'd wanted information from me, I was still doubtful that I could possibly share everything that had happened with both Hunter and Sebastian and not have her be disappointed in me for my lack of truthfulness when it came to relationships.

"You know you can always talk to me," she assured. "I know...I know your dad was the one you tended to confide in. But I just want you to know, you don't have to keep things from me."

"I know."

"Okay then."

We sat there quietly for a moment, the crashing of the waves the only sound between us. Katrina's voice played in my head, urging me to be honest about what I felt instead of keeping it inside. I decided to test the waters.

"Sometimes I don't know if I really want to be a lawyer."

I looked out at the ocean as I said it. The sight of the ocean was slightly amusing to me given that I had started the year on track to be an Oceanography major because I couldn't just be honest with the academic adviser. When my mom didn't respond, I looked over at her.

She gave me a smile.

"That's fine. I just want you to be happy. Also, you have a lot of time to figure it out."

"It doesn't feel like I do," I countered. "I don't have to declare anything until next year, but I feel like everyone else I saw at those pre-law informational meetings knew exactly what they wanted to do and already had a plan for taking care of all their pre-reqs. They all knew exactly what major to pick to make them good candidates for law school."

"Well, what makes you happy?" She shifted my focus. "That's always a good place to start."

My mom wrapped her blanket around her tighter, looking attentive but relaxed. I could tell she was enjoying this moment. Not because of my own uncertainty, but simply because I was sharing with her, trusting her.

"Eating and drinking wine," I said flatly.

"Well, I guess the apple doesn't fall far from the tree," she laughed.

"To me," she looked at me lovingly, "you seem most happy when you're taking care of others. I saw it the minute you became a big sister. I saw it when you used to make sure Hunter studied for his tests. I saw it when your dad got sick and you—" she sighed, "took care of so many things around the house for me, for him.

"And what's great about that is there are plenty of things you can do with your life that involve taking care of people, not just being a lawyer. Yes, despite popular opinion, I do think lawyers help people." She paused to grin at me. "There are so many jobs and professions out there...believe me, you've got time to figure it all out. And it will come to you," she assured. "Undergrad is more about the experience than the actual answer," she added wisely.

"More than anything, I want you to make choices based on what you want and not what you think will make other people happy." She made sure to look me in the eye. "And that includes your dad."

We both stared out at the waves crashing, letting her advice sink in.

"Lucy, he was so proud of you and would've been proud no matter what you chose to do." She paused, probably amazed I hadn't run away from the conversation yet. "I love you."

My mouth curled into a half-smile, feeling months of anger and resentment loosen their grip, knowing I would remember this moment forever.

"I love you, too," I said quietly.

She smiled back, clearly pleased with how her morning was going.

We spread Dad's ashes into the ocean later that day, waiting until sunset. Afterwards, we huddled together on the beach, crying and wrapped up in blankets, watching the sun go down.

It was sad. But it wasn't overwhelming. It hurt in a different way than before. Despite the continued sense of loss, my heart was full of gratitude that I had had such a wonderful dad, even if it wasn't for long enough. I was grateful I still had my mom and sister. We all felt the loss differently, but in sharing it, I decided, it was a little more bearable.

Chapter Twenty-Two

Returning for spring quarter left me more excited than anything. I was finally starting to feel like I was getting the hang of the whole college routine. The Seattle weather gifted us with more sunny days, made only more perfect by the cherry blossoms in the quad. The girls from the floor and I made a point to shift our afternoon studying to the iconic location whenever we could. I began to understand more why my dad had loved this place so much.

I decided that I wasn't ready to rule out law school completely. As a result, I sat down with an advisor again. We narrowed down potential majors to English or History. These left flexibility for different grad school programs and also fit with my ability to easily remember facts, as well as my strong essay writing skills. What Sebastian had previously labeled 'bullshitting' from our time in AP Lit together was actually considered an attribute by the advisor when they looked at my work.

Although I had signed up for the cushion course of American Pop Song, I threw my hat in the ring for the more challenging Medieval History, and a Social Issues Composition class. The latter was likely going to frustrate me, given that social issues involve some sort of conflict and injustice, but it also had a service component, so I hoped that would balance out any negative feelings.

There was so much reading and writing, I was glad I didn't have the extracurricular activity of curating a fake relationship on Instagram on top of it. Truthfully, I was grateful for the distraction all my assignments gave me.

Sebastian had been equally busy with his course work, deciding to sign up for four classes because that was just the type of overachiever he was.

He had shared his logic during a brief conversation I had with him after running into him in the dining hall. He seemed happy, and it perplexed me how anyone could be happy taking two math classes on top of physics and engineering. I imagine it had something to do with being back together with Amelia. Which I made a point to ask nothing about and continued to deliberately avoid both of them on social media.

Sebastian and I never spoke again about the night we kissed. I also refrained from saying anything to the other girls about it. I was well-trained and knew the information would just perpetuate drama. It helped that they had moved on to being distracted by their own love interests. Everyone had accepted Operation Fake Girlfriend as a success and they were none the wiser to the time when I had wanted more from Sebastian. It made it easy to pretend like nothing had ever happened.

Four weeks into the quarter, I had also kept my birthday a secret. Mostly because no one had ever asked. It wasn't like I hated my birthday, but I wasn't one to go around exclaiming to others that they needed to make a big deal about it.

In high school, however, Hunter had made a point to do just that. Showing up with flowers and balloons I would have to carry around all day long. Of course, this gesture only endeared Hunky Hunter to all the girls more. It didn't upset me, but I felt like he got more out of it than I did.

If someone had told me that Hunter was once again planning to do something to acknowledge my birthday, I wouldn't have been surprised. It was the grandness of the gesture, or rather the event, that I never expected.

It was a regular Thursday and I was at my desk reading one of the thousands of pages that had been assigned to me for History that week. Danica was also at her desk studying.

There had been no scrunchy sentencing since my drunken scene of assertiveness the previous quarter. Regardless, our exchange of words remained limited. While the silence was often awkward, knowing that I wouldn't be kicked out of my room for indefinite amounts of time was delightful.

There was a knock at our door.

"It's open," I called out.

"Hey, I'm looking for an almost-nineteen-year-old."

I looked up to see an unexpected Hunter grinning widely in my doorway, flowers in hand.

"I was wondering if you could help me find her?"

My mouth dropped. I wasn't sure if what I was seeing was real. He started laughing at my response. I jumped up from my chair, squealing, running and wrapping my arms around him before he could even come inside.

"You're here! You're here!"

He looked down at me, both of us still smiling,

"Yeah, I'm here," he laughed.

"What're you doing here?" I exclaimed, still in disbelief.

"It's your birthday on Monday, duh," he said.

I let go of him, unable to stop my smiling.

"I got a hotel a few blocks away. Just for the weekend. I fly out Sunday."

"You flew up here and got a hotel for my birthday?" I repeated in shock.

"I might have told my parents that I needed to see you for the weekend just to make sure I wasn't really straight," he admitted.

Of course, he did. I shook my head.

"Hey, it worked." He shrugged. "I can't help it if they are still hoping you'll be their daughter-in-law someday."

Veronica and Hattie had joined us in the hallway after hearing all the noise.

"Surprise!" Veronica cheered.

"You knew about this?"

"Ronnie and I have been conspiring for the past month," Hunter informed proudly. "Hi, I'm Hunter, by the way. Nice to meet you in person."

He stepped over to shake her hand. Veronica and Hattie were visibly taken by the sight of Hunter in person. I think I might have even seen Hattie blush. There was no denying he looked handsome with his perfectly disheveled surfer hair. I knew the grey North Face zip up he was wearing was chosen purposefully to blend in amongst the PNW crowd.

"So, the plan is, you're going to come with me tonight. We'll hang out Friday and then Saturday," he stopped to look at Veronica and then back at me, "we're throwing you a party!"

"I have class tomorrow."

"I know for a fact you only have one seminar at ten tomorrow."

"Wow, okay, stalker," I teased.

"The hotel is not that far from the campus, if you still want to go to class tomorrow like a nerd, you can," he teased back.

I mulled over the idea. Hunter sensed me softening.

"Come on, Luce, it's Thursday. That's pretty much Friday when you're in college."

He turned to look at Hattie and Veronica. "Do you see this? She's honestly considering making me spend the night alone in my hotel after I flew all the way up here to see her and I even brought her flowers."

"Come on Lucy, don't make the boy sad," Hattie chimed in.

"And you haven't really had any fun this whole quarter. You've been so busy reading," Veronica pointed out.

Hunter was holding my hand and giving me puppy dog eyes while mouthing the word please.

"Okay," I agreed with a sigh.

"Yay for Fun Lucy!" he exclaimed, triumphantly holding my hand up in the air victoriously with his.

"But," I said sternly, "I am bringing my reading with me."

"Oh yeah, of course," he feigned the same level of seriousness, before pulling me in for a hug, wrapping his long arms around my shoulders.

"Go pack, Beautiful." He kissed my forehead before sending me back into my room.

Unsurprisingly, Hunter invited himself into Veronica and Hattie's room to pass the time while I packed my things. Intermittently, I called out for a few specifications on what I would need. He remained somewhat vague, but did acknowledge that I'd probably want something "nice-ish" for dinner with just him on Friday.

Danica remained uninterested in what I was doing. I imagine she was probably excited that she was going to have the room to herself for the night.

Once all my clothes and toiletries were collected along with my school stuff, I rejoined Hunter. He was looking over all the photos and knick-knacks Veronica and Hattie had on their shelves. Always the charmer, he was getting to know them better through various questions he asked, and of course making them laugh. He was such a natural with people. Seeing their reaction to him reaffirmed what I had always known: he was just so easy to love.

"Okay, I'm ready," I announced.

"Splendid," he smiled back as he handed a picture frame back to Hattie. "Thank you, ladies. We will see you at the party Saturday night."

He walked over to me and held out his arm. "Are you ready to go cause some trouble, m'lady?"

"If that includes having a snack and going to bed in the next hour, then I am. Here. For. It."

He shook his head at my answer.

"It's like you don't even have to bother getting older; you're already there."

"Not going to lie, I'm legit excited about the non-dorm mattress and thread count," I grinned widely at him before I said my goodbyes.

We walked by Sebastian's door that was closed—a relief. Hunter still had no idea about everything that had happened behind the scenes of the posted photos. I knew I would tell him soon—but the thought of being in the presence of two former fake boyfriends was less than appealing.

The next morning, Hunter came to my History seminar with me. It was a five-hundred-person lecture, so his presence went unnoticed. Well, at least in the sense of the professor noticing a new student. There were at least five sorority girls who kept staring at him throughout the lecture. He stupidly made a point to smile back. Only to be met by a death stare from me because of how distracting the silent flirting was.

"What?" he whispered with a boyish grin.

"You are totally leading them on right now," I scolded back in a hush.

"They smiled first," he defended. "I don't want to be rude."

"You just like knowing that people think you're pretty."

"Maaaaaybe," he playfully admitted. "But not as much as I like you."

He kissed the back of my hand placatingly. I shook my head and went back to taking notes. My disapproval managed to make him behave for the rest of the lecture.

"Is that your favorite class?" he asked afterwards as we walked to an early lunch.

"I think it's interesting. But there's like fifteen different books assigned. I could do without all the reading. My Pop Music class is super easy. The tests just consist of the professor playing sound clips of the songs and then we answer multiple-choice questions about them"

"You realize not everyone can remember ten different facts associated with a song selected at random."

I shrugged.

"We all have our talents. What about you? You like your classes?"

"They're all right," he sighed. "My dad wants me to declare business or finance. I've been thinking about physical therapy though. Jonathan pointed out it would be a good way to stay involved in sports."

"Oh? Jonathan?"

"Yes, Jonathan." He looked back at me sheepishly, while he walked with both hands in his pockets.

"Not Trevor?"

"No," he shook his head. "Not Trevor."

"Well, I can't wait to hear about this."

I led him into the HUB food court.

Once we settled in with our food, Hunter teased me by stalling the conversation, saying he was doubtful the pizza from Pagliacci was going to be anywhere near as good as Pizza My Heart. He demanded silence after he took his first bite, considering the merits of the pizza.

"Seriously?" I asked, vexed.

He continued to chew, holding his finger up for a moment as he took a drink of his soda.

"Ahh," he sighed dramatically.

"It's decent," he reviewed, smiling at my glare. "I'm sorry, did you have something you wanted to talk about?"

"No, not anymore. I'm officially uninterested," I lied.

He bit his lip like he had exciting news.

"I have a boyfriend," he sing-songed happily.

"Shut up!" I swatted his arm across the table. "Tell me everything! How are you just telling me now?"

He laughed, backing away from my intensity.

"I knew I was going to see you in person, so I decided to wait."

"How long?"

"A few weeks. The first weekend back after Spring Break," he specified.

"So..."

"So...?" he mimicked.

"My God, Hunter, just tell me the whole story of how it happened." I had very little tolerance for his delayed report.

Hunter finally humored me with his very long—and very detailed—story that dated all the way back to January.

While he had been casually dating Trevor when he first came out on social media, he remained friends with Jonathan. Hunter said he knew that Jonathan was interested in dating him, but he had been hesitant because Jonathan was two years older and already looking into applying to different med schools. Hunter didn't want to end up having a serious boyfriend who was going to just end up leaving in a year. However, Hunter kept noticing he was happiest when he was around Jonathan.

A few weeks after Valentine's Day, things gradually fizzled out with Trevor. Hunter said he hung out with Jonathan a few times before finals but he didn't know if they were dates or not. During one of their hang-outs, he even ended up embarrassingly asking Jonathan if it was a date. To which Jonathan replied, "Well, what do you want it to be?" Hunter knew I would find this detail notably swoon-worthy.

Jonathan had been part of the group who had gone to Puerto Vallarta with Hunter. During the trip, some drama erupted where Jonathan finally called Hunter out. He said he needed to make a decision and not let fear of the future keep him from an opportunity to experience love. Hunter said it would have been the perfect moment to kiss Jonathan, but he chickened out. Then Jonathan declared he needed to move on, because he wasn't going to sit and wait for Hunter.

Luckily, Hunter got a second chance once back at Santa Barbara when they both ended up at a house party the first weekend of spring quarter.

Hunter made sure to set every single detail of the scene. What he was wearing, what Jonathan was wearing, how they had been trying to avoid each other all night. Until finally Jonathan asked him to go talk outside on the porch.

"Then," Hunter said intently, as he looked directly into my eyes, "we go outside. And Jonathan looks at me. He starts to apologize for Puerto Vallarta. I start to apologize, too. And then from inside the house we hear 'Wonder' playing. You know, by Shawn Mendes?"

I nodded. Hunter paused, knowing he had me completely enthralled.

"And I look at him and he looks at me, both of us realizing the song is saying everything we're feeling, and then he pulled me in and we kissed."

Leave it to Hunter to have a big cinematic moment for when he got together with his first boyfriend. With anyone else, I might have rolled my eyes, but I was too happy for him to let my pessimistic nature take over. Also, I was incredibly happy he picked the steady guy he had originally labeled as boring.

I sighed contentedly at the conclusion of his story.

"I'm happy for you," I said.

Hunter smiled back at me. We went back to our food for a moment.

"Does he know about us?"

"You mean how we dated or how we 'dated'?" He put the second 'dated' in air quotes.

"The second one."

"Yeah, otherwise I'm sure he would've had a lot more questions about me coming up here. He wants to meet you."

"Ditto. You know I have to make sure he's not just an older boy taking advantage of you." I grinned at him and he rolled his eyes.

"Okay," I sighed, "so what do you want to do now?"

"We are going to head downtown and I'm going to help you pick out a dress for tomorrow. Later, I made dinner reservations and I may or may not have smuggled some wine in my suitcase."

"You know you didn't have to do all of this."

It felt kind of weird now that he officially had a boyfriend. He should have been directing all his fanfare to Jonathan now.

"Nonsense, I wanted to," he dismissed. "I like you and I love you."

He poked at my face, in an endearingly awkward way. I swatted his hand away.

"Plus, I don't really trust your judgment on picking out a dress."

"Whatever," I rolled my eyes. "Let's get some coffee before we go."

After I ordered both of our high-maintenance coffees, I stood off to the side, waiting. Hunter had gone off to look through the magazines. The barista called out my name and I stepped up to gather the drinks. I turned around and was met with an unexpected sight.

Sebastian.

Although it shouldn't have taken me by surprise. We did go to the same school. It was just that being around Hunter for less than twenty-four hours had left me wonderfully distracted. I tried my best not to look dumbfounded. I was not doing a very good job.

"Oh, hey."

"Hey," Sebastian smiled. "Fancy meeting you here. I figured you had successfully reclaimed your room for studying since I never see you around here in the afternoons anymore. I already have a table if you want to join." He motioned behind him.

"I, uh..." I tripped over my words awkwardly. The thought of Sebastian and Hunter being together when I wasn't prepared for it caused my anxiety to spike. Before I could explain that I was about to be leaving, Hunter walked up behind me.

"So, we're in agreement that Beyonce's new *Vogue* cover is some of the fiercest shit we've ever seen, right?" Hunter said adamantly while grabbing his coffee cup from me.

He looked up to see who I was staring at, as I stood frozen.

"Oh, hey, Sebastian," he greeted cluelessly.

"Hey," Sebastian raised a brow, showing his confusion.

"Hunter flew up for the weekend to surprise me," I somehow managed to form words.

Sebastian nodded.

Nobody spoke. I could feel Hunter staring at me and reading me like only he knew how to.

"Okay, well..." Sebastian started.

"Yeah, see you around," I managed to spit out.

Sebastian walked back to his table with his coffee.

I turned to see Hunter staring at me wide-eyed.

"Okay, just—" I preemptively defended against what his expression was implying. "Just stop, okay. It's not."

"Oh, but it definitely is," he argued. "We are so talking about all of that, that just happened," he insisted as we walked out the door.

All through dinner at the insanely delicious, but also insanely expensive restaurant, I was able to successfully dodge Hunter's demand for an explanation regarding my encounter with Sebastian. I not only had the four-course meal Hunter's dad was paying for to thank, but also the impressive views of Lake Union we took in at our table. People twice our age probably had to wait months to get reservations for the breathtaking spot. Having pretended to date Hunter for three years, I also knew exactly what topics to bring up to distract him; surfing, various sports, and almost any show on Bravo.

After managing to make it through the whole meal appearing more mature than we were, we took an Uber back to the hotel in the U-District.

After returning to Hunter's room for the night, we changed into our respective sweatpants and t-shirts, poured the petit verdot he'd brought, and settled into bed. I curled up next to him as he cued up the godawful Netflix romcom we had decided on.

"Don't think I didn't notice that you kept distracting me this afternoon and at dinner," Hunter announced.

"Okay, fine," I relinquished, knowing his questions were unavoidable. "What? What do you want to know?"

"I want to know what happened with Sebastian," he stated obviously.

"Nothing," I said as convincingly as I could. I was still unsure if I was entirely ready to admit to him that he had been right about me needing to be careful.

"Lies!" he declared with a laugh.

"It was a successful partnership that ended with him getting back together with Amelia, like I had planned all along."

Hunter inspected my face.

"But why the awkwardness at Starbucks today?"

"What awkwardness?" I feigned cluelessness.

"The long pauses. It felt like if we were dating and you ran into someone that you cheated on me with," he evaluated.

I shifted my eyes away from his gaze, knowing I was done for.

"Ohmygod! You did cheat on me!" he exclaimed.

"That's ridiculous. We're not dating. We never were," I reminded him.

He stared at me, contemplating his next move. I remained silent.

He started poking at my side. "Luuuucccyyyy...Luuuuccccyyy...tell me what happened."

I swatted his hand away.

"Luuuuuuccccyyy. This is going to turn into tickling," he warned.

"Okay, fine," I shouted as his fingers were about to start their attack. "We kissed!" I confessed. He dropped his hands down.

"Yeah, but like, how did you kiss? Kiss like we kiss, or like kiss, kiss, you know?"

I sighed, rubbing my forehead, not nearly as excited to talk about the situation as he was.

"Oooooo," he crooned. "Did you guys make out? How far did you get? Is he a good kisser?" Hunter fired off questions, excited by the gossip.

"Whatever, it was nothing," I dismissed. "It was just something that happened. And it's stupid. And he's back with Amelia now."

Hunter paused his teasing for a second when the tone of my voice registered. He leaned into my back to offer comfort. He propped his chin up on my shoulder.

"And how do you feel about that?"

Willing myself not to cry, I turned my head back and peered down at his bright blue eyes as they looked up at me.

"Sick," I said quietly with a frown.

He sighed and then repositioned to sit with his back against the head-board. He pulled me into his chest. We sat there in the quiet for a moment and then I finally recounted everything that had happened with Sebastian.

"Just for context," Hunter broke the brief silence when I was done spill-ing my guts, "how many times have you listened to 'Cardigan'?"

"I lost count," I admitted.

"Well, that's some high-level heartache."

"I feel like such a loser. Who makes out with someone they know has absolutely no interest in dating them?"

"Um, only, like, most people our age," he pointed out.

"I just wanted to have something be real for once, you know?" I shared quietly, appreciating that at least in that moment I could be held by Hunter.

"We were real," he argued. "In our own way."

When I didn't respond, he knew that wasn't enough anymore.

"Well, fake girlfriend or not, I think Sebastian is pretty stupid for not knowing how great you are. I mean, I would know. It's not like I would let just anyone pretend to be my girlfriend for three years, right? Especially since girls are kind of gross," he attempted to get me to laugh.

It didn't work.

"But more importantly, boys are stupid."

"Agreed."

"Except for Jonathan," he qualified.

"Except for Jonathan," I allowed, finally giving him a small smile.

Chapter Twenty-Three

Hunter remained very tightlipped about the birthday party he and Veronica had planned for me. They had rented a private dining room at a restaurant in U-Village, and Hunter—really his parents—had picked up the tab on all the catering. I knew this was probably one of the last times that Hunter was going to spoil me, now that he had come out and was officially in a relationship.

He knew it, too, which was probably why he made a point to do it. We both knew he enjoyed orchestrating and pulling off the large gestures way more than I enjoyed being on the receiving end of them. That said, it was far too soon in his relationship with Jonathan for a show this big. I mentally reframed it as a celebration of his coming out, more so than my own birthday, and it made the attention a little bit easier to handle.

Hunter did deliver on helping me find a new dress I looked good in. It was a black halter that had an ombre gold sparkle detail from the waist down. At first, I was worried about being cold all night, but the small banquet room filled with heat as guests arrived and started mingling.

I had been anxious that some people would be disappointed since there was no alcohol, but I guess given the free food and the fact that a couple of people had fake IDs, people managed to enjoy themselves.

It was hard not to slip into old Hunter and Lucy mode, meaning his hand kept ending up around my waist or holding my hand. Part of me thought he was probably doing it because in his own weird way, he was trying to make up for the rejection I felt from Sebastian. At one point, Veronica pulled me off to the side, looking somewhat concerned.

"So, what's the deal?"

"What deal?"

"You and Hunter. Are you back together?"

"No," I laughed. "He's gay. You know this."

"Are you sure he's not bi? He flew all the way up here to throw you this party and you spent the past two nights in a hotel room together."

"Completely platonic." I shrugged.

"You're not the least bit confused? I mean, you guys did date for three years and were anything but platonic during that time."

I really wanted to tell her that it had always been unromantic, but knew what I had agreed to...even though unbeknownst to Hunter, I had already broken that promise by telling Sebastian the truth.

"I don't know what to tell you." I shrugged, deciding to keep it honest and vague.

Before she could ask more questions, Sebastian walked in. I froze, Veronica turned to see what I was looking at.

"I ran into Sebastian yesterday and invited him. Lucy, you guys are still friends, right?"

I barely nodded before Sebastian made his way to me.

"Happy birthday," he smiled.

I felt butterflies in my stomach. He was holding a gift in his hand.

"I wasn't sure if people were doing gifts, but here you go."

He handed it over to me. I unwrapped it. Laundry detergent.

"You got me laundry soap?" My confusion was evident.

He smiled proudly. "Yeah, it's the one that I use. Now all your stuff can smell like eucalyptus, too."

I couldn't help but laugh. It was thoughtful, but it was also definitely random. I remembered when he'd boasted about how he always managed to make Amelia's gifts meaningful rather than cliché. There was nothing cliché about this gift for sure.

"Well, thank you."

I set it down on the table. Turning back to him, I crossed my arms. I felt slightly exposed in my fitted dress in front of him.

"So, how have you been? I haven't seen you much this quarter."

"Oh, good, just lots of papers and reading for History and English." I refrained from telling him there were about fifteen different facts I had learned about Medieval culture that I had wanted to tell him, just to see if he already knew them.

"How's Amelia? I stopped following both of you on Instagram because I thought that made the most sense. But that means I never found out how Spring Break went," I informed. It was satisfying to give him the impression that his official status with her wasn't something I had cared enough to follow up on before that moment.

"Yeah, uh..." Sebastian paused and furrowed his brow as he thought about his answer. "Spring Break was good...but a few weeks ago we decided it just wasn't going to work."

"Oh?" I tried to sound neutral.

"She wanted me to transfer and I didn't really want to. Turns out I kind of like it here."

"Despite the subpar Mexican food?" I joked.

"Well, someone told me I might have been making that claim too early before examining all my options."

He looked intently into my eyes and I started to question whether he was just talking about Mexican food. Sebastian opened his mouth to say something else, but stopped just as Hunter walked up to us.

"Hey Luce, you okay?" Hunter asked, putting his hand on the small of my back.

His concern was obvious. Sebastian raised his eyebrow. Before I got a chance to answer, Hunter said under his breath. "I'm sorry, I didn't know Veronica invited him. Do you want me to ask him to leave?"

Apparently, Hunter hadn't made the offer quietly enough.

"Really? You want to play like you're the chivalrous one right now?" Sebastian mused.

"Excuse me?" Hunter gave a look of warning to Sebastian.

My muscles tensed when I heard Hunter's tone. Thankfully, no one was yelling yet, but the exchange was still enough to get the attention of a few people nearby, including Veronica.

"Oh, don't think for a second I don't know everything she's done for you, and what a selfish prick you've been about it." Sebastian once again proved himself lacking in the area of tact.

"You definitely need to leave now." Hunter took a step forward. I pushed myself in front of him, preventing him from getting in Sebastian's face.

"Why? Because then she might actually find out all the shit you said about her behind her back?"

"Shut up!" Hunter raised his voice.

One look at Hunter's face and I knew. I knew there was some sort of truth to what Sebastian was saying.

"Lucy, why don't you ask him? Go ahead and ask him who started the rumors about you sophomore year when you guys started dating."

"Shut up," Hunter repeated. "Lucy, it's not—"

Sebastian interrupted before Hunter could continue his defense.

"Because I have the unfortunate memory of being stuck in a locker room with you and all of your idiot bros. Having to hear you recount in vivid detail the type of things your new girlfriend would do, how easy it was to get her to do all of those things, because you were so much more popular than her."

My mind started to feel fuzzy as Sebastian's words registered. He had opened a wound I had tried my best not to think about for years.

When I first started dating Hunter, the two months before I knew he was gay, there had been extremely nasty rumors about me at school. In hindsight, I probably should've told an adult about it, but I just sucked it up, not wanting it to wreck the fairytale of getting to date the most popular boy in school.

Hunter had been adamant that he had no idea where the rumors had started. He hypothesized that they might have come from Olivia or one of the other girls out of jealousy. He had been so convincing, and I'd liked him so much—I never thought twice about believing him. From that moment on, we agreed not to waste time on the stupid things other people said. As long as we knew the truth from each other, that was all that mattered. It was how I'd tolerated him being my fake boyfriend for so long, because I knew despite the façade we put on for others, I was the one person he had always been completely truthful with.

"And after all this time," Sebastian shook his head, "she's still protecting you even after you ruined her reputation. It takes a special type of asshole to let someone do that."

"Stop it! Stop it," I yelled before Hunter could punch him.

My eyes were starting to sting. Hunter went to touch my shoulder, attempting to console me. I backed away, shaking my head. Luckily, Veronica had the foresight to grab my purse. Without saying anything, she and Corine followed me out the door. All the heartache I had been feeling about Sebastian was superficial compared to the absolute betrayal and devastation erupting in my core at that moment.

"So, are you going to tell us what that was all about?" Corine finally asked as we drove back to the dorm.

"Corine, I don't think she wants to talk about it right now," Veronica interjected quietly.

Thankfully, I had kept myself from crying, but the anger and embarrassment still burned brightly in my chest. Much like I had wanted to avoid having to talk about my dad when I moved away to college, I had also hoped I would've never had to share the pain that had come from choosing to date Hunter, despite how picture perfect he and I had managed to make it all look.

"Hunter was more popular than I ever was in high school. Like, a lot more," I said softly. "People were confused about why he asked me out when we were sophomores since he could've dated anyone else at the school. The first few weeks we started dating, these really horrible rumors broke out about all these things I did with him. None of them were true. When I asked him about it, he denied ever saying anything. And I guess...according to Sebastian, Hunter was the one that started it all."

"What did Sebastian mean when he said 'after all she did for you?'" Veronica finally asked.

I contemplated not telling them the truth for fear of how pathetic they would think I was, but at the same time, I was so tired of holding on to Hunter's lie. Especially when it was obvious now how little Hunter had actually cared about me for the past three years.

"I knew Hunter was gay after two months of dating him," I confessed. "He was terrified about coming out and didn't want to keep hooking up with girls, pretending like he was attracted to them. He decided to date me because he was hoping if he tried dating someone he was friends with, it might change him, which of course it didn't. After he came out to me, we decided to stay together and pretend it was romantic. No one ever knew but us."

"You did that for three years?" Corine exclaimed.

"Yep," I sighed.

"Why didn't you say anything when he came out?"

"His parents really like me. He said it made it easier for them to accept that he was gay by thinking that he had really tried to be in relationship with me." I paused. "It's all so stupid."

"But Sebastian knew?"

"He didn't believe I could successfully make Amelia think we were dating each other over Instagram. So, I ended up telling him to prove a point. He always seemed so hostile towards Hunter. I guess now I know why."

"But why did Hunter ask you if you were okay with Sebastian being at the party?"

I let out another sigh. Explaining messes was never fun.

"Because Hunter knows that I made out with Sebastian before he got back together with Amelia."

Veronica and Corine's eyes widened.

"See, Lucy, I always knew you were a lady of mystery," Corine joked with a wink.

"I can't believe you kept all of the stuff with Hunter a secret for the past four years," Veronica exclaimed.

"You weren't at all sad that you missed out on actually dating people?" Corine asked with disbelief.

"At the time, no. I mean, you've both met Hunter. He's so fun and caring, I really didn't think I was missing out on anything," I explained. "But now I don't know. It's not like I could've dated anyone else...seeing as how he ruined my reputation," I repeated Sebastian's words and then felt sick.

"Why are we on the Ave? I thought we were going back to Lander," I said as Veronica parked the car on the busy street.

"Nonsense," Veronica declared. "If ever a situation called for ice cream, it was this one."

She stepped out of the car, Corine and I following her.

I didn't disagree, but the whole experience of being comforted by girl-friends over boy trouble was unfamiliar. Especially since the last group of girls I'd hung out with weren't really friends at all.

"I wonder why the whole thing upset Sebastian so much?" Corine asked once we settled in with our respective orders. I shrugged.

"I mean, think about it," she started. "Those rumors were from the tenth grade. He's held on to that for a long time to just suddenly call Hunter out tonight."

"Well, in all fairness, he probably thought that it was true until recently."

"Yeah, but why didn't he tell you about it when you told him that everything with Hunter was fake?"

I shrugged again.

"Why did he decide to run off to see Amelia for Spring Break after mak-ing out with me the night before?" I posed a question back. "I guess there are certain things about Sebastian Torres that we will just never understand."

"If Sebastian told you he wanted to be with you right now, what would you do?" Veronica asked me seriously.

It wasn't that I hadn't considered the question. I literally had numer-ous times before Spring Break. Wishing he would show up at my door during finals week with a high maintenance coffee, telling me that he was happier when I was around, and that he'd much rather kiss me than Amelia.

But he never did.

He chose her.

In all fairness, he did not choose her for very long, but still, he chose her. And when he got back from Spring Break, he waited to tell me they weren't back together, and it was only after I asked about her.

He had made no real effort to see me besides the occasional hello, even though he had my phone number and lived literally eight doors down from me. And maybe I didn't know what I wanted, but it was a fair argument to say it seemed like Sebastian was clearly communicating what he wanted. And it wasn't me.

Veronica and Corine looked at me expectantly.

"I think that question is irrelevant," I avoided.

"Then what do you want?"

"More ice cream," I said flatly, making them laugh.

At least in that moment, as horrible as it was, I knew my first year in college hadn't been a total waste socially. The genuine female friendships I had made with Veronica, Corine, and the other girls on my floor was something I had never thought I would be lucky enough to find. There was no doubt in my mind that it would never have happened had I not broken away from Hunter.

Chapter Twenty-Four

On Sunday morning, I was trying to get caught up on the homework I had neglected during Hunter's 'Big Birthday Weekend of Fun' that instead had turned into a big weekend of bullshit. My attempt to complete the assignment was going poorly because I had left two of my history books at the hotel along with all my other stuff.

Rationally, I knew I would need to coordinate getting it back, but the thought of texting Hunter left me too angry, so I put it off. I figured he would be smart enough to leave it all at the front desk and I would pick it up later.

As I attempted an essay for the third time by trying to piece together what I could from notes and internet searches, I heard a knock at the door. I got up and looked through the peephole to see Hunter waiting.

He knocked again.

"Lucy, I know you're in there. I already got it out of Veronica."

I would decide if I was upset with her later.

"I came to apologize, please..."

A pause.

"I have all your stuff," he reasoned.

He waited and then sighed.

"Okay, I'm about to go get on a flight and since you have a personal understanding of how fleeting life can be, I would hate to have something happen where I die and you have to live with this being the last interaction we ever had."

He waited. I opened the door.

"That was manipulative," I evaluated as I walked back to rest against the windowsill. My arms were crossed.

"Resourceful," he reframed.

I looked at him expectantly. He walked my things into the room as he held on to his own bag. We stood there, with at least ten feet between us. I had never felt further away from him.

"I'm sorry," he said softly.

"So, it's true? Say it's true."

"It's true," he nodded and looked away shamefully.

"Lucy, I was fifteen. I was an idiot. I was scared," he started to defend himself. "I swear, everything I said was before I came out to you. I stopped once you agreed to stay with me. I had always hoped that by us staying together through senior year, it would make it less bad."

"You know that's why people thought we were together, right? Like there couldn't have been any other reason for someone like you to be with someone like me. You don't remember how it was all over social media anytime we posted a picture?"

"It went away after a while," he argued.

"It didn't change the fact that they all still thought it. I lied and told myself it didn't matter, because you needed me, and at least I was with a guy who would never hurt me—"

"Lucy, I'm sorry," he interrupted, not wanting to hear me voice his wrongdoings. I didn't stop.

"—and then, when you finally come out, you won't let it be over for me. People still think I did all those things with you that I never did. Why? Because you're scared of what your parents will think. I used to think I got some benefit from this, still being your person that no one else could be, but it just doesn't work anymore—not when everything is only about what you want."

My voice cracked, scared by the honesty that finally came out of my mouth.

"That's not fair. What the hell do you think this whole weekend was?"

"You trying to keep up appearances as the perfect guy and make up for the fact that you completely forgot to say anything about my dad in February or March," I accused bluntly.

Hunter looked at me and the shame reappeared.

"Don't think I don't know that all the grand gestures have always been more about making you look good than about anything I would ever want."

His eyes didn't hide the fact that my words cut him. But he knew it was true.

"Everything for the past four years has been dictated by you being selfish and scared and me being too nice to call you on it. And stupidly, I thought it meant we had some great friendship, but all it means is we're a bunch of cowards manipulating people...and each other."

Part of me worried that my honesty might cost me the one friendship I'd had in high school. One that I had thought I would never be without.

Hunter sighed, continuing to stare at me with his wonderful blue eyes. He cautiously made his way over to the windowsill and sat down next to me, crossing his arms. I didn't back away, but stared at the floor. For several moments, we sat there silently.

"But," Hunter began quietly, "doesn't that kind of make us like the Real Housewives?" The hope that he would make me laugh was evident in his tone.

"No. You are not allowed to make me laugh right now," I ordered.

"I don't know what else to do," he admitted, a sadness in his voice. "Everything you said just now is true. And I wish I could go back and change it. I know I hurt you. But, Lucy, please believe me when I say you are my best friend and I would do anything for you. And that will never change."

"I think you should probably head to the airport," I said simply, knowing if he stayed longer, he would charm me into not being mad at him anymore.

He nodded.

"I'm sorry, Lucy. You know I love you."

I nodded, but I couldn't bring myself to accept his apology. It was the first time in four years I didn't give him a hug when we said goodbye.

The next day, I woke up to see a notification that Hunter had tagged me in a post. He put up a picture from my birthday party (before it turned into a disaster).

We looked gorgeous in it. There was also a picture from sophomore year—our first picture together as a couple. We looked so young. There was a slight sting of anger when I realized it had probably been taken within days of when he'd started those horrible lies about me. Regardless, I read the caption.

Happy Birthday to my best friend, Lucile Consuelo Allen! @luce.c.a

I was 10 when I first realized I wanted to kiss boys instead of girls. I had told myself it wasn't ok because I was good at sports. I spent the next five years trying to make myself attracted to girls. I dated girls, made out with girls, did other things with girls—all it brought was guilt that I couldn't be different and led them on. When I was 15, I had a ray of hope. Maybe if I dated a girl I was actually friends with, it would change me.

It did change me. Not in the way I had foolishly hoped at 15 #stillgay but in a way I had never imagined. I came out to Lucy after dating her for 2 months. She responded with only love, acceptance, and a promise to protect me until I was ready to come out. She weathered horrible rumors (most of them stupidly started by me trying to sell myself as a player) and all sorts of other hate from people. She did it all with grace, because I was scared and not ready to be myself.

There is no doubt in my mind that my relationship with Lucy kept me alive when I was in high school. Having her in my life reminds me that unconditional, selfless love is possible. I hope one day I can do it as well as she does.

Thank you, Luce, for always being my person. You deserve nothing but the best and I'm so lucky to have you in my life.

For the first time, I didn't bother to read the comments. Hunter's words were enough.

Of course, in true Hunter fashion, given his public confession, it took him less than forty-eight hours to win back my favor. Since it was our first real fight, I chose to believe that he was truly sorry for the stupid things he'd said four years ago and forgave him.

"I am sorry about February too, Luce," he said during my birthday phone call. "I was so distracted with what was going on with Trevor and Jonathan, and it was really shitty of me to forget. You were right...I went into this whole overcompensation mode when I realized what I did. Hoping it would make you forget that I didn't say or do anything...and it's like," he sighed, "it's like it was the first sign of me not being close to you anymore, and that's the last thing I ever want."

"You do realize we will eventually have our own lives apart from one another?" I rationally pointed out.

"No, we're going to live next door to each other and coach our kids in youth soccer together," he stated his delusion half-jokingly.

I sighed, still finding him slightly loveable.

"You know, I talked to Jonathan about all of this," he shared.

"Oh really? And what did Jonathan say?" I asked, imagining that Jonathan probably thought it was ridiculous that his new boyfriend was so attached to a straight girl.

"He said fear of growing apart never made any relationship stronger."

"I would have to agree with him."

"Why do I have the urge to sing 'I Will Always Love You'?" Hunter joked, taking a break from the reality that our relationship was going to change from what it once was, whether he was ready for it or not.

"Because you have a weird fixation with romance movies from the nineties."

"You can never tell anyone."

"Maybe, we'll see. I don't have to keep secrets for you anymore, remember?"

"Fair enough," he granted. "So, where did things fall with Sebastian?"

"What do you mean?"

"You haven't talked to him since Saturday?"

"Nope."

"You don't want to?"

"I don't know," I sighed. "What's one more interaction where I overanalyze everything going to do for me?"

"Well, maybe you can ask questions and then you won't have to overanalyze things," he suggested obviously.

"Ugh, that seems like too much potential for getting hurt."

"I think we both signed up for that after we broke up and I came out."

"Well, that was stupid," I joked dryly.

"I know, almost as stupid as knowingly dating a gay guy for three years."

"Touché."

The opportunity to get the answers that everyone—except for me—seemed to crave happened later that day when I was in my room studying.

"I saw your door open, and decided I should bring you my peace offering," Sebastian walked into my room and handed me a latte. "Also, you left your awesome birthday present behind at the restaurant." He held up the bottle of laundry detergent.

"Imagine that," I responded flatly.

"I know, it's almost like some jerk came in and caused a whole bunch of drama that made you want to get the hell out of there as quickly as possible."

I didn't correct him. He stared at me, waiting for me to say something. He folded before I did.

"So, do you want the explanation or just the apology?"

"I'll take the explanation *and* the apology," I said coolly as I turned to face him.

My arms were crossed. Admittedly, I enjoyed that I was in a bit of a power position as Sebastian stood before me, ready to present his case.

"I've never been a huge fan of Hunter Davis," Sebastian started.

"Shocking," I interjected.

"Please, no interruptions," he said seriously.

"I feel like he is the type of person to coast by in life on good looks and using people. In fact, I'm fairly certain most of the AP teachers passed him because it made the program look more appealing to have him in there."

"That's not—" I started to argue. Sebastian held up his hand, stopping me.

"I will acknowledge that my opinion of him was not the highest from the beginning. Especially after hearing how he and all his idiot friends talked about girls behind closed doors. I may have even been a little disappointed when you two started to date, because—" he stopped himself.

"Anyway, that's not the point," he restarted. "I will tell you that the only time I personally heard him say things about you was that one time sophomore year after you first started dating. Not sure if this should redeem him at all, but I will acknowledge that I never heard anything else directly from him again."

He paused.

"When I saw him Saturday night and how he was acting like he needed to protect you from me, it pissed me off." He sighed. "I guess you could say I have a low tolerance for hypocrisy."

I sat there, expecting more. Sebastian knew it.

"I see him continuing to interject himself into your life, and it just bothers me. I mean, I know you guys are friends, but high school's over. You're not together. Why does he need to come up here and keep putting on a show? At what point does he let you move on?"

Sebastian crossed his arms, signifying the end of his point. I nodded, knowing that only months ago, these critiques against Hunter would've triggered immediate defensiveness from me.

"I said an explanation *and* an apology," I specified, holding a slight smirk.

"I am sorry I ruined your birthday party with a stereotypical show of testosterone and machismo."

I nodded, considering his apology. Before I could respond, he began another apology.

"And I'm sorry for what happened before Spring Break. I know I said that I wasn't going to do that again after the first time it happened, but when Amelia didn't respond to my message right away and you didn't seem against it...I didn't think...I didn't think through how it was..." he started fumbling.

"Sebastian," I stopped him, knowing I couldn't take him explaining how to him it had just been physical and not something more.

"Anyway," he went on, "obviously, seeing how you've been avoiding me and how Hunter seemed to think there was a need to protect you from me, I misread the understanding of the situation, and I'm sorry about that, too."

He tripped over that apology more than the first one, seeming more disappointed in that decision than calling Hunter out at my party.

"Do you know why I dated Hunter?" I asked.

Sebastian furrowed his brow, confused by the direction I'd taken the conversation.

"Yeah, the whole beard thing. To protect him until he was ready to come out. Why?"

"Yes, that's partly it. But a big reason was because it was easy and convenient," I admitted. "I set myself up to be in a relationship with a boy who couldn't hurt me."

Sebastian raised an eyebrow.

"Well, at the time, to the best of my knowledge, I didn't think he could hurt me," I clarified. "Anyway, I avoided all the heartache that can come with dating someone and still got to experience most of the best parts. And he got to have that, too.

"I don't blame him for being scared about moving on. I mean, I am, too. We are both phenomenal at knowing how to make a relationship look perfect from the outside, but the reality is that neither of us has any experience when it comes to all the real stuff.

"I mean, I can't even have a straight boy do a couple of nice things for me without it messing with my head." I referenced how I misread his kind gestures while we were fake dating. "I appreciate you wanting to look out for me when it comes to Hunter. And I am extremely disappointed and hurt that he was the one who started those rumors, but please don't think of me as someone he's forcing friendship on.

"I don't deny that the whole thing between him and me is weird to those on the outside, but that doesn't mean it doesn't feel comfortable and safe."

Sebastian sighed, looking thoughtful.

"Comfortable is probably the biggest reason I fought so hard to get back together with Amelia," he admitted. "I guess you guys have more in common with us than I thought."

"Please, Hunter and I are way cuter together than you two ever were," I joked.

He gave me a half-smile.

"You know, you're not the only one to get confused by things," he hinted.

That would have been the perfect time to ask those questions Hunter told me to ask. But I let it go. The cost-benefit ratio did not favor taking the risk.

"Well, if you are looking for anyone to help you study for midterms, please let me know," he offered quietly.

"Ditto," I mirrored.

"I really don't think I'll need your help with engineering and math, but thanks," Sebastian said smugly, trying to hook me as he headed for the door. "Enjoy your coffee, and happy birthday."

He left and I tried my best to not think of all the answers I still didn't have.

Chapter Twenty-Five

I made it through the rest of the school year without ever asking Sebastian any of those clarifying questions. We continued to not see each other as much as we had over winter quarter when Operation Fake Girlfriend was in full effect.

To me, the lack of interaction and seeking me out was enough information to answer all those questions everyone else said I should've asked. My hard-fought conclusion was that it was for the best anyway. If Sebastian had come to me and told me he had feelings for me, I would have had to figure out whether I wanted to try dating someone.

The truth was, I was only nineteen and most of my adolescence had been tied to a boy. Not necessarily a boyfriend in the traditional sense, but it still meant that I had spent very little time being independent. In my heart, I knew immediately attaching myself to the first boy I ever really kissed would only lead to temporary fulfillment. There were so many more important things to figure out besides whether I was in love with someone or not.

Most days (usually the days I didn't see Sebastian come back from a run covered in sweat), I was content having my questions go unanswered... just like the lady of mystery I had established myself to be (according to Corine and Veronica).

I went on to wrap up my finals flawlessly, anticipating a three-point-seven or higher in each class. My confidence in my cumulative GPA was a drastic change from what it had been in October. Although I was going to miss the independence and girls from the floor, I was looking forward to home and a less tension-filled summer than the previous one. Time and, I will begrudgingly admit, counseling with Katrina, could be credited for my altered appreciation for being around my family.

A day after my last final, Veronica had been kind enough to help me move most of my things into storage for the summer. We returned to the dorm, sweaty and sticky from the PNW summer humidity I was just becoming familiar with and was more than happy to leave behind. Of course, she and the other girls had already made fun of me for my sensitivity to the climate.

"What time do you need to leave for the airport? I can take you." Veronica asked before I headed back into my room.

"Four, but you don't have to. I can just get an Uber," I offered.

"Nonsense, Lucy. Everyone knows free trips to the airport are why you make friends with someone with a car."

"Damn, you caught me. I've been planning this since Day One," I joked.

"Just come get me when you're ready," she said before heading back into her room and leaving me to clean my dorm and pack my two oversized suitcases.

Even though I was leaving for the summer, I wouldn't have much time to miss Veronica. She and Hunter had already planned her summer visit to Modesto for the Fourth of July. I tried my best to prepare her for being underwhelmed, but Hunter, ever the hype-man, did not help. At least she was flying out of Oakland, allowing a visit to Corine to make up for the lack of excitement that awaited her in Modesto.

There wasn't that much to clean since Danica had already moved out the day before while I was in the middle of taking a final. There had been no goodbye, but at least she had been considerate enough to clean her side of the room before leaving. I was thankful that for next school year I had arranged with the other girls on my floor to live in Steven's Court, the nearby student apartments, and could avoid any more roommate horror stories.

Just when I had finished wiping down the desk and windowsill, I turned to find Sebastian standing in the doorway.

"Hey," he greeted.

"Hey."

"How'd your finals go?"

"As far as I know, good. You?"

"One more to go tomorrow."

I nodded.

"So, you're heading home this summer?" He motioned to my suitcases.

"Yeah. You're not?"

He shook his head.

"Nope, summer school."

"Glutton for punishment," I evaluated.

"More like a glutton for trying to establish residency and get in-state tuition," he corrected.

"Ah, I see. Smart."

"I know, I get that a lot," he quipped back. "So how will you be passing your time in the land of water, wealth, contentment, health?" He asked, referencing the town slogan, which was ancient. More evidence that he was an old man on the inside. "More raucous parties at Emily Mason's house, I imagine?"

"Probably not. I don't really need to keep up appearances anymore."

It was freeing to say it out loud.

"That's probably for the best," he sighed. "I mean, we all know the malbec she serves isn't that drinkable anyway."

"Exactly," I smiled. "My mom actually set me up with an internship at her firm," I shared. "So, I'm expecting that will keep me pretty busy."

"Being around daily conflict all summer? You're going to be exhausted. Hope you can handle it."

"I think I'll do all right. I mean, I have to start somewhere. They don't just let a person into law school just for being prom queen, you know." I reminded him of his tactless statement from one of his first tutoring sessions.

He gave me a half-smile.

"Well, have a safe flight and a good summer." He tapped his knuckles on the door, but remained standing there.

I laughed at his awkwardness.

"What?" He furrowed his brow at me.

"You know you can hug me goodbye," I said coolly. "Or are you worried you'll cry?" I teased.

"I'm not the one here with a habit of crying," Sebastian argued as he walked up to me.

He wrapped his arms around me and squeezed me briefly. Admittedly, I just wanted to take in his scent one last time. That laundry detergent he had given me for my birthday seemed to have a missing ingredient that left me wanting.

It was momentary, but it was nice. When he backed away, we made eye contact.

I felt the need to thank him for how he had been there for me when I needed someone...but I didn't. I told myself he wanted to thank me, too. But I still didn't know his expressions well enough to be confident in that belief.

"I'll see you around in the fall," he said before walking to the door.

"Sounds good," I agreed.

He turned and grinned.

"Peace, bitches. Modesto out." He mimed dropping a mic, giving me one last smile before he walked away.

Epilogue

Sebastian and I did run into each other a few times over the next three years. At first it was planned, meeting for coffee to study every now and then. Unsurprisingly, he started dating one of the girls in the aerospace program towards the end of sophomore year. We both knew there was no reason for him to keep studying with me at the risk of harming his new relationship. After that, we would only occasionally run into each other at the HUB.

It was always a bright spot in my day to see him, followed by an hour of what-if, and then I would refocus on my academics or latest plans with my other friends.

I never refollowed Sebastian on social media. Since my days of presenting false narratives were over, I refrained from going on there very much. It seemed like too much of a potential risk when thinking about applying to grad school and future jobs. Though, occasional lurking and analyzing was done when I was called upon by my friends, of course.

At the end of sophomore year, I declared English with a minor in History. Over the next three summers, I maintained the internship at my mom's firm, and bumped up my college resume by studying abroad in Puerto Rico for a quarter. There were times when I wanted to show off to Sebastian how much better my Spanish accent had gotten. But the opportunity never presented itself.

Along the way, there were other crushes and kisses with a few guys, but nothing ever turned serious. Honestly, none of them ever seemed worth the effort that was involved with a committed relationship.

In the end, I did decide to go to law school, but opted for Berkeley Law over UW Law, because I wanted to be closer to home. My mother was ecstatic even though it wasn't her or my father's law alma mater. It was a decision that did not involve me trying to make anyone happy but myself. Which might not seem like much, but to me it was one of my greatest accomplishments over those four years.

Acknowledgements

Thank you to Ben for his unending belief, encouragement, and patience. Thank you to Shannon and Bridget for humoring my first attempt at a YA novel, even though you both hate Hunter. Thank you to Rachel T for giving me the detailed backstory of the Real Housewives of Beverly Hills at the ready, no questions asked. Thank you to Travis for standing around, waiving his hands, and trying to look useful...and for the help writing calculus into dialogue (but thank you mostly for introducing me to Ben). Thank you to Becca for her free, yet priceless, consultation. Thank you to Andrea for her benevolent technical editing, as well as Erica for being a sounding board, again. And finally, to those in the Bookstagram community with whom I have forced friendship upon, thank you; you make this journey more enjoyable.